SUNDAY DINNERS

To Mum and Dad, who gave me so many happy Sunday dinners growing up and to Kristin, Charlotte and Jack, who continue to give me many more.

About the author

JON RANCE writes novels about love, family, relationship, and all the messy bits in-between. His novels have been described as hilarious, romantic, heart-warming, and perfect for fans of *Mike Gayle* and *Beth O'Leary*. His first book *This Thirtysomething Life* was a self-published Amazon top-ten bestseller and subsequently published by Hodder and Stoughton. Since then, he has written numerous novels including, *Sunday Dinners*, *About Us*, *Dan And Nat Got Married*, and *The Notecard.*

Jon grew up in England and studied English Literature at Middlesex University, London, before travelling the world and meeting his American wife in Australia. He now lives in California with his wife, two kids, and a dog called Pickle, where he writes full-time and drinks far too much tea.

Also by Jon Rance

This Thirtysomething Life
Happy Endings
This Family Life
A Notting Hill Christmas
Sunday Dinners
Dan And Nat Got Married
About Us
The Summer Holidays Survival Guide
Good Grief
The Notecard

Prologue

(Muswell Hill, London
Autumn 1999)

Greg Wilde

My son, Matt, has unfeasibly pointy elbows. You wouldn't know it to look at him but put him at the table next to his sister Lucy and he's like a James Bond car. His elbows suddenly extend, sharpen, and become weapons of mass annoyance to anyone within a one-foot radius.

It's Sunday and we're all around the table for our weekly roast dinner. From Monday to Friday, life's a bit like the London Tube map, and I feel like the bemused foreign tourist staring at it with a pained expression on my face, trying desperately to work out what all the coloured lines mean. The Sunday roast gives us the chance to come together, to reconnect, and, of course, for the kids to fight about their personal elbow space.

'Dad, Matt's doing it again,' moans Lucy.

'Matt, stop doing the thing with your elbow,' I say, for the fourth time.

'I didn't do anything,' protests a disgruntled Matt.

Matt is ten and Lucy is fourteen. It's hard to believe I have two children in double figures. Matt is the spitting image of me with his pale blue eyes, mop of unruly brown hair, and lanky frame, while Lucy is just like her mother with her wavy auburn hair, soft round face, and obsidian eyes. It doesn't feel like five minutes since they were crawling around the house, leaving foul smelling presents in their nappies, or eagerly rushing downstairs at the crack of dawn to watch cartoons in their pyjamas. I remember the day we brought Lucy home from the hospital, terrified we were going to somehow break her. I'll never forget Matt's first tentative steps in the living room. Even Lucy cheered her little brother on, prouder of him than anyone, before she decided she'd had enough and slyly pushed him over. Now we're more afraid that Matt's going to break Lucy than us and Matt's tentative steps are earth shattering leaps from his bed as he prepares for life as a Teenage Mutant Ninja Turtle.

'He did it again,' says Lucy, and I catch a glimpse of his elbow inching away from her.

'Matt, please,' I say.

'But I didn't do anything,' mumbles Matt.

'I just saw you.'

'I'm being victimised.'

'You're not being victimised, Matt, you just have very annoying elbows.'

'I demand a recount.'

'This isn't an election.'

'I learnt about this at school. It happened in that war.'

'Which war?'

'The big one.'

'The big one?'

'With that man with the funny moustache.'

'Hitler?'

'And the man with the large hat.'

'Mussolini?'

'And it happened to Jesus. Don't forget Jesus.'

'Sorry, Matt, but I don't think we can compare the plight of your elbows to the son of God.'

'Matt, please just stop,' says my wife Lizzy, as always firm but kind and getting Matt to do exactly what she wants. He adores Lizzy and she dotes on him.

Lizzy and I met at university in the eighties. Lizzy with her dark permed hair, the palest of faces, which to some people might have been the epitome of bland, but to me has always been the most beautiful face in the world. We left like a lot of people at that time, eager to change the world. Lizzy wanted to be a playwright and me a novelist. We fell in love over Shakespeare, Oscar Wilde, and Virginia Woolf, but while I ended up wandering into the world of academia and landing a lecturing position at a university in north London, she gave it all up to stay at home and be a mother.

Although she's always quick to remind me that she got a First at university while I only got a 2:1. Housewife or not, she'll always be cleverer than me and she has the certificate to prove it.

'What's that?' says Holly, pointing at the meat in the middle of the table.

Our youngest, Holly, is only five and unlike Lucy and Matt, she wasn't planned. We were done having kids after Matt, but then, and despite Lizzy being on the pill, along came Holly. It's just one of those things, but now she's here I wouldn't have it any other way. Although, I did get a pretty swift vasectomy to be on the safe side. Holly is the mirror image of my mother as young woman. She has the same almost white, blonde hair, piercing blue eyes, is stick thin, and is terrifyingly independent and strong willed.

'It's lamb, sweetheart. Smells delicious, doesn't it?' I say.

'Like the lambs I see when we drive to the country?'

'Not those actual lambs.'

'But it's one of those lambs? The ever so cute fluffy lambs?'

'Well, yes, but—'

'I don't want any of that. It's murder.'

'It's not murder, sweetheart.'

'Yes it is,' says Holly defiantly.

'You ate beef last week,' says Lizzy.

'But that's different,' says Holly, very matter of fact. 'Cows are black and white and boring, not cute like lambs. Cows just moo and do big poo pats.'

Only five and already the moral centre of our family. Unlike Matt, who doesn't care enough about anything, or Lucy who picks her battles with surgical precision, Holly throws herself into every cause, every last mangy pony that needs saving or tree that needs protecting. She's always asking questions and demanding we answer them. It's exhausting.

'I talked about this with Charlotte's mummy,' says Holly.

'About what, love?' says Lizzy.

'Charlotte's family are vegenarians and her mummy said it's wrong to kill faceless animals.'

'I think you mean 'vegetarian' and 'defenceless animals',' says Lucy, correcting her little sister.

'And that people who do are murderers,' says Holly obstinately.

'But Daddy isn't a murderer,' says Lizzy. 'He bought you that nice red bicycle for your birthday. A murderer wouldn't do that, would they?'

We all look at Holly, who seems to be giving this a great deal of thought.

'Fine, Daddy's not a murderer,' says Holly finally.

'Glad we cleared that up,' I say.

'But someone killed that faceless baby sheep and I'm not eating it,' says Holly, and she stubbornly folds her arms across her tiny, five-year-old chest in defiance. 'I mean, you wouldn't eat a puppy, would you?'

'Well, no, of course not,' I say.

'But lambs are cute like puppies.'

'Well, yes they are, sweetheart.'

'Dad's what you call a hypocrite,' says Lucy.

'That's not fair,' says Lizzy.

'Why not?' says Holly. 'Why's Daddy not a happycrit?'

'It's just … different,' I say.

'Happycrit!' shouts Holly, standing up and pointing at me. 'Daddy's a happycrit!'

'Right, that's it!' says Lucy, picking up a gravy sodden roast potato and throwing it at Matt. The roast potato hits Matt directly in the face, droplets of dark brown gravy dripping down his nose.

'Food fight!' yells Matt, springing up, and holding his fork aloft like a young Spartacus.

'No!' Lizzy and I shout in unison, but it's too late. A Brussels sprout hits Lucy in the head. Holly launches a carrot at Matt, which doesn't make it and ends up on the floor, and then before I know what's going on its all-out war. Lucy gets up and runs away, Matt hot on her heels, then the next moment I hear screams and feet stomping up the stairs. And in the middle of the table there's a melange of half-eaten Sunday roast.

Admittedly, our family roasts aren't like the commercials they have on television (the Oxo family we are not) but like I said, I wouldn't change a thing. This is my family. I love them all to bits and a part of me wants to keep this, just as it is now, like one of those tiny ships in a bottle, but I know I can't. Right now life is good, but one day all this is going to change and so I intend to enjoy it while I can: warts, elbows, food fights and all. Because that's the thing about life, it doesn't matter how happy you are or how happy you think you're going to be in the future - without warning it can all change in a second.

Part One

(Thirteen years later)

October Roast

Greg

It's a Sutton Hoo, organic, free-range chicken, not some mangy old bird from the supermarket. You can't (as Matt so ridiculously suggested) just "bung it in the oven". It needs care, attention, and a great deal of love. It lived its short but happy life in Suffolk, allowed to roam free in acres of beautiful English countryside. I intend to give it the send-off it so richly deserves. I'm going to smear it with a delicious herb butter, insert an organic lemon, a whole bulb of garlic and some fresh rosemary, and then slow roast it in the oven. Why does no-one else in my family care how moist the chicken is?

Holly isn't even here yet (whereabouts unknown). Matt is lying (as per usual) on the sofa. My wife, Lizzy (in a huff about something) is talking to Lucy and doing the whole Jane Austen bit (arms flapping about dramatically). Meanwhile, Mum is dozing off in the living room, her snores like shifting tectonic plates creating seismic vibrations around the house. It's our monthly Sunday roast and as usual I'm the only one putting in the effort.

One Sunday a month is all I want. Is it too much to ask? It used to be weekly when the kids were little, but gradually over time all our lives became too chaotic. Lucy moved out, Matt went to university (and then came back again), Holly was and still is too busy and so now it's once a month. One day out of thirty to get together, sit around the table, and talk about nice normal things. Maybe we could talk about the success of my book 'Wilde on Wilde' (would it kill them?) or Lucy's life at the BBC. Matt could update us on his promised (not promising, unfortunately) photography career, without that boorish face he always makes whenever I mention the possibility of him getting a job. And perhaps Holly could join in with the conversation instead of spending the entire afternoon tapping away on her phone, as if it's the most interesting thing in the universe, Mum will do her best, but since Dad passed away she's fading badly.

I suppose the thing is that it's important to me and so I think it should be important to them as well. Us sitting around the table together isn't going to last forever. As much as I want it to, as much as Lizzy and I perhaps need it to, it's not. The kids are almost all grown up and this is one of the last remnants of their childhood. Whatever happened when they were young, no matter who had football practice, ballet, or gymnastics, we always sat around the table on Sunday. It was the one constant in the ever-changing tapestry of our life. I feel like I missed out on large chunks of their childhoods because of work, but the Sunday roast was always my thing. I made it every week without fail and it still stands like a pillar of something important and meaningful and it's slowly slipping through my fingers.

A girl from The Telegraph newspaper came to university on Friday to interview me about my book; a lovely young reporter called Milly, with a photographer in tow. She was a gorgeous young thing, late twenties, all blonde hair, white teeth, and enthusiasm. My book 'Wilde on Wilde' has been an unexpected success and is even being hailed in some circles as "the definitive book on Oscar Wilde" (The Guardian). The university is getting quite excited, I'm being lined up to give a lecture, and there's even been tentative talk of a university tour. I'm fifty-four years old and finally getting some professional recognition, although much like the roast, none of my family seems to give two hoots about it.

'Wine?' says Matt, breezing into the kitchen, dressed as though he's been living rough on the streets as part of a Channel Four documentary.

Matt, twenty-three, a graduate, and today he's sporting grey jogging bottoms with a hole dangerously close to his groin and a manky old white t-shirt. His scruffy brown hair looks like it hasn't been washed in days and I don't know when he last shaved. I thought he'd go away to university and grow up, but if anything he seems to have regressed. I'm worried about him. I keep trying to tell him that life is fast and he's already twenty-three. He needs to do something now before it's too late, but my words are met with the same disdainful, benevolent face that seems to have become his trademark.

'Excuse me?' I say.

'Can I have some wine? Nan's snoring. I can't hear the telly and Mum and Lucy are bitching about you.'

'Did you hear what they were saying?' I enquire.

'No, but you're definitely not in their good books. I'll tell you what, give me some wine and I'll find out what's going on.'

Matt's always been the same. All his school reports were basically subtle variations on the same theme. Miss Norris at primary school said that Matt was a bright boy who spent far too much time pretending he wasn't. Miss Stapleton at middle school said if Matt spent as much time on his work as trying to make people laugh, he'd be the best student she'd ever had. And Mr Barraclough at secondary school said Matt lacked focus and dedication but showed real promise when it came to getting away with doing nothing to the best of his ability. I was relieved when he started showing a real interest in photography and I've never told him this, but he's actually pretty good. The problem with Matt is that he lacks drive, direction, and any sort of desire. Like most of his generation, he seems to think that one day he's going to wake up and be a successful photographer without doing any of that annoying thing called "work".

Matt seems happier spending his time lounging in the pit he calls his bedroom, going to sleep in the middle of the night, and waking up as if mornings don't exist. I haven't been in his bedroom for months, afraid of what I might find lurking beyond the door. The wooden barrier that once bore a 'keep out - genius at work' sign because he was busy building something with Lego, now seems to house more unsavoury items. Like I said, I don't venture to the other side, but walking past the other day, the door slightly ajar, a cacophony of smells hit my nose and I could see the floor was an uneven pile of rubble; clothes, boxes, and who knows what else. It was like a post-apocalyptic vision of a nuclear ravaged world. I want to cordon off his room with some cones and maybe some police tape, but I don't want the fight it would inevitably cause. Lizzy, despite her annoyance at any mess I might leave around the house, or the occasional stray sock that fails to make it into the laundry bin, defends Matt and his bedroom to the ends of the earth because he's a sensitive boy who needs our love and understanding. The only thing I understand is that Matt's a lazy bugger who seems to get some sort of warped pleasure from making my life miserable.

'Half a glass now and the rest when you find out why your mother's angry with me,' I say, filling up his wine glass halfway.

'Deal,' says Matt, and he saunters off towards the living room.

I really need to know why Lizzy's angry with me. Since going through 'the change' Lizzy has actually changed. I'm sure she used to be more relaxed and fun-loving, but now every tiny thing is the biggest deal. I can come home from a hard day at university, five hours of lectures behind me, and students begging for extensions because they've been too busy getting pissed to write an essay, and all I want is a glass of wine, something nice to eat, and to put my feet up. And most days this is what happens, but on Wednesday I came home to a raging mentalist who called me a "useless, vacuous, thoughtless, piece of shit!" All I did was ask what was for dinner. I ask you, are those the words of a rational human being?

It feels like everything I do at the moment annoys her. During the first few tantalising months – maybe even years - of a relationship, nothing about the other person bothers you. You pedestal all you see, and you ignore all the imperfections because you're in love. The way they chew their food or slurp their tea, the endless snoring, the way they throw their coat on the bedroom floor instead of putting it away in the cupboard you specifically bought for coats, none of it touches a nerve. But over the years the imperfections start to grate. None of it seemed to matter before. I loved Lizzy and Lizzy loved me, we loved our children, and it worked. We had our peaks and troughs like any other couple, but now it feels like I'm on trial. Like I'm auditioning for the same job I've had for the last thirty years, and it's not going well.

'What the hell's wrong with you?!' shouts Lizzy, storming into the kitchen while I'm julienning carrots. Matt and Lucy shuffle in behind her and Matt's looking a bit sheepish. Lucy has her arms stoically folded across her chest - sides have obviously been taken. 'Sending your son to sort your mess out.'

'Oh.'

'Not "Oh", Greg,' says Lizzy, snapping at me. 'It's completely unacceptable. You made your bed; you can lie in it. Poor Matt shouldn't have to come in there, bribed with alcohol, to find out what his useless father's done wrong.'

'But that's the whole point, Lizzy. I have no idea what I've done wrong.'

'You have absolutely no idea why I'm annoyed? Really? No idea?'

'No.'

'There's nothing you can think of. Nothing at all during the first week of October that could possibly have pissed me off?'

I hate these moments. Obviously there's something I've forgotten, but I can't for the life of me think what it is. I've been so busy at work and everything with the book has taken up so much of my time. I wish Lizzy understood. I'm at the pinnacle of my career, the kids will soon have all left the coop, and it's almost time for Lizzy and me to start enjoying ourselves. Instead of rejoicing in this she's in a constant state of annoyance as though I go out of my way just to piss her off. Like I have nothing better to do with my time.

'I've been really busy,' I say, but before I can say anything else she starts crying. Her body shakes, her eyes well up and then tears start marching down her face. Each one a reminder that this is my fault. I did this.

'Our wedding anniversary. It was on Wednesday, and you forgot,' she sniffs.

'I didn't mean to forget, love, but,' I start to say, but before I can finish she stops me.

'No buts, Greg. I'm tired of buts because sometimes there just isn't an excuse.'

'It's pretty shit, Dad,' says Lucy with an accusatory frown.

'Pretty shit,' reiterates Matt.

The thing is, yes I forgot and it's bad, I know, and maybe it's just me, but I don't think it's that big of a deal. We're in our fifties, surely the odd slip up is allowed. Why is she making such a big deal out of this? What terrifying monster is lurking beneath the surface of this argument? Is this like the time she refused to let me see her naked with the lights on because I made that one off-the-cuff remark about her thighs? I apologised for weeks and told her how much I loved her legs, but it was months before I was allowed near her thighs again. The joy of sex isn't so joyous when it's below the knees and above the thighs only. I need to stay quiet though. Take the hit, apologise and move on. But this is the problem. I should be able to tell my wife how I feel, but I can't because Lizzy, Lucy, and Matt are stood staring at me like judges on one of those awful singing shows on the television.

'Look, love, I know it's bad. I do and I'm sorry,' I plead.

'But?' says Lizzy sharply.

'But I've been busy and when you think about it ...'

'Yes?' says Lizzy.

'It's just a day,' I say, realising straight away that I've said probably the worst thing I could possibly have said. With every single word I utter, her face contorts into greater degrees of annoyance and frustration.

'And that just about sums it up,' says Lizzy, wiping the tears from her soft, pale cheeks, before she turns around and walks out, closely followed by Lucy.

'Wine?' says Matt after a moment, shaking his empty glass at me, a momentary hint of veiled amusement in his eyes.

'What's the racket? I was sleeping,' says Mum, slowly trundling in behind Matt, her ever decreasing wire brush of grey/blue hair sticking up where's she's been asleep, and the tangle of cardigans falling off her depressingly frail body.

'Dad forgot their wedding anniversary,' says Matt with a sort of pantomime grimace.

'I was asleep, and all the shouting woke me up. I'm seventy-nine,' she says, as though this covers all possible reasons for her annoyance.

'Sorry, Mum.'

'Sorry, Gran.'

'Humph,' says Mum, before she turns around and staggers back to the living room. The salted water for the potatoes boils over with a damning hiss.

Lizzy

I'm not just annoyed about our wedding anniversary. I'm not stupid. Greg's a man. The list of things he's forgotten over the years is biblical in length. The fact he hasn't forgotten before now is nothing short of a minor miracle. Greg forgetting our anniversary was just the last straw in a series of last straws. It wasn't only him. It's everything.

I'd had lunch with one of my best friends, Stella Blackwell, earlier on our wedding anniversary. Stella's been my friend for years, but it's impossible to keep up with her. She and her husband, Paul, only have one child, Louise, who went to boarding school, then onto Oxford University, and now she's working for one of the big PR firms in London. Stella and Paul are constantly on holiday somewhere exotic, they have a summer house in Italy, and to top it off, they still have an active and exciting sex life - which I hear about in oh so graphic detail. If I hear another story that starts "Paul came home from work the other day with his sex face on," I'll be forced to jam pencils in my ears.

After coffee, an expensive lunch, and her going on about their latest holiday to South Africa, I went home to my own jumble sale mess of a house, dreading the giant pile of detritus awaiting me at the bottom of the stairs. I felt deflated, unattractive, and a complete failure. In comparison to her, my life feels about as exciting as folding laundry, which I have piles of to do in case you're interested. The only bright spark on the horizon seemed to be that Greg was going to come home from work with a big wedding anniversary surprise. He hadn't mentioned it before he left in the morning so foolishly I assumed he was pretending he'd forgotten. Then he came home talking about his day as though it was just another Wednesday, kicked off his shoes, put his feet up and turned on the telly. When he asked what was for dinner, I blew my top.

The thing is, I'm fifty-three, but that isn't old these days. I'm at my peak in so many ways and now the kids are all grown up I want to travel, I want to live, and I want a bloody orgasm! I just read Fifty Shades of Grey and I'm clearly missing out. Not that I want Greg to tie me up and the thought of him cracking a whip across my bottom doesn't do much for me, but something slightly sexy would be nice. Anything remotely sexy would be nice. Maybe Greg's forgotten what it's like, but I'm still a sexual woman. It's been two years since my last proper orgasm. Two long, barren, orgasmless years in the sexual wilderness and despite what Greg says, this isn't anything to do with the menopause. Why do men think that whenever something's wrong, it can be blamed on periods, and when they go, the menopause? Maybe it's you that's the problem and not our bloody hormones, did you ever consider that, Greg?

Losing your sex life is strange because it happens so gradually you don't even realise until it's too late. It's a bit like the wrinkles on my face. It wasn't like I woke up at fifty and went, "where did they come from?" It's been happening slowly, gradually for years. The same thing has happened to our sex life. We used to have sex frequently, and it was good, great on occasion, but over time it slowed down, got delayed, was put off because we were too tired, too busy, had children, or something better was on TV, and now it's gone. No one cared enough to start a campaign to save it and it became extinct. My orgasms went the way of the dodo. Where's Sir Bob Geldof when you need him? Sex Aid - it could bring a whole new meaning to the word "relief".

When you think about meeting the love of your life you imagine fireworks. You think of long lingering stares across a crowded room and your breath being taken away by the overwhelming passion of it all. You think that when you meet The One you'll just know.

It wasn't exactly like that for us.

At university Greg was physically awkward. Tall and

gangly, he hadn't grown into his body yet. It would be another ten years before he looked like he knew what to do with it. His hair was always a complete mess, and he didn't have any of the physical qualities of my previous boyfriends. Before Greg, I'd always gone for bad boys and creative types; singers, artists, the typical enfant terribles of sixth form. I met Greg in the union bar at university where he was arguing with the barman about his change. I was behind him in the queue, and I got so bored of waiting that I handed over the seventy-six pence they were squabbling over. It was hardly a life changing moment. The heavens didn't open, and I'd never have believed then that I'd have ended up marrying him. It happened because the more I knew him and talked to him, the more I realised how similar we were and how much we wanted the same things. He made me laugh, we always had fun, and he was a great kisser. We used to snog for hours back then. I slowly fell in love with him and together we created a life. A wonderful, beautiful life.

'Are you all right?' says Lucy, giving me a supportive squeeze on the arm.

I didn't mean to start crying in the kitchen. I was trying to keep it together and not be the 'typical female emotional wreck' Greg so obviously perceives me to be, but when I reminded him about our wedding anniversary, I'd hoped for a different reaction. I expected guilty grovelling and instead I got laconic indifference, which sums up our marriage at the moment.

'I just need a moment,' I say, and head off upstairs to the sanctuary of our bedroom (where orgasms go to die).

I slump down on the bed and stare up at the ceiling. The same ceiling I've stared at so many times in my life. With Greg just after we bought the house, post-coital and ever so young. With all of my babies asleep on my chest, not imagining I could ever be unhappy again because I had children and I'd never felt love like it. On Sunday mornings, listening to the sound of the house already in full swing; the children running and shouting, while Greg tried to keep order and make breakfast. Crying my eyes out the night Lucy left home for university. After Mum's funeral, alone, while downstairs the rest of my family ate small sandwiches and made even smaller talk. So many moments spent lying here, staring up at the same spot, thinking, wondering, and now for the first time feeling sad not because of anyone else, but sad because of my life as it is now. Because I'm unhappy.

Eventually there's a knock at the door and Greg (looking apologetic but failing to completely convince in his role as 'sorry husband') trundles in and sits down on the bed. I sit up and shuffle along a bit to put some distance between us.

'I'm sorry, love,' says Greg eventually. 'I shouldn't have said that thing about it being just a day.'

'You're right, you shouldn't.'

I don't think Greg even knows why I'm annoyed. He's oblivious. He probably thinks this is just about the anniversary. That I'm being overly mawkish. Bung the old girl some flowers and a box of chocolates and everything will be fine.

'I'll tell you what. Next week I'll take you out. A proper slap-up meal wherever you want. How about that Italian place you like so much? How about that, love?'

How about that? Is that the solution to our problems? A meal out at an overly expensive Italian and all my worries will go away. If only it was that easy. How can I explain to Greg that I feel like life is passing me by? That I'm worried all the dreams and things we talked about doing at 'some point in our lives' are in danger of becoming just youthful folly. I'm bored and tired and I need something to change otherwise I feel like I'm going to implode. How do I bring all of this to the conversation when Greg is offering me a nice meal and a hopeful smile? I'm having a full-blown midlife crisis and Greg's proposing bruschetta.

'You think that will make everything all right, do you?' I say eventually.

'It's a start, love.'

'It's a meal.'

'And wine?' says Greg with a tentative smile, before he reaches across and tries to put his hand over mine and I quickly pull it away.

'This isn't just about our anniversary, Greg.'

'I know.'

'What do you mean, you know?'

'Well, you've been a bit …'

'A bit what?' I say sharply, trying to keep all of the anger and frustration inside of me.

'A bit touchy.'

'Touchy?' I say, feeling the bubble of annoyance begin to breach the surface.

'You know what I mean, love. Recently you've been really ... sensitive.'

'Touchy? Sensitive? That's what you're calling it? So when men have a midlife crisis and start banging their secretary, buying sports cars, or getting hair implants its fine because it's acceptable for men, but when women start asking questions, we're just being overly sensitive? It's always our bloody hormones.'

'You're having a midlife crisis?' says Greg suspiciously.

'No, Greg, I'm not having a midlife crisis. I'm just unhappy.'

'Oh,' says Greg. 'I didn't realise.'

'I know.'

'Sorry,' says Greg, moving his hand across and giving mine a squeeze. This time I let him. 'It will be fine. The meal will be nice. Maybe we could stay in a hotel for the night.'

'Maybe,' I say, but all I can think is that this is just another plaster. Greg likes to keep putting plasters on problems, piling them up, hoping they'll eventually fix the pain, but they don't. Plasters hide it, but the wound is getting deeper and deeper, and I don't think Greg realises how bad it's become. You can't keep putting plasters on everything and hoping it won't fall apart.

Greg smiles at me and I smile at him. He pats me on the leg and then walks off to cook his roast and all I feel is sadness because the one thing I never thought I'd end up being, was one half of an unhappy marriage. Greg and I were for life. We were going to grow old together. We were going to change the world, but instead the world changed us.

Greg

We're at the dinner table waiting for Holly. Lizzy's obviously still annoyed with me. I keep trying to smile at her across the table, but like an eclipse she won't look directly at me. I can't believe she's having a midlife crisis. I know she said it wasn't, but it certainly sounds like one. I realise she's been unhappy of late, but I just put it down to the menopause and the kids. They're all leaving us one by one, and Lizzy's been a stay-at-home mum for the last twenty-seven years. She probably feels a bit useless. No, not useless, that's the wrong choice of word. Lost. She probably feels a bit lost. As for all this talk of going on adventures and "really living" it isn't that I don't want to, it's that I don't have the time. Before we had kids we talked about all the places we'd like to visit "one day" and I still want to, but she needs to realise that I can't drop everything and bugger off to Peru to trek Machu Picchu just because she's feeling a bit mawkish.

'Has anyone heard from Holly?' I ask.

'I got a text,' snaps Lizzy.

'She didn't text me. I thought we had a family text group thing set up,' I say.

'No, thank God,' says Matt.

'What's that supposed to mean?' I say.

'It's easier if we deal with Mum,' says Matt, a sarcastic smile slapped across his face.

'Is that the door?' says Lucy, as the front door opens and then closes. Keys are put on the hook in the hallway, and a moment later Holly comes into the dining room and slumps down in her chair next to Mum.

Holly is eighteen and in her last year at sixth form. Next year she's off to university to study Drama and I have a feeling she won't be moving back again. Unlike Matt, who's always at home, moping about in his room, or taking baths as though water bills don't exist, Holly is hardly here. Between college, her various drama commitments and going out with friends, I catch the occasional glimpse of her as she's leaving the house or coming back. She's my Hi/Bye child. With Matt it's like we have a lifetime lodger, but with Holly it feels like a part of her is already gone.

'Sorry,' says Holly to Lizzy (without looking at me). 'I got caught up.'

'Well, you're here now. Let's eat, shall we?' I say. 'Lizzy, do you want to start?'

'You're actually thinking of me? That's a first,' says Lizzy taking a sip of wine. Holly looks at me, then at Mum and shakes her head despondently.

Lizzy starts serving herself, followed by Lucy, Matt and then Holly, while I get a small plate together for Mum. She doesn't eat much these days, so I serve her a tiny piece of chicken, a small puddle of gravy, a solitary roast potato, and a couple of vegetables. It's a pathetic looking meal. I pass it to her, and she smiles at me and for a moment there seems to be a glimmer of my old mum, but it's soon gone.

I visit her at the home once a week, sitting down with all the other old people, having the same conversations and watching the clock until it's time to leave, then I kiss her bony cheek and wonder if it's the last time. At least at the home she has the musical delights of Fred Strang and his Festival of the Fifties. Last week one of the old folk got so excited when Fred played Great Balls Of Fire that he tried to get up and dance, attempted a wildly ambitious spin, and ended up putting his hip out. It was the day Rock 'N' Roll died at Roseview Retirement Home.

'How are the potatoes, darling?' I say to Lucy.

'Epic. Best ever,' says Lucy.

'Kiss arse,' mumbles Matt.

'She's not a kiss arse. She just appreciates good food. Lucy probably eats at a lot of nice restaurants with her BBC mates,' I say.

Lucy joined the BBC straight from university on a graduate scheme and she's been there ever since. I'm so proud of her. I remember when she was sixteen and first told me her plans to work there. I encouraged her to work hard and follow her dreams and she made it. There's no better feeling as a parent than watching your children achieve their goals. Two years ago, with our help, she bought a small flat in Notting Hill and she hasn't looked back.

'Sometimes, but it's usually just something quick,' says Lucy.

'Too busy kissing arse,' says Matt.

'No,' says Lucy. 'Too busy working because I actually have a job.'

'Please you two,' I say, tired of their bickering. 'How's the chicken, Hols?'

'I'm not really hungry. I already ate,' says Holly.

'What?' I say, rather offended. 'Why would you eat? Today's family roast day.'

All eyes are on Holly, who puts her knife and fork down and looks at us intently.

'I have an announcement,' she says.

Holly is always making big announcements. When she was five she stood up and announced she was a vegetarian. At seven she announced she was eating meat again, but only the less cute animals. At ten she decided to become an actress. At eleven she told us she'd stopped using shampoo because she'd read somewhere that hair was basically self-cleaning. And at fifteen she announced she'd joined a band called 'Aggravated Noise' as lead singer/songwriter, but quickly unannounced it because the band had split up due to creative differences without performing a single gig. I can't imagine what's next.

'As you know, Charlotte goes to church every Sunday and I've been going with her for the past few months,' says Holly.

'You're …?' says Matt with a salacious grin.

'A Christian,' says Holly smiling. 'I have been for a while, but I didn't want to tell you because, well, you know.'

'No, why?' I say.

Everyone looks across at me.

'Because of you, Dad. I know how you feel about religion, and I didn't want an argument about it,' says Holly.

'I'm open minded about it,' I say, and Lizzy snorts her wine back into her glass.

'I'm sorry,' says Lizzy. 'Did you just say you were open minded about religion?'

'Not about religion. I'm an atheist, but if Holly wants to investigate it for herself, try it on for size—'

'You see, there you go,' says Holly, bristling with annoyance. 'Try it on for size. It's not a new coat, Dad, its God!'

'Would someone please pour me some gravy?' says Mum. 'I haven't got any gravy and the chicken's dry.'

'It's not dry, Mum, it's a free range, organic, Sutton Hoo chicken,' I say.

'I don't care what it's called, it's dry,' says Mum, as I drizzle more gravy on her plate.

'And I don't care what you say, it's my life and my choice and I choose God,' says Holly.

'Praise the Lord!' says Matt, raising his arms to the heavens like an Evangelical pastor.

'Not helpful, Matt,' I say. 'I realise it's your life and your choice, Holly, and of course, your mother and I will support you whatever you decide.'

'I definitely will,' says Lizzy.

'But?' says Holly to me.

Everyone is looking at me. This is a key moment and I'm on a sticky wicket. I raised my children to look at the world rationally. 'Science' and 'fact' were two words I used all the time when they were growing up. You can't believe something blindly without proper reason. I'm an atheist and not because I don't believe, but because I do. I believe in intellect, art, humanity, nature and science. How can I believe in a God that is based purely on blind belief without anything factual to back it up? This is probably just a phase like her sudden interest in Tarot cards last year, and the time she joined that left wing political group (The Commuchists - an amalgam of communist and anarchist. I always thought they sounded more like a pop group than an anti-establishment political movement). Holly's always been a phase-ist and this is just another one to add to the list. The best thing I can do is pretend to be fine with it and then wait for her to find something else to be passionate about.

'You're eighteen, Holly, you're going to experiment. You need to find your own path in life. You know my feelings on religion, but you need to come to that conclusion yourself,' I say.

'Typical Greg,' says Lizzy. 'Sitting up all high and mighty, and sanctimoniously looking down at anyone who doesn't agree with you.'

'I don't do that.'

'You do,' says Matt.

'Lucy?' I say, looking towards the one person who's usually on my side.

'You do a bit,' says Lucy.

There's an uncomfortable moment of tension at the table and everyone is looking at me. Probably waiting for me to get all "high and mighty", but I'm not going to give them the satisfaction. I'm not sanctimonious and I don't look down on anyone. I'm going to let this go. I'm going to be the bigger person.

'Let's just eat, shall we?' I say, looking down at my plate and feeling everyone's eyes burning into the top of my head.

I don't want to argue with Holly. She isn't going to be living with us for much longer and I don't want her last memories of me to be bad ones. I wouldn't have minded if she'd confessed to smoking a bit of pot, or even if she'd got one of those awful tattoos all of her friends seem to be getting, but religion? She knows it's the one thing I can't abide and so, of course, she has to do it.

We eat in a heavy silence. Lizzy's still angry with me, Holly's giving me some very un-Christian stares across the table, and even Lucy's against me.

These are the times when I wish my father was still here to take the tension away. It's been just over a year since he died of Alzheimer's. He would know what to say. Not the sick version that would sit there like a hollow shell not knowing what day it was, but my real father. The man who always made us laugh, who told the same tales too many times, but somehow as though you were hearing them for the first time. Dad was the life and soul of the family and I miss him terribly.

It was a Tuesday when Mum rang me in a panic. Dad had popped out to take a couple of books back to the library and hadn't come home. It had been nearly five hours and Mum was on the verge of calling the police. I didn't think much of it at first. Dad had always had an awful memory. It was just how he was and so when it started to get slightly worse, none of us really noticed. "It's just your father, you know what he's like," Mum would say lovingly. "Brain like a sieve," was the running joke in the house, although suddenly it wasn't funny anymore when Dad came home in the back of a police car. That was seven years ago.

There was a day near the end when Dad and I went out together. He wanted me to take him to Plumstead where he grew up. As we sat in the car, driving through London in the early morning rain, I had my doubts about whether this was a good idea or not. He hadn't been doing well and was going through a difficult patch, his memory fading in and out like a dying light bulb. He was in the car in a heavy wool coat and scarf that drowned his frail body. He wasn't saying much, so I turned on the radio and we listened together in silence.

We parked outside the house he grew up in. It was a typical working class London street; small, generic terraced houses sitting on top of each other. I vaguely remember going there as a boy. The cramped living room full of cheap ornaments, the curtains pulled tightly together, the acidic smell of beer and the woody aroma from Grandad's pipe. We drove to his old school and watched children running around the playground. We stood, leaning against my car, him gazing off into the distance, occasionally smiling, but not saying why.

After an hour, I could sense he was fading so I suggested we make our way home. Dad nodded, but once in the car he asked if we could pop to one last spot. We'd only driven a short way when Dad asked me to pull over near a park. We found a bench and sat down, the rain coming down in a faint mist, covering us in a thin layer of moisture.

'Right there,' said Dad, pointing at a small clump of trees.

'What's that, Dad?'

'Sally Grimley. She had her hair in these little pigtails. Blonde it was and she was always chewing bubble gum. She used to blow these big bubbles,' said Dad, smiling and looking across at me. 'My first kiss. I was fifteen.'

I didn't cry much during the Alzheimer's. I didn't cry on the day he wouldn't see me at the hospice because he thought I was trying to hurt him. I didn't cry on the day he sat at the dinner table and wet himself for the first time. But as I looked at my father and realised he was remembering something for the last time, I reached down, held his hand, and I wept.

On the drive home, I told him I was glad he took me there and that I'd never forget Sally. Dad just stared at me, his eyes red and glassy, his face pale and sunken in.

'Who's that?'

'Sally Grimley, Dad. Your first kiss. The girl you just told me about.'

Dad looked at me, his face blank, and he was gone again. He looked out of the car window at the rain as we drove back through London, and he never mentioned Sally again. He died six months later and after the funeral I went back to Plumstead. I walked among the trees and thought of fifteen-year-old Dad. It made me smile because it was one of his last memories and I'd shared it with him, and in the end it was one of my last memories of him too.

I try and smile at Lizzy, but she doesn't smile back. Holly is playing on her phone and Mum is lost inside her own world. Matt and Lucy are eating, but none of us are talking. We're all disconnected from each other. Sitting together, yet alone, and I want to say something light-hearted to break the tension just like Dad would have done, but I can't think of anything. And so I sit here eating, hoping it'll get better - because it has to. I'm the luckiest man in the world. A perfect wife, three wonderful children, and a job I love. Isn't that what we all want? The dream? The perfect life?

November Roast

Lizzy

When Greg and I first started dating, I remember going to restaurants and seeing older married couples sitting in silence, looking around as though they'd rather be anywhere else in the world. We used to scoff at them and wonder how it happened. Why were they still together if they had nothing to say to each other? What terrible thing must have happened for their marriage to turn out like that?

Greg and I were still in the honeymoon phase of our relationship. We hadn't heard all the stories we'd hear time and again over the years and we'd barely scratched the surface on politics, religion, or top ten films. We had the world to talk about and we never imagined in a million years we'd become one of those couples. Sometimes we'd sit in the student house he shared with three other boys and read in silence, but it was fine because it truly was a comfortable silence. A nice, soft, woollen jumper sort of silence that fitted over us, enveloping us both in its warmth. The silences at our anniversary dinner weren't comfortable, they were itchy and sharp, and they dug into us making us both shift in our seats. They made me wish I was at home where I could get up and leave if I wanted to. Pop the kettle on and make everything seem fine.

As wedding anniversary celebrations go, it was about as sad and depressing as it's possible to be. We went to the nice-but-over-priced Italian restaurant Greg had suggested. The food was fantastic, the ambiance romantic, and everything was as it should have been. Everything except us. We sat and looked at each other, smiling hopefully, but neither of us had anything to say. I wanted to talk about important things and get everything out in the open and I suspect Greg wanted to talk about anything else. In the end we did what every married couple does when they run out of things to say; we talked about the kids.

We'd both made the effort. Greg was in his best suit, his hair was about as un-messy as it's ever been, and he'd spent a good thirty minutes in the bathroom beforehand getting himself ready. I'd gone all out too with a new dress, makeup, haircut, and I'd even (rather optimistically as it turned out) put on some sexy underwear. It's slightly ironic because over the years I've acquired a fair amount of frilly, lacy underwear in a variety of colours, but the number of opportunities I get to wear them has dwindled. When Greg and I were young, when the need for such things was called for on a regular basis, I couldn't afford it, but now I have the money, the demand is gone. I'd even deliberately picked something particularly uncomfortable because it looked fabulous and the bra gave me quite a boob lift, although I soon regretted it as I sat in the restaurant with sequins wedged up my bottom. Greg did give me the once over when I appeared at the top of the stairs, eyeing me as though the only thing he wanted to do was cancel dinner and head to the bedroom. But once we'd had dinner and were sat in uncomfortable silence, having eaten our own body weight in carbohydrates, the idea of anything vaguely sexual happening was as likely as Greg and I starting an interesting conversation.

And so we ate, got the bill before dessert because we were too full, and headed home. We both said it was nice, had a cup of tea, got into our pyjamas, watched television, and before we'd even gotten into bed, it was like the whole thing never happened. The spark of adrenalin I felt as I'd put on my underwear for the date, imagining Greg tearing them off later in a fit of uncontrollable desire, was gone, and all that was left was a feeling that life, that Greg and I, were as sad and sorry as it was possible to be.

Today is Joan's eightieth birthday. We bought her a present and a small cake, but I don't think she cares to be honest. I wished her a happy birthday when she came in, but she just looked at me and said, "Is it?" I don't know if she was asking me a rhetorical question, or whether she was asking me because she didn't know if it was her birthday or not.

I understand. I imagine it's probably one-part wondrous achievement she's reached eighty, which is an impressive milestone, but probably two parts, 'bugger I'm eighty', which means she's bored, old, her husband's dead, and she's ready to join him. Eighty is great if you're still healthy and still living at home with the love of your life, but it's probably a bit shit if one or both of these isn't true. It's definitely a good thing we decided to go with one candle on her cake. Greg wanted to go with eighty, but that might have pushed her over the edge/started a fire and the last thing you want on a birthday is for the birthday girl to puff herself to death.

I'm actually less concerned about Joan's birthday and more concerned with Holly. She's been in her bedroom all morning and she didn't go to church today. Greg is hoping she's finally come to her senses and in his words, "realised it's all a fictitious sham. An institutionalised delusional cop out". Typically Greg's greater concern is the moral high ground, while all I'm worried about is whether my little girl is all right.

Holly's a complicated girl and there are times when I worry about her. I know she's eighteen and it's a horrid age, all hormones, trying to find out where you fit in, and what you're going to do with your life etc., but religion? I must say I was surprised. We've never taken her to church, and she's never had any inclination to go herself. I'm guessing it's got something to do with her friend Charlotte, who comes from quite a religious family. Maybe we've let our children down by not talking about it or taking them to church, but just because we don't believe, it doesn't mean they don't or can't.

I knock on her bedroom door and wait.

'Go away,' mumbles Holly after a moment.

'It's your mother,' I say hopefully. 'Can I come in?'

'If you must.'

I walk in and she's lying on her bed staring stoically up at the ceiling. She's still in her pyjamas and it looks like she's been crying. Her normally pale cheeks are puffy and red, and her eyes are bloodshot. It's easy to tell when Holly's been crying. She might be a good actress, but she can't fool me. I walk over and sit next to her on the bed. My first reaction is to take her in my arms and give her a hug, squeeze away all of the pain like I did when she was little, but she's eighteen now and I don't think that's going to cut it.

'You all right, love?'

'Yeah,' says Holly unconvincingly.

'No church today?'

'Didn't feel like it.'

'I thought you were really into it these days. Kumbaya and all that.'

'I think that's the scouts, actually, Mum.'

'Oh yes, so it is,' I say with a tense giggle.

'It isn't church anyway.'

'Then what is it? It's nothing to do with your father, is it? Because if it is, you shouldn't give two hoots what he thinks. Your father is a typical middle class, fuddy-duddy. He loves you and wants what's best for you, but when it comes to religion—'

'I don't want to talk about it,' says Holly, before she rolls away.

I always thought I'd be a great mum, and I don't mean that in a conceited way, but whenever I put my mind to something I put my whole self into it. It's the only way I know and so when I became a mum, I did the same. I never got on with my own mother, who was cold and distant, so all I wanted was a close relationship with my own children. I've always tried to talk to them like they're my equal. I never judged them or hopefully made them feel afraid to talk to me, and yet now they're all grown up, I'm not as close to them as I thought I would be and especially not with Holly. She's the youngest and I want to help her and be the person she can go to for advice. I just don't know if she needs me for that. There are moments when I feel like she does and is reaching out for my help, but at other times I feel as though she needs me less than Matt or Lucy ever has. Sometimes it feels like I'm becoming the annoying, clingy ex-girlfriend who won't admit the relationship is over.

I reach out a hand and place it lightly on her shoulder, feeling the soft tickle of her hair on my skin.

'You know, whatever it is, maybe I can help.'

'I doubt it,' says Holly dismissively.

I think about walking away, but I want to help her. I need to help her. She'll be off to university soon and the chance will be gone.

'Try me, you might be surprised.'

Holly turns on the bed and looks at me, her big, blue eyes sullen and ever so sad. My little girl. All grown up and yet somehow not at all.

'Do you really want to hear about it, even though there's nothing you can do to help?'

'Of course, love, even if that's the case, which it probably isn't.'

'Which it definitely is because you can't help me. No one can.'

'It sounds serious,' I say, getting worried. What could possibly be so awful that she's beyond help? All the worries and irrational thoughts of a parent flash through my mind. She's in trouble with the police. She's pregnant - God, please don't let it be this. I have similar thoughts whenever she's five minutes late coming home from the pub. She's been kidnapped, hit by a car, or sold into a prostitution ring- all thoughts I have on a weekly basis. It's the curse of being a parent. When they're young you worry about all the things you can control and when they grow up it's all the things you can't.

'It's the most serious thing in the world, Mum,' says

Holly, looking at me on the verge of tears. 'I'm in love.'

I'm in shock. Holly's never had boyfriend issues because she's never had a boyfriend. Lucy had a boyfriend at sixteen, who lasted for three years before he was dumped for another long-term boyfriend, and Matt's had a few short-term girlfriends, a couple of flings, and then there was Lindsey. Holly's always been so into her acting and moral crusades that she's never had time for boys. I've always been quite relieved about it to be honest. It's much easier dealing with Holly's beliefs than having to cope with her feelings because they kept her young. Now I have to accept that she's growing up. That she isn't my little girl anymore.

'Oh, Jesus, Holly, that's all,' I gush happily.

'What do you mean, "That's all"? Its love, Mum, the most painful thing in the world. How can you be so blasé about it?'

'I'm sorry, love. It's just that when you said I couldn't help and you seemed so sad, I thought it was something really awful.'

'Something more awful than being in love with someone you can never be with?'

'Obviously, that's terrible too,' I say, trying to stop Holly from rolling over again and thinking I have no idea what I'm talking about. Of course I know what it's like. I've had my heart broken too. 'I'm sorry. I didn't mean to make light of it, and I do know how you feel.'

'I doubt that very much,' says Holly obstinately.

'And why do you doubt it? Do you think your generation invented love?'

'No, but you're with Dad. You got your happy ending.'

'I had a life before your father, you know. I've had my heart broken.'

'Really?' says Holly incredulously, as though the idea of me before Greg seems utterly implausible. I understand because sometimes I feel the same. It's hard to imagine myself when I was still single, still just me, searching for the life I would eventually have.

I was sixteen when I met Daniel. He was the most gorgeous boy I'd ever seen and when we met, it was like something exploded inside of me. I'd never felt anything like it. He had long dark hair, sizzling blue eyes, was tall, and seemed so exotic and adventurous. I'd grown up in Leicester, probably the most central town in England. Literally in the middle of everything. I'd never gone anywhere exciting or met anyone remotely interesting. Daniel had travelled. He'd been to South America, which to me might as well have been the moon. He was worldly, spoke several languages, had a taste for strong alcohol, and always had a French cigarette hanging from his lips. He had a languid way of standing, as though his life was a continual photo shoot, and from the moment I saw him, I knew I wanted to be a part of it.

We met at a party, me trying to pretend I wasn't sixteen, and him casually sitting in a corner looking about as moody and deep in thought as a person can. After the first night we kissed and arranged to meet again the following day - for coffee, of course, and this was before everyone drank coffee. I'd never even had a cappuccino before, and it all seemed so glamorous. Within a week I was convinced I'd met the love of my life and so followed six heady summer weeks of traveling across England in his old Triumph Spitfire, camping on the beach. Sex, drugs and rock 'n' roll. It was probably a little more provincial than that, but it felt like my whole world had changed. Everything I knew and thought was different, and Daniel and I would be together forever. That was before he went off to university, a tearful goodbye, a whole list of reasons why we couldn't be together, and then weeks of me crying uncontrollably in my bedroom.

'I was a mess. It was pathetic and my mother didn't understand and probably like you, I thought I'd never get over it and no one could help me. I know love hurts, Holly, I do, but I also know the pain passes and we heal.'

'But this is different.'

'Why?'

'Because,' says Holly, trying to stop the tears from leaking out. 'Because it just is.' And then she lets go and the tears come streaming out. I grab her and hold her in my arms, and she lets me. I squeeze her body as tightly as I can, pushing her into my chest. I don't know what to think. Holly isn't usually like this. She isn't vulnerable. She's passionate and I've seen her cry on stage, but she doesn't sob like this. For some reason this makes me happy. I'm happy my daughter is crying into my chest. Holly's always been a closed book when it comes to me. She's always shared the big things, but never the little. She tells me about global warming and how to end third world poverty, but never anything about her own life.

'Oh, Holly,' I say, stroking her hair. 'You're so beautiful, clever, and wonderful. Whatever happens with this boy you're going to be all right.'

'You have to say that you're my mum,' says Holly from beneath me, sniffing up tears.

'But it's true,' I say, realising it doesn't matter how much I tell her what I think, she still won't believe me.

Holly is probably the best looking of all my children. Lucy is the most like me physically with her auburn hair, dark eyes, and fuller figure. Matt is just like his dad; tall, skinny, unruly brown hair, and lovely blue eyes, while Holly is slim, blonde, with the same piercing blue eyes. She's gorgeous and I know in a few years once she grows into her body, she's going to love how she is. At the moment, she's more worried she doesn't have breasts (as if that's the be-all-and-end-all of being attractive). I think it comes down to her friend Charlotte, who quite frankly has an enormous pair of tits. Unfortunately, teenage boys rarely see beyond them - it's hard because they are bloody gigantic. If only I could make her understand that in the long run she's far better off and in a few years, her slender figure and beautiful face will bring its own rewards.

'I know I'm just your mum, but you need to tell this boy

how you feel. Maybe don't start with "I love you", you don't want to terrify him, but why don't you ask him out at least?'

'Because I can't.'

'Why not?'

Holly looks at me with an expression that says something like, "Mum, are you like properly mental?"

'Because you can't just go up to someone and ask them out.'

'Well then,' I say, trying to sound authoritative and knowing. 'We'll just have to get them to ask you out.'

'And how are we going to get them to do that?' says Holly, who seems to have come to the conclusion that yes, I am properly mental.

This is the one giant flaw in my otherwise brilliant plan. I have no idea how to get them to ask her out. I have to try though. I have to be the parent who she knows will always be there for her, who will never give in, and who she can talk to about anything.

'I don't know, love, but we'll think of something,' I say with very little conviction.

'And in the meantime?'

'In the meantime, you have me,' I say with a comforting smile, but she doesn't look very comforted. She just looks young, heartbroken, and lost.

Matt

I've never had much of a clue what I want to do with my life. The question, "So Matt, what do you want to be when you grow up?" always stumped me, so I always gave the same comedic answer: "bigger". A degree in photography is only useful if you want to teach it or you plan on being a photographer, and although I do want to be a photographer, it isn't as if there are actual jobs. You can hardly walk into the job centre and ask about openings in the photography field, and if you do all you get back is a blank stare from someone called Tracey who says, "Have you tried Snappy Snaps?" I haven't quite figured out what sort of photographer I want to be yet and so (in Dad's eyes at least) I'm wasting my time. But that's Dad. When I graduated from university, instead of congratulating me, he looked at me with that special kind of disapproval he's always kept just for me and said, "So what now?"

I always planned on living back at home post university. Mainly because I didn't have any other choice. I met my now ex-girlfriend Lindsey at university and we both grew up in the same part of north London, so it seemed logical. We'd spend a year or two at home with our respective parents, we'd get jobs, save up as much money as we could, and then we'd go traveling. I was going to take my camera around the world and capture our year and Lindsey said she wanted to become a born-again hippy. She was happy and I was happy. Everyone was happy. I didn't tell Mum or Dad about it for different reasons. Mum because she'd start crying immediately, "My little boy gone for a whole year". And Dad because he'd no doubt think I was wasting yet more time, "poncing about the world," when I should be doing something productive. He wouldn't understand and Mum would be inconsolable, so I didn't mention it.

Then (while I was wrapped up being in love and planning the trip of a lifetime) Lindsey's friend, Jo, showed up and I was soon dumped for the flimsiest of reasons (Just not feeling it. I'm not sure we want the same things anymore. We've grown apart. Blah blah blah), and before long all the plans Lindsey and I had made, were theirs. They left from Heathrow airport (presumably in a whirl of evil plan laughter) while I was left alone to cry pathetically into my own pity bucket. The question about what I wanted to be when I grew up suddenly became even more difficult to answer and even the funny answer didn't seem funny anymore.

My life plummeted from promising to pointless very quickly and I spent the last year wallowing in despair. But then everything changed. Last week I was walking along Muswell Hill High Street when I saw a sign in the window of Olive's Cafe. They wanted an Assistant Manager. Olive's Cafe is one of those uber trendy places that looks like a vintage living room. It's all stripped wood floorboards, reclaimed or upcycled furniture (I'm never sure which is which), and bunting as far as the eye can see. I noticed the sign and was about to keep walking when something stopped me. It was Dad, not literally, but I heard his voice calling me useless, lazy, and bone-bloody-idle, and I realised I needed this.

I wasn't really dressed for an interview. I had on an old pair of faded blue jeans, a creased green shirt, my leather jacket with the fur collar, and an old pair of blue desert boots. At least I'd put on a splash of aftershave. I didn't really look the part, but I was ready to move on. What's the saying? Every journey starts with a single step. This was my first step.

I wasn't expecting what happened next to happen. I was going to go in, head held high, most impressive interview voice on, ready to talk my way into a job I had no prior experience of, but as soon as I walked in, the only thing I saw was The Girl. She was the most gorgeous thing I'd ever laid my eyes upon. She had long, tousled blonde hair, beautiful big brown eyes, and she was wearing a really nice blue flowery dress that led down to perfect, wobbly knees, and then slim legs that finally gave way to some flat black shoes. My sudden confidence that I was going to get this job and that it was going to be the tipping point in my otherwise unsuccessful life, quickly melted into a boyish crush. My heart fluttered with excitement and adrenalin.

'Hi,' she said in a bright American accent. 'Can I help you?'

She was probably mid-twenties and up close she was even more beautiful. Long eyelashes, just the right amount of makeup to suggest she was girly (but it wasn't the most important thing about her), a pair of antique looking earrings, and a small tattoo on her wrist that said 'love' in a flowery, lyrical font.

'I-I-I-I,' I started, which obviously wasn't the best first impression. My tongue felt like a giant sponge, sucking up all the moisture and making it impossible to talk without it sounding like I'd been gagged. 'Job,' I eventually said, pointing at the sign in the window.

'You're here about the Assistant Manager's job?'

'Yes,' I smiled inanely. Crazy with a huge tongue sponge wasn't the impression I was going for, but whether she felt sorry for me or not, she didn't turn me away.

'Come through. I'm Saskia, the Manager.'

I shook her hand and immediately felt the spark. The magic. We walked through to the back of the cafe and sat down at a small table. I'd never really been all the way inside the cafe before and up close it was even more pretentious and upmarket than I'd thought. It definitely put the V in vintage, although having a quick look at the menu behind the counter (handwritten on an upcycled (?) blackboard) the prices were definitely very modern. Every chair in the place was different and hand painted in a variety of colours, the wooden tables looked like (and probably were) old school tables, and the walls were adorned with a plethora of pictures and artwork. There was even an old wooden wardrobe against the wall, presumably to add to the overall effect, either that or Narnia was just a few feet away.

'Do you want a coffee?' said Saskia.

'Oh, no, I'm fine, thank you,' I said, finally regaining some composure, the sponge in my mouth shrinking slightly and some moisture returning. 'And it's Matt. Matt Wilde and I'm sorry about before. I was nervous.'

'No need to be nervous,' said Saskia. 'It's just you and me.'

'Yes, I suppose it is,' I said, looking deep into her eyes and knowing she probably didn't mean it the way I wanted her to. Just YOU and ME.

Saskia went on to explain about the job. Despite having zero experience in the cafe world, it didn't seem too difficult. Basically I'd be Saskia's number two and we'd be working closely together. I liked the idea of being her second in command. I started drifting off while she was talking in her lovely American voice and imagining us together. We'd join forces and take the cafe to the next level. We'd be the toast of Muswell Hill, one of Time Out's best places to eat in London, and in time, and inevitably working so closely together, we'd be unable to resist each other and would become more than just Manager and Assistant.

Eventually, Saskia stopped talking and all my dreams and thoughts were put on ice because it was my turn. I suddenly had the feeling that amongst all the trendy furniture and artwork, I was the elephant in the room.

'So, Matt, what experience do you have of running a cafe?'

Time to come clean. For a brief moment, I thought about lying or telling her about my ill-fated two months in charge of the school tuck shop, but I couldn't do it. She deserved the truth. Also the school tuck shop incident is still something of a family embarrassment.

'Truthfully, none, zero experience, actually.'

'Oh,' said Saskia, her face dropping in a sort of confused

disappointment. I could see the opportunity slipping from my fingers. All the dreams of us working side-by-side, becoming partners and then lovers, began to vanish as quickly as it had come to me. 'You do realise it's a managerial role and experience is sort of vital?'

'Saskia, the truth is, I need this for so many reasons. Since I graduated from university I've been living at home with my parents and my dad's driving me bonkers. He thinks I'm lazy and bone idle, but I'm not. I'm a hard worker, quick to learn, and I want this, probably more than anyone else that's going to come through those doors. I know all of them will have more experience than me, but I'm smart, creative, and really good with people and if you give me a shot, you won't regret it. I promise,' I said without taking a breath.

Saskia looked at me for a moment and then she smiled.

'Trust me, I know what it's like trying to prove something to your parents, but look Matt, I need someone I can rely on. It's not rocket science, but the hours are long and it's hard work.'

'Saskia, I promise if you give me a chance, I'll work harder than anyone you've ever seen. I'll be the first in and last to leave. I'll work through lunch. I won't let you down. I'd never let you down.'

I was getting a bit carried away, but I really wanted this, and I was hoping it would come across as passionate and not creepy.

'Okay, Matt, I get it, you really want the job,' said Saskia with a lovely smile. 'Let me ask you this. It's on the form so I sort of have to. What would you say is your biggest strength?'

'Probably my abs. I've been working really hard on my core recently.'

'I meant at work,' said Saskia with a smile and suddenly I was blushing like a fool.

'Yes, right, of course, me too. You said the hours are long and it's hard work so good core strength is vital,' I said.

'I'm also a great team player and super organised.'

'Good save,' she said with a smile. 'And what about your weaknesses? And please don't say you care too much and work too hard. I've already had two of those today and honestly, it's just annoying.'

Weaknesses? The truth is I have many weaknesses. Despite my desire to do something amazing with my life, I'm often clouded with fear and self-doubt. I give up on things too easily. I'm messy. I fall in love too quickly. I spend far too much time talking and thinking about things rather than doing them. Despite getting my degree in photography more than a year ago, I haven't done anything since to turn it into a career. I swear too much when I'm drunk, I eat far too many Pot Noodles (unless five a week is part of an approved diet I'm not aware of) and I've been known to wear the same pair of socks for three or four days too long. Of course, Saskia doesn't need to know any of this or that I think she's the most beautiful girl I've ever seen. All she needs to know is why she shouldn't hire me for a job I have no business interviewing for in the first place.

'My main weakness would be that I haven't ever worked in a cafe, but then again that might be my biggest strength.'

'And how might that be a strength?' said Saskia, holding her pen and form and looking across at me expectantly.

'I'm a clean slate, Saskia. I'm not going to come in and have different opinions and ideas about how to run a cafe. I'm fresh, new, and …' I run out of adjectives.

'Sparkly?'

'Exactly,' I said, and we both laughed. 'You can mould me.'

'Noted,' said Saskia with what seemed like a definitely coquettish grin.

The rest of the interview was straightforward, and she asked me a few more obligatory questions. We had a nice, casual chat at the end, and she told me she'd definitely call me on Sunday, and I left clutching onto a small nugget of hope that my life was about to change. I've been on cloud nine since the interview, but my main fear is if I don't get it, I'm going to be heartbroken again. My life feels like it's been stuck in a holding pattern since Lindsey left me and I've been waiting for clearance to start living again. This feels like it's my moment, but then again, maybe it's just me getting ahead of myself because that's one of the biggest weaknesses Saskia definitely doesn't need to know about me. Fingers crossed.

I'm in my old bedroom, still decorated circa before I left for university, and so it feels like I'm a teenager whenever I'm here. I'm waiting nervously for Saskia to call about the job. I know this is what I need. It's time I grew up a bit. Despite Dad's obvious failings as a human being, I know he just wants me to be happy, and he's right about me getting a job. Maybe I've been too pig headed or lazy, or maybe I was afraid of more failure after Lindsey, I don't know, but sitting on my bed, I know I want this job more than anything I've wanted in my entire life.

Eventually my phone rings and when I look down I see Saskia's name staring back at me. This is it. Maybe the tipping point in my otherwise unsuccessful life.

'Hello?'

'Hello, it's Saskia, the Manager from Olive's. Is this Matt?'

'Yes, hello, hi, guten tag' I say, sitting down on my bed. 'Sorry I don't know why I said that. I'm not German and neither are you.'

'It's fine, Matt, no worries. How are you?'

'Yes, brilliant, thanks,' I say, my heart racing with tortured anxiety. 'Nervous now, obviously, so I apologise if I start blabbing because I tend to blab when I'm anxious. I'm a blabberer. Hence the German.'

'Then I'd better cut to the chase before you start blabbing in Swahili or something,' says Saskia. 'So, as you know, we had a few more interviews after you.'

'Right.'

'And you didn't really have the experience we were looking for.'

'Oh,' I say, my heart sinking. It's obvious I haven't got the job.

'And we had people with years of managerial experience, Matt.'

'I understand, I didn't get the job. It's okay, Saskia, thank you.'

'But,' says Saskia, and suddenly I'm alive again. I'm the contestant on the X Factor who thinks their time is done, but it's not. It's bloody not. 'I gave you the job anyway.'

'What?! No! Seriously? Shut the fuck up! Oh, fuck, sorry, I didn't mean to tell you to shut the fuck up. Obviously I wouldn't say that to my new boss because that would be fucking, and fuck I keep saying fuck.'

'Matt?'

'Yes.'

'It's fine, although you should probably stop saying fuck.'

'Right.'

'Can you come in tomorrow morning at say ten o'clock?'

'Yes, yes, I can't wait. I can come earlier if you want?'

'Normally I'd say yes. I'm usually in at seven, but I have this thing with my boyfriend in the morning,' she says, leaving the word hanging in the air. B.O.Y.F.R.I.E.N.D.

She has a boyfriend. Of course she does. She's beautiful, and smart, and funny, why wouldn't she have a boyfriend? My momentary excitement at getting the job is suddenly shattered because I feel like an idiot. I had all of these ideas about Saskia. I thought we had something, but it was all in my head. I can't help but think about Lindsey. People told me it wasn't going to work, that I was a lot more into her than she was into me, but I didn't believe them. For a beautiful moment when she told me I had the job, everything seemed to be clicking into place. For a second, the daydreams I had about Saskia, and I were coming true and the nightmare that was Lindsey was fading into my past.

'Matt? Are you still there? Matt?'

'Yes, yes, sorry, still here. I'm just in shock.'

'See you tomorrow at ten?'

'Yes, definitely, with bells on,' I say, as light-hearted as I can, while the dull ache in my heart sits like a heavy weight.

'And Matt, I'm taking a big risk on you, so please don't let me down.'

'You have my word,' I say, and then Saskia is gone, and I flop back on the bed and look up at the ceiling at the Cheryl Cole poster I put up when I was sixteen. As I'm staring up at Cheryl, I can't help but feel a sense of sadness because for a moment I had this feeling of happiness, of that tipping point finally going in my favour. At least I have a job though. It's a start and who knows where it might lead. This morning I was just Matt Wilde, the person who had the school tuck shop closed down over claims of pocket money laundering, and this afternoon I'm Matt Wilde, Assistant Manager at Olive's Cafe. Every journey.

'Matt, we're going to blow out the candle on Mum's cake,' Dad shouts up the stairs.

'Coming,' I say, taking a deep breath, before I get up and start the walk downstairs, finding myself smiling because for the first time in a long time I have a reason to be hopeful.

Christmas Roast

Jon Rance

Lucy

Why hasn't he rung yet? He said he'd call in the morning and it's now one o'clock, which definitely isn't morning. The worst part though, and the bit that's driving me to drink, is how much it's consuming me. I can't stop thinking about him. It's pathetic. Don't get involved with people at work. Everyone says so and I'm starting to think they're right. But it doesn't matter, does it? I already love him. Like I said, it's pathetic. Utterly, completely, and appallingly pathetic.

You see the thing is it's Christmas. Probably like most children, it was my favourite day of the year growing up. The decorations, the feeling in the air that something magical and altogether ethereal was possible. The promise of presents, delicious food served up around a raucous dinner table while Christmas songs played on the radio. And yet, this year all I can think about is him. The man who's at home sharing all of those wonderful moments with his own family. His own wife. His own children. Never fall in love with a married man. It's the simplest thing to know and yet, actually, the most difficult thing not to do once you start.

I saw him last night. A fleeting moment, stolen kisses around the back of a pub in Covent Garden. Promises that things will change, that it won't always be like this, as we stood in a dank alley trying to avoid the passing drunks. Despite what he says, I know he'll never leave his wife and deep down I don't want him to. I can't stand the thought of his children lying in their tiny beds in their little kid pyjamas, crying their eyes out because their daddy isn't there to tuck them in at night. I couldn't do that to them. I'm not the sort of girl to break up a family. I despise those people. How could they? How could anyone break a child's heart, and for what? Because they can't keep their knickers on? I can't be that girl. And yet I am. And I hate myself for it.

'Games!' says Mum suddenly, clapping her hands excitedly during a lull in conversation. 'We should play a game.'

'Do we have to?' says Matt.

Dads in the kitchen cooking Christmas dinner. He and Mum are arguing again. I wish they'd stop. It's Christmas and maybe it's because of what's happening with me, but I need them to be happy. They're my parents and if they can't make it, if they can't be truly happy, I don't hold out much hope for myself. My future lies in their hands, and they don't even realise. Dad seems more concerned with the moistness of the turkey and Mum's getting non-festively drunk. The something magical and ethereal is slowly disappearing along with my hopes that Richard's going to ring. God, that's so terribly sad, isn't it? Despite everything I've said, despite the horrific and irretrievable damage it might cause, I still want him to call.

'It will be fun. Just like the old days,' says Mum, with a wistful/pissed look on her face. 'How about Charades? I love a good game of Charades at Christmas.'

'It's the only time we play Charades,' says Matt. 'And eat nuts. Seriously it's like no nuts all year and then Christmas comes around and suddenly a giant bowl of nuts appears as though we've all really been missing nuts.'

'Come on party poopers,' says Mum over-enthusiastically. 'You kids today, no sense of adventure.'

'It's Charades, Mum, not base jumping,' says Matt dryly.

'I'll play,' I say, looking down at my phone, at the same screen I've been seeing all morning. No Calls. No messages. No Richard. I need something to take my mind off it. 'We should get Holly too.'

'I'll go and get her. Matt, you're on alcohol duty. Lucy, you're in charge of pens and paper,' says Mum, and she jumps up and heads off upstairs to get Holly. Matt walks off to get more alcohol leaving me alone with Gran.

I feel awful for Gran. She and Grandad were proper soul mates. You could tell being around them how much they loved each other. If ever two people were meant to be together, it was them. I used to love watching them. The expressions on their faces when they looked at each other, or when one of them walked into a room and you saw their whole being change because that's how strong their love was. It could melt your heart. Now her face is blank. She's staring at the TV and I'm not even sure she's watching it. Grandad could always light her up, but without him it's like the lights have gone out and I'm not sure they'll ever come on again.

'You all right, Gran?' I say.

She slowly turns and looks at me and smiles a thin, gaunt smile.

'Yes, love. I was just thinking about Paul.'

'Do you mean Grandad?'

'I think I know who I mean. Paul.'

'Who's Paul?'

'Oh, you know, the nice looking one. Lovely voice. My old friend Jenny Dunn, dead now, of course,' she says without a hint of sorrow. 'She preferred the other one.'

'The other who, Gran?'

Gran looks at me as though I'm the senile one.

'You kids today. The Beatles.'

'Oh, right, now I'm with you. So you preferred Paul McCartney?'

'There was just something about him, wasn't there? A sweetness.'

'Yes, I suppose.'

'You know,' says Gran, a wistful smile on her face, 'your Grandad and I each had one person we said, it was silly really, but we said the other one could have dinner with. Sort of like a date, I suppose. Just one person each and only once. Someone famous. Paul was mine.'

'Oh, Gran,' I say, and Gran chuckles quietly to herself. 'And who did Grandad have? Who was his one night off?'

'I can't remember now. Someone American, I think.'

Gran smiles and looks off towards the TV and I can't

help but think about Richard and me. What we have is nothing compared to them. What they had was so pure, and lovely, and perfect, but what I have with Richard is just dirty sex in Premier Inns, stolen moments, and empty promises. We're the one night off Gran joked about with Grandad, but what I really want, what I crave more than anything is to have all the other nights. The nights that matter.

'Right, Matt, you have three minutes,' I say. 'Holly, start the clock. Go!'

It's me and Holly against Matt and Mum. Matt's standing in the middle of the living room doing the signal for a film. Holly and I should win this easily. For an intelligent, middle-aged woman, Mum is ridiculously awful at Charades and Matt isn't a lot better. The rule for Charades in the Wilde household is never end up with Mum.

My mind isn't on Charades though because all I can think about is Richard. I started working with him six months ago. He's in his forties, is married with two young children, and is a genius Script Editor. From the moment he walked into the room I had a silly crush on him, but I didn't think for a moment that anything would happen. It didn't happen overnight, but gradually, like a feeling you can't quite put your finger on, then you wake up one day and realise what it is. Even at the beginning it took a while to take hold, but soon he was all I could think about. My days seemed taken over by him and he said he felt the same. Despite the age difference, the pull of attraction was too strong. We couldn't help ourselves and suddenly work wasn't about work anymore but about him. From my choice of outfit in the morning, to what I was doing for lunch, what time I got home at night, all of it was about Richard. He consumed me and still does.

'It's a film. One word,' says Mum, as Matt holds up one finger and then does the pinchy fingers together thing. 'A short word.'

We all look at Matt, who stands for a moment looking a bit confused. He finally decides to go for the 'sounds like' gesture.

'Sounds like?' says Mum, on the edge of her seat. Matt still stands there. 'Sounds like?' says Mum again. Matt shakes his head. 'Oh, come on, Matt, do something.'

'Two minutes,' says Holly.

'Just do something,' says Mum.

Matt starts jumping around and acting like a lunatic.

'Idiot?' says Mum, and Matt shakes his head. 'Crazy? Umm, bird of paradise?'

We all stop and look at Mum.

'I saw a documentary about them last week. They do this incredible mating dance—'

'The clock's still ticking,' I say.

Matt's still jumping around and making the funniest faces.

'French person?!' shouts Mum and Matt just stares at her.

'One minute,' says Holly.

Matt continues jumping around like a maniac.

'Monster?' says Mum, and Matt finally nods and gestures for her to keep guessing. 'Monsters Ball?' Matt shakes his head and does the one word again. 'One word, oh, right.' Matt seems to have a small epiphany, does the 'sounds like' gesture again and then points to his neck. 'Gun?' squeals Mum. 'Gun monster?!'

'Forty-five seconds,' says Holly.

Matt does the 'sounds like' symbol again and then points to his neck again.

'Oh, you mean it sounds like neck?' says Mum and Matt nods. 'Fleck!' says Mum and Matt shakes his head. 'So it's a monster film that sounds like neck.'

'Thirty seconds,' says Holly.

'I don't know,' says Mum. 'Neck? Neck? Something that sounds like neck, and it's not fleck. Is it cheque? Monster Cheque?' Exasperated, Matt does the one-word symbol again. 'Oh, yes, only one word.'

'Ten seconds,' says Holly.

Matt is standing with his hands on his hips now and looking quite frustrated.

'Umm, Czech? Blech? Yeck?'

'Five seconds,' says Holly.

'Schmeck!' shouts Mum, jumping up from the sofa, caught on a tidal wave of her own deluded triumph.

'Time,' says Holly finally.

'Schmeck?' says Matt. 'I don't think I've seen that one, Mum. Was it straight to DVD?'

'I don't know,' says Mum laughing. 'What was it?'

'Shrek,' says Gran from across the room.

'Next time Gran's on my team,' says Matt, and we all laugh. Then my phone starts ringing.

I pick it up, my heart racing, my face suddenly flush, and every ounce of my soul hoping its Richard. I need to hear his voice. I look down at my phone and see his name staring back at me and a smile immediately breaks out on my face. I answer and then rush out of the living room and upstairs to my old bedroom. I fall onto my bed, feeling sixteen again.

'Merry Christmas.'

'I can't talk long,' says Richard. 'I managed to sneak away for a few minutes.'

'Right,' I say, my heart falling a thousand feet. I imagine him at home telling his wife the lie that he needs to pop out for a moment, and it makes me feel sick. 'I miss you.'

'You too. I wish I could see you.'

'I know, it's just horrible.'

'Love you.'

'Love you back,' I say, knowing and thinking as I'm saying it, just how ridiculous it is. And this is the problem. I know it's ridiculous. He probably knows it's ridiculous, and yet we're trapped in this spiral of need. We think we need each other. Whether we do or not seems irrelevant to the fact that we think we do. It's an addiction neither of us is willing to admit to.

'What are your lot doing?' says Richard.

'We're playing Charades.'

'It's a bit early in the day for Charades, isn't it? We're usually a lot drunker before we tackle the dangerous world of Charades, especially with Wendy, she …' Richard suddenly stops at the mention of his wife. It's one of the rules of having an affair. You can't mention the wife. It's a bit like Fight Club. The first rule of the affair: You do not talk about the affair. The second rule of the affair: You never mention the wife. There's an awkward silence and neither of us seems sure what to say next.

'I love the necklace,' I eventually say.

'Oh, good, that's good. I hoped you would.'

Another tense silence.

'Do you have to get back?' I say because I don't know what else to say. I've been waiting to talk to him all morning, but now we are it's just awkward. I suppose this sums up our relationship perfectly; the outcome never matching the expectations.

'Yes, probably should, you know.'

'Right,' I say, feeling the unwanted attention of a few tears beginning to struggle up behind my eyes.

'Merry Christmas, Lucy.'

'Merry Christmas, Richard.'

'See you in a few days. Maybe we could do a night away before new year.'

'That would be nice.'

'It would,' says Richard, his voice suddenly a little hoarse. 'I'd better.'

'I have to get back to Charades anyway.'

'Oh, right, have fun.'

'Will do.'

'Bye then.'

'Bye then.'

'Love you.'

'Love you.'

And then he's gone and I'm all alone in my old bedroom.

I don't feel sixteen anymore. I feel old and tired. I feel like life just got far too complicated and far too much like hard work, and all I want to do is get under the duvet and stay there.

You imagine the sort of women who cheat with married men. Desperate, sad, lonely women who can only find happiness where there's also sadness. They must have had some sort of trauma growing up, or come from a broken family because otherwise why would they do it? Why sleep with a married man when there are so many perfectly good single men available? You probably think she's pathetic or trying to get a promotion at work. All of these clichés have run through my mind since Richard and I started sleeping together. I'd become a cliché, but the thing is that none of the clichés are true for me. I come from a brilliant, strong family. My life's been nothing but perfect. I've had great boyfriends, I'm not lonely, sad, or pathetic, and I'm definitely not using Richard to get ahead at work. I'm none of the things on the list, so why do I do it? The truth is I don't know.

I wipe the tears from my cheeks, get up, walk out of my room and straight into Matt.

'Just going for a wee,' says Matt, and then he sees my face. 'You all right, Sis?'

'Fine,' I say with a pretend smile.

'You've been crying. Who was on the phone?'

'No one, it's nothing.'

'Lucy, listen,' says Matt, and he's holding my arm. 'I know I'm just your stupid little brother, but if there's a problem, if you need anything, you know you can always talk to me.'

'I'm fine. Honestly. Just being silly.'

Matt gives me a supportive smile, which makes me feel about a million times worse, before he skulks off towards the toilet. Downstairs I hear the sound of Christmas music and the smell of dinner filling the air with warmth. I stand for a moment trying to compose myself, trying to wedge all the Richard shaped thoughts into the smallest compartments at the very back of my mind where they'll be safe and far away, and where they can't ruin the most wonderful, magical day of the year.

Greg

'What's going on?' says Lucy.

She's standing next to me in the kitchen with her accusatory face on, which is really clashing with her festive tinsel necklace. I'm cooking and listening to some Christmas songs on the radio. The kitchen is full of vegetables waiting to be sliced and cooked. The organic, free-range turkey is already in the oven, seasoned, basted, and smelling fantastic. The homemade stuffing is in the fridge, the roast potatoes are parboiled, and I'm in my own little world.

'With what, darling?'

'With you and Mum, obviously,' says Lucy, taking a sip of wine. 'It's Christmas and you aren't talking.'

'Nothing's going on. We're fine. I'm just busy with dinner.'

'I'm not stupid.'

'How much have you drunk today?'

'It's Christmas Day, Dad, the one day of the year when you're allowed to drink as much as you want.'

'Maybe you should slow down a little.'

'I didn't come in here to talk about my alcohol consumption. I came to talk about—'

'About me and your mother, I know, and like I said, nothing's wrong.'

'Fine. If you won't tell me, Mum will,' she says, her face stiffening up. She obviously isn't going to let this go.

Lucy always knew how to play her mother and me against each other. Matt either doesn't have the natural curiosity or doesn't care enough to intervene. Holly is, well, Holly, but Lucy always takes it upon herself to get involved in our relationship. Maybe it's because she's the eldest and feels like it's her place. She's always been a classic first child.

The argument with Lizzy started last month, but I've

been at work, so it's been easy to put it to one side. Pop it away and pretend it isn't there. Now I'm off work and we're forced together, the same issues have been jamming and inserting themselves into every look and conversation, and so it isn't quite so easy to ignore. It all began when Lizzy brought up the idea of going away on holiday.

For the past few years, Lizzy's been talking about doing more adventurous things, taking more "us time", and "really living" in her words. I don't know what her version of "really living" is, but apparently what we're doing isn't it. She seems to have it in her head that I'm against holidays, which is absolute nonsense. I love a good break as much as the next man, but at the moment I'm so busy with the book and work that I can't just take a week off so we can gallivant off to Tunisia. And that's how this whole argument started. Because I used the word "gallivant", which is apparently the sort of word that really pisses Lizzy off. Who knew? Not me, obviously.

The thing is, the rumblings about a book tour finally became a bit more than just rumblings. It's definitely going to happen. I've been having preliminary meetings with the university about a full-scale tour. It might start off fairly small, but the possibilities are there for it to get a lot bigger. I tried to explain to Lizzy that this is my moment. I have to grab it with both hands. She said she understood and was happy for me, but she was worried her life and our marriage were being "put on hold" so I could achieve my dreams. I said we could go on holiday during the summer, but she said, "Tunisia wasn't just a holiday, Greg, but a chance for us to reconnect". After a few more minutes of going backwards and forwards about why we should or shouldn't go to Tunisia, it ended with Lizzy shouting that I was, "a dull, middle-aged workaholic, who cared more about making money than fixing his marriage!"

Maybe I'm being selfish, but a holiday isn't high on my list of priorities at the moment. Why can't we just go away during the summer like everybody else?

'We just had a bit of an argument, that's all, darling,' I say.

'That's all? Jesus, Dad, the atmosphere in the house is frostier than a trip to Iceland.'

'The country or the shop?' I say with a smile.

'It's not funny, Dad.'

'I know, I'm sorry, but it's fine, darling, really.'

'It's not fine, Dad, its Christmas,' says Lucy. 'The season of goodwill. The day when we're supposed to put aside our differences and get along. Christ, if the British and German soldiers during World War One could down arms and have a game of football between the trenches, then I'm sure you and Mum can do the same.'

'I don't think your mother fancies a kick about in the garden.'

'That's not what I meant, and you know it. Just fix it, Dad,' says Lucy, taking another swig of her wine. 'Please don't let things fall apart.'

Lucy turns away from me sharply, looking off into the distance. We stand for a moment, until I hear the unfamiliar sound of tears. Lucy, like me in so many ways, isn't one to show her emotions. She's good at keeping it all in, battening down the hatches, and stiffening the upper lip. I reach across and put my hand on her shoulder.

'What is it, darling?'

'You've been arguing a lot recently and I'm worried.'

'Don't be a silly sausage,' I say, using the expression I always did when she was a child, the familiarity of it catching me by surprise. 'Your mum and I are fine. It's nothing serious.'

'Promise?'

'Promise.'

Lucy smiles sweetly, before she gives me a hug and then walks out leaving me with 'We Three Kings' on the radio.

One of the last things Dad said before I lost him was, "live each day in a happy way and never take anything for granted". I always remember that and for some reason when

I think about it, it makes me think about my family and especially my children. Being a father has never come easily to me. I'm so different from my own father who was easy going, light humoured, and prone to moments of reckless abandon. Growing up, I remember countless days when we'd be at home and Dad would say, "Right, let's go somewhere fun!" And we'd jump in the car, our faces brimming with excitement, and Dad would always, without fail, take us somewhere fun.

I often wonder what my own kids will remember of me when I'm gone. Not particularly my recklessness or humour, but instead my heavy handedness and lack of adventure perhaps? What Dad said stuck because I knew he was talking directly to me. I want a better relationship with my kids and especially so with Matt. We're fine, we banter, and I know that under the layers of repression, we love each other, but we've never really said it. We're too afraid to be honest and open with each other and I can't put my finger on why. Yes, we're English and we're men, and English men aren't supposed to be emotionally open with each other, but he's my son and if the truth be told, I don't know him awfully well and I want to know him. I should know him.

For the past year or so, after the business with his ex-girlfriend Lindsey, he's been wallowing in self-pity, and I was always the first one to have a go at him. I suppose in my mind I was trying to help, but I don't think he saw it that way. Now he's got a job and he's trying to do something with his life, and I want to tell him how proud I am of him. I want him to know that despite the bickering, and the constant arguing, I love him and all I want is for him to be happy. I want to say this, but I can't. The thing is, with Lizzy and I at each other's throats, Holly barely talking to me, and Lucy crying because she thinks the family's breaking up, when I think of Matt I realise how easy it would be to fix our relationship. Just a few kind words and maybe everything would be all right. I want to live each day in a happy way, and I don't want to take anything for granted.

Especially not my family.

I walk out of the kitchen and as I do, Lizzy is walking along the hallway towards me, empty wine glass held loosely in her hand, face of Himalayan annoyance at the ready. We both stop and look at each other like two Wild West gunslingers. Lucy's words suddenly rattle in my ears. "Don't let things fall apart".

'Lizzy, look,' I say, breaking the silence. 'We need to talk.'

'Do we?' says Lizzy. 'Don't you have some organic, hand reared giblets to tend to?'

'Please, love, I don't want to argue.'

I look at Lizzy and she looks at me. My wife. I want us to be happy again. I'm tired of the bickering, the arguing, and the tension. I suppose that's the thing that's most difficult to deal with. The tension. The simmering annoyance that's always there. Lying in bed at night next to my wife and knowing she's unhappy. That we're not okay. I look at her face and it's the same beautiful face I've always known. The same dark hair, the same eyes, the mouth I've kissed a million times, yet underneath something is different, and I can feel it.

'Maybe you should have thought of that before you laughed at going to Tunisia.'

'I didn't laugh.'

'Fine, you scoffed, same difference. Don't try and wriggle out of this with semantics.'

'Come in here,' I say, grabbing her by the arm and dragging her into the cupboard under the stairs. I close the door, lock it from the inside, and turn on the little light, which gives us both a strange ethereal glow.

'What the hell are you doing?' says Lizzy, her fruity, alcoholic breath stronger inside the confines of the cupboard.

'I said we need to talk and here's as good a place as any.'

'Under the stairs?'

'Yes, under the stairs.'

Being so close to her in the semi-darkness, it reminds me of a moment from a Christmas long ago. It was before we were married. Lizzy and I went to her Uncle Colin's house in Bath. We went for a family party on Christmas Eve, and we stayed the night. Lizzy's parents were there and a few other members of her family. It was the first time I'd met a lot of them. Uncle Colin was quite old fashioned, and we were warned beforehand that he wouldn't take any funny business. Despite Lizzy and I being together for over a year, we weren't married so that meant separate sleeping arrangements and no public displays of affection. We had to be 'just friends' at Uncle Colin's house.

The night was long and despite our very best efforts (and quite a few drinks), Lizzy and I were finding not touching each other impossible. We ended up eloping to Uncle Colin's shed. It was freezing cold and snowing outside, but we stood together in the darkness, a small amount of light from the house breaking through the window, and we kissed. I remember because it was so intimate and romantic. We were young and in love, but now, so many years later, standing together again, everything just seems so much more difficult.

'Lizzy, look, I'm sorry.'

'Do you even know what for?'

'For Tunisia, for whatever I've done that's made you angry. I don't want to argue. It's Christmas, can't we just put everything aside and get along?'

Lizzy looks at me through the darkness. In the background the Christmas songs are still playing in the kitchen, and I can hear the children in the living room.

'You don't think I want that too?' Lizzy says eventually. 'I don't want to be arguing either, but it isn't that easy, is it? Problems don't go away just because you want them to.'

'But we can try, can't we?'

'I don't know,' says Lizzy, and I can feel the tension between us, flickering like a flame, illuminating the both of us.

'Do you remember that Christmas when we went to your Uncle Colin's house?' I say after a moment, hoping the memory of us back then might awaken something in Lizzy. Maybe it will remind her of how things were between us then and how they can be again. As I look at her face, the hardness becomes a little bit softer and whether it's the alcohol, Christmas, or the cupboard, I don't know, but I feel like I have a chance to make this right.

'The year it snowed, and we took refuge in the shed?' she says.

'Because we weren't married, and Uncle Colin thought we were living in sin.'

'Which we weren't.'

'Which we weren't.'

'So we eloped to the shed,' says Lizzy, and through the miniscule amount of light, I can just make out a faint smile.

'And we had a good snog amongst the gardening equipment until Uncle Colin opened the door, hands on hips, demanding we stop, and I'm fairly sure he used the word, "fornicating" and he told us to get back inside.'

'I'm surprised you remember that,' says Lizzy.

'How could I forget?'

'Things were so much simpler back then, weren't they? Before we were married and had kids. Before you were a grumpy old fart.'

'Look, Lizzy, I'm really sorry about everything. I know it's not an excuse, but I've been so busy. But I promise that nothing is as important as our marriage. As us.'

Lizzy looks at me through the semi-darkness, and then below me I can I feel her hands searching for mine. She finds them and holds them in hers. We're so close I can feel her warm breath tickling my face.

'Kiss me,' she says.

'Sorry?'

'Just shut up and kiss me.'

I squeeze her hands and then I lean forward and kiss her. We haven't kissed each other properly for weeks. It's horrid how time can so easily consume itself, and before you know it weeks and sometimes months have gone by, and all the things you meant to do and meant to say haven't been done and nothing has changed. Yet things do change. The kiss is sweet, tinged with wine and it feels like it always has. Immediately I'm back in that shed, the snow coming down and Lizzy next to me. Eventually we part and stand looking at one another.

'This doesn't mean anything's different. Sometimes saying sorry isn't enough. You have to show me you mean it. I still need more adventure. Our marriage needs more excitement,' says Lizzy.

'And we shall have it.'

'Promise?'

'Promise.'

'Then let's have a very happy Christmas,' says Lizzy, and for the first time in a long time I don't feel the tension between us and instead all I feel is love.

The turkey is in the centre of the table like a golden, juicy mountain, surrounded by fields of potatoes, vegetables, and gravy. The Christmas crackers are laid out by each setting. The wine glasses are full, and the cutlery is shining like jewels set upon the special tablecloth that's been passed down through generations of Lizzy's family. We're all here and outside faint freckles of snow are beginning to fall on the ground. This is the moment I love most on Christmas Day. Sitting with my family, about to have a wonderful dinner. Together. Perfect.

'Before we start, I'd like to say something,' I say, looking out across the table at my family.

'Speech!' says Matt, clinking the side of his glass with his fork. 'Speech!'

'Thank you, Matt. I just want to say merry Christmas. I know it's been an up and down year, but we're still here together, around the table, eating a roast dinner, and that makes me very happy. So thank you and let's eat.'

'Before we start,' says Holly. 'I'd like to mention the person who's responsible for all of this. Without him, we wouldn't be here today.'

'Hols, there's no need,' I say, thinking she's referring to me.

'Jesus,' she says brusquely. 'Today's his birthday.'

'To the birthday boy!' says Matt with sarcastic triumph, raising his glass in the air.

'Matt don't be annoying,' says Lucy.

'I know that none of you believe in God, but maybe for me you could at least acknowledge it,' says Holly, lowering her head. I think she wants us to pray. 'Thank you, Lord,' says Holly.

I look around the table, Matt is trying to stifle a laugh, Lizzy is looking at me with a sort of 'just be quiet' face, Lucy is gently hitting Matt on the arm, and Mum is either praying or she's completely dozed off.

'Are you going to allow this nonsense?' says Matt to me.

'Matt, please,' says Lizzy.

'But it's ridiculous. It's Christmas, not some sort of religious ceremony,' says Matt.

'But that's exactly what Christmas is,' says Holly. 'You've probably all forgotten the real meaning of Christmas, among the rush for presents, and Dad's obsession with which celebrity chefs' meal to cook, and oh, what's going to happen on EastEnders. Yet the whole point of this day is to celebrate Jesus. Why can't you, for one moment, put aside your own feelings and do this for me?' Holly is almost shouting now, and her face is bright red and trembling with rage. I don't want to say it, but she looks like one of those crazed American ministers you see on television, peddling their ridiculous, fundamentalist views on the poor, uneducated masses.

When Holly was little, she wore the same expression on her face just before she blew her top. She's always been a very emotional person. Tears, laughter, and breakdowns were never far away. Her face now takes me back to when she was little. She's chewing the corner of her lip, her cheeks are red, her eyes are glistening, on the verge of tears, and she's rubbing her hands on her thighs. The only difference between then and now is that then, when I saw her on the verge, I could stop her by tickling her or throwing her over my shoulder and dumping her down on the sofa. The anger would subside and be taken over by laughter.

'Steady on, Hols,' I say after a moment.

'No I won't steady on,' says Holly. 'Why don't any of you take me seriously?'

'We do, love. Of course we do,' says Lizzy.

'No you don't. Dad dismisses everything I say as childish nonsense. Matt treats me like I'm a joke, and Mum, you never say anything. Keep quiet and let Crazy Holly spout her rubbish.'

'To be fair, Hols, today you're a Christian and next week you might be a Buddhist. It's hard to keep up with whatever new idea you're trying on for size,' I say, and for some reason this really sets her off.

'Oh and because I don't agree with you, I must be wrong, is that it?'

'No, it's because you flip flop between so many ideas, Holly, it's impossible to agree and listen to all of them with the same degree of enthusiasm, that's all,' I say.

'Excuse me for having a curious fucking brain!' screams Holly, and then she gets up, walks out of the room and stomps upstairs. After a moment, I hear her bedroom door slam shut. I look across at Lizzy and shrug my shoulders in disbelief. There's a momentary quietness across the table as none of us seem sure what to say.

'Something's got her knickers in a twist,' says Mum eventually.

'What just happened?' says Matt.

'I don't know,' I say.

'You could have been a bit more sensitive,' says Lizzy to me.

'So this is my fault now, is it? It's my fault Holly's a fundamentalist Christian?'

'Don't be so ridiculous, Greg. She's not a fundamentalist Christian, she's just in love.'

'In love?' says Lucy. 'With who?'

'I don't know, someone at church,' says Lizzy.

'At church, is that?' I start to say, but Lizzy's face gives it away. 'So that's why she's suddenly all religious, because of a boy?'

'Maybe. I don't know,' says Lizzy. 'But I do know she's confused and needs our support.'

'I should go and talk to her,' I say, getting up and putting my napkin down.

'Don't, Greg, please,' says Lizzy. 'Give her some time. Let her calm down.'

I sit back down at the table, and we start eating. The food, the decorations, the music are all perfect, but with Holly upstairs this isn't the Christmas I was hoping for. It's not perfect.

It's a few hours later and the girls are in the living room drunk and dancing badly to 'Merry Xmas Everyone', Mum is working her way through a chocolate orange, and dinner is all cleared away. I'm in the garage with Matt putting up the table tennis table. After all the work was done and it was time to sit down, I had a thought: Table tennis! It was something Dad and I used to do all the time growing up. If I couldn't tell Matt how I felt, how proud I was of him, then maybe this might be enough. It's Christmas and I need to do something with one of the kids that doesn't end up with them shouting at me or crying.

'It's a bit chilly out here,' says Matt, rubbing his arms with his hands to keep warm. 'Can we just go back indoors?'

'You'll be fine once we get started.'

'If you say so,' says Matt, as we finally get the table all set up and ready to play.

Dad and I played on this table when I was a kid. Dad would always let me win. From the age of five until eighteen, I always somehow managed to just beat him. Dad would go for ridiculous trick shots, when he could have beaten me with simple strokes because I was never very good. I used to play with Matt all the time until he was about thirteen. Maybe it was his age, or my career, but it feels as though when we stopped playing table tennis we gave up talking too. When he was a boy, it seemed easier to be with him, to answer his questions, and talk to him, but then at some point it became difficult. Maybe table tennis is the key to all the male relationships in my family.

'Play for serve?' I say, putting my wine down on the side.

'Take it away, old man, but be warned, I'm not a kid anymore,' says Matt with a smile.

I smile back and for a moment I can see my father across from me in his trousers, shirt and tie, with his sleeves rolled up, and his glasses slightly askew.

'One moment,' I say, rolling up my own sleeves. 'Right, Matt, do your worst.'

Matt looks at me with a steely determination, but it really doesn't matter because I know that whatever happens, I'm going to let him win. Just like my own father had done with me. From inside the house, I hear Christmas music, and the girls singing at the top of their voices, while Matt and I start playing table tennis as snow falls across London.

January Roast

Jon Rance

Lizzy

When I was younger, in the throes of late adolescence, I wanted more than anything to be a writer. I used to spend hours in my bedroom reading Sylvia Plath and Virginia Woolf and dreaming that one day I might follow in their footsteps. Greg's probably forgotten, but I got a First at university, while he only got a 2:1. I used to have a very capable and creative brain, but years of neglect and parenting have turned most of it to wobbly mush. Instead of contemplating deep philosophical and literary questions, my brain has become used to wondering why Matt's smelly socks always end up underneath the sofa and how to cook four different things in the oven at four different temperatures for varying times.

The other day I dug out the play I wrote after university. Greg and I were still living in our old rented flat on the Caledonian Road. It was a bit of a hole, "not big enough to swing a cat" were most people's first words when they walked inside, closely followed by, "smells like we're in Bombay". It was nestled unappealingly above an Indian takeaway, which meant cheaper rent, but also that I smelt like 'Eau de Rogan Josh' for two years. It was badly furnished with mismatching furniture, the fridge worked about half the time, so food was always tepidly cool instead of cold, and milk was always a bit of a gamble. The very elaborate paisley wallpaper was in a state of constant peeling, like a badly sunburnt English tourist, and the toilet was permanently blocked. Despite the conditions, I loved that little place.

Historians often proclaim that certain times are golden periods. If this is true, then this was our golden period. Greg and I were so happy in that poky little flat and I wrote my first play there. I had interest from a few local theatres and even met with a director, but then I got pregnant with Lucy, and it all fizzled out. We moved to this house with a big mortgage, Greg had to work harder, I became a mother, and life was never the same again. For the short time we were in that flat, Greg and I were as close to the us I'd imagined when we met than we have been before or since. Greg bought an old espresso machine from the market, and he'd make us cappuccinos. We'd make love at random moments, sometimes in the middle of the night or in the first light of morning. In that little flat for the shortest time, Greg and I were really happy, and it isn't as though we were suddenly unhappy once we left, but something changed. I kept my play in a cardboard box and it moved with us to this house. It's remained under the bed ever since. A stolen moment from another life.

It's absolutely chucking it down outside. I've never seen rain like it. It's coming down vertically, horizontally, and in all shapes and sizes. The clouds are threatening and charcoal black and it's making the day very gloomy indeed. Luckily, I have four lovely, colourful, and shiny holiday brochures to work my way through. So while outside it's looking a bit like Armageddon, inside my head it's more like paradise. I'm lying on a beach somewhere hot, sipping a cocktail, and working my way through some light holiday reading. I am not, I repeat not, at home on the wettest Sunday since the beginning of time.

Things between Greg and I have been so much better since Christmas. We talked about everything, he's been attentive and understanding, and we even had sex. Admittedly, I didn't have a proper orgasm (more Earl Grey than Fifty Shades), but that's probably because my vagina was so confused. It's been such a long time since Greg and I had sex, I think by the time my body remembered what it was supposed to be doing the whole thing was over. Still, we did it, we're talking, and all the tension and anger we had seems to be gone. Greg's also agreed to a holiday so after my Pilates class yesterday, I picked up some brochures. I've started going to Pilates three times a week with Stella Blackwell. I adore Pilates, although I've started aching in some much unexpected places. I didn't know you could pull muscles in your bum and even my breasts are hurting.

Stella has an amazing body. It's all so tight, toned, and tanned. Compared to her my body looks like a value pack of ham squeezed into a too small piece of Clingfilm. I saw her naked in the changing room and she's hairless downstairs too. I don't think I've ever seen such a lack of hair on a human being. I was a bit shocked at first. She caught me having a sneaky peek and she said with a saucy smile, "Paul likes to see what he's doing down there". To be honest, mine looks like the last days of Rome at the moment, although it is winter, and I haven't had the need to keep things up.

I wonder if Greg would appreciate a little waxing. He's never mentioned it, but I suppose it might spice things up a little. Either that or it will terrify him. I haven't seen my vagina in a hairless state since I was about twelve and I'm sure Greg's never seen a bald one either. They're not that attractive, especially at my age and after three kids. I think it needs the hair to give it some semblance of dignity - like a nice woollen hat.

Not that it matters today. Greg went out last night with work and he's really feeling it. He's so hungover he's letting Lucy and Matt cook the roast. I would have cooked it myself, but Lucy and Matt seemed quite keen to give it a bash. I'm a bit concerned because the last time we let Matt loose in the kitchen he almost set fire to himself. And he was only making boiled eggs. I also had to pick up Joan this morning, which went about as well as can be expected. "Where's Greg? Why isn't Greg here? I like it when Greg picks me up. He drives nicely. You drive too fast on the corners. Greg knows how I like the corners".

'I think I'm dying,' groans Greg dramatically. 'Literally.

Dying.'

'You're thinking of me,' says Joan with a chuckle.

'Really?' I say. Greg's lying on the sofa, his head underneath the holiday brochure on my lap. 'One night out and this is the result?'

'It's embarrassing,' says Holly. 'And I heard you throwing up last night. It was so gross.'

'I shouldn't have touched the vodka. It happens every time,' says Greg, his hands cupped over his stomach as though he's expecting it to burst any moment.

'Then why do you do it?' I say, flipping the page. 'If it happens every time.'

'Holly, could you get me some more Resolve and a big glass of water?'

'What did your last slave die of?' says Holly. 'Oh, yes, I forgot, atheism.' Holly gives Greg a smirk and carries on looking at her phone.

'It's on. Can you turn it up?' says Joan looking quite excited.

'What's on?' I say.

''The Dam Busters',' says Joan. 'It was George's favourite film.'

'No it wasn't,' says Greg. 'Dad's favourite film was 'Bridge on the River Kwai'.'

'I don't think so. Can you turn it up? I can't hear it,' says Joan.

'It's already on forty-nine, Joan. It's quite loud,' I say.

'I can't hear it with all the groaning,' she says, looking across at Greg.

I turn the volume up so it's on the verge of being ear bleedingly loud instead of just ridiculously loud. Joan smiles and settles in to watch the film.

'It was definitely 'Bridge on the River Kwai',' whispers Greg to me.

'I heard that,' says Joan.

I feel so energised looking at the holiday brochures. Greg and I have been on quite a few holidays over the years with the kids, but recently it's been quick weekends away or family holidays to the West Country, which is fine, but eventually wet and windy ice-cream and damp holiday cottages start to lose their appeal. It would be lovely if the first thing I packed was a bikini instead of a pair of wellies. It's been years since I've left the country, which is quite depressing when you think about it. My mother only left the country once her whole life, seven days in Spain, which Greg and I paid for. She didn't like the food, the weather, the water, the people, the hotel, or the flight, and she said afterwards with her usual expression of superciliousness that she'd never bother with it again. And she didn't.

My parents weren't adventurous people. They didn't get a microwave until about twenty years after everyone else because Mum "didn't trust them". And they used to eat the same meals on the same day every week without fail. Growing up I always dreaded liver and onions Wednesday. And we never ate anything that could be construed as "foreign food". When I went off to university and discovered that other people ate pasta, curry, and heaven forbid, chilli con carne, my culinary world exploded. I remember when my parents came to visit and I took them out to an Italian restaurant, my mother ordered a margarita pizza, but only because I explained that it was a bit like cheese on toast. It was the first time she'd had pizza, olives (which she didn't like), and mozzarella cheese (why can't they just use cheddar like everyone else?). My parents were the archetypal little Englanders. Growing up, holidays were always the same caravan site strategically far from the beach, so we hardly ever went. The most exciting it got was when Dad would let me have a double cone ice cream or gave me twenty pence for the arcade. Hardly Livin' La Vida Loca.

When I had my own family I wanted to show them the world. We ate different foods from every corner of the globe, we holidayed all over Europe, and they were encouraged to try new things and be adventurous. It's important to me because growing up I felt like everyone was having more fun than me. I grew up in a house where anything slightly different or exotic was considered a threat and I didn't want that for my children. Recently though something's changed – or rather, nothing's different - and it scares me because the last thing I want is to end up like my own parents.

'Nigger?!' says Holly suddenly.

'Excuse me?' I say, rather taken aback.

'On the film,' says Holly. 'They just said "nigger".'

'It's the dog,' says Joan. 'The dog's called Nigger.'

'But you can't say that. It's racist,' says Holly.

'I don't think it was back then, love,' I say.

'What? It was fine to call a dog Nigger?' says Holly.

'What's wrong with it?' says Joan.

'It's a derogatory word for black people, Joan,' I say.

'But that's nonsense,' says Joan. 'It's a dog.'

'But its racist,' says Holly.

'I don't think the dog's racist,' says Joan.

'No, I meant … it doesn't matter,' says Holly.

'Things were a bit different back then, love,' I say. 'Gay people were just happy.'

'And dogs were racist,' says Holly, and we both giggle.

'I can't hear the film,' says Joan.

I look across and smile at Holly and she smiles back at me.

I feel so guilty I couldn't help her with the boy from church. I can tell she's still upset about it, but I couldn't think of a way to get him to ask her out and now he's seeing her friend Charlotte. I tried to comfort her and make her realise that if this boy doesn't feel the same then it's his loss and not hers, but she's in the throes of her first love and nothing I say is going to help. Although maybe after today she'll be a bit happier. I've organised a surprise. Greg thinks it's a terrible idea, but I think it's just what she needs. A bit of a pick-me-up. I'm nervous to get involved in her life, but I can't just sit back and do nothing.

Greg rolls around beneath me, holding his stomach and

groaning as though he's been shot. He's as bad as those Italian football players that get tackled and spend five minutes rolling around on the ground, clutching at some phantom wound.

Why is it that men have no capacity for pain or discomfort? Greg is absolutely useless when he has as much as a sniffle and with a hangover he's incapacitated for days. However, being the matriarch, I'm expected to troop on through all minor colds, painful periods (before I went through the menopause), any sort of headache, tiredness or hangovers. Last year when I got that awful stomach flu and spent five days squatting over the toilet, I was allowed some time off (which has since been referred to as my holiday. Yes, it was lovely. I felt so refreshed afterwards), but in my absence the house fell apart. On Sundays, Greg likes to take centre stage and cook his famous roast, yet any other day of the week and it's like he can't toast bread. This is typical man behaviour. They like to do the grandstand cooking that everyone remembers, but when it comes to midweek dinners they don't want to know.

'What do you think about the Greek islands?' I say, showing him the photo in the brochure, which looks absolutely gorgeous. I don't think I've ever seen an ocean so clear and turquoise before. 'Look at the colour of the water? Doesn't it look amazing?'

Greg looks briefly at the brochure and then groans.

'At the moment, love, I couldn't care less if we spent a week caravanning in Wales,' says Greg. 'I'm in a great deal of pain and discomfort.'

'So am I,' says Holly. 'Listening to you.'

'That's not very Christian of you,' says Greg.

'And neither is drinking so much you turn into an annoying git,' says Holly.

'Okay, you two, back to your theological corners,' I say, stepping in before things escalate.

I look across at Holly and put my finger to my lips and then her phone starts beeping. She quickly glances at it, looks a bit fretful, gets up, and walks out of the room.

'That was probably God telling her to be nice to me,' says Greg.

'I doubt it. God's a woman and has no time for men who can't handle their booze.'

'Could you turn up the film? I can't hear it with all this racket going on,' says Joan, and so I turn it up again. The TV only goes up to seventy and it's currently at fifty-eight. Greg wiggles around before resting his head on my lap and I get back to my brochure. I start dreaming about lying on a tropical island in the sunshine, while outside the rain comes down harder, smashing against the windows and drowning out some of the noise from the TV.

Holly

I think it might be the total and complete end of my life. Seriously. Everything is so messed up, it's not even funny. Why does life have to be so complicated? Why does nobody understand me? Why don't I understand myself? Ugh.

I just got off the phone with Charlotte. I don't know how much more of this I can take. She was going on and on about her and Josh. He's getting too heavy, it's too much, she's too young, she's going off to university next year and doesn't want a serious boyfriend, blah, blah, blah. I listened and listened, every word punching me in the heart. By the time we said goodbye, I was a complete and utter mess. I hate it.

I thought going to church might make my life easier, but to be honest it's just made things even more confusing. I thought being a Christian might change me. That it might take away all the bad parts of me and the bits that don't work, but it hasn't. It's just made me hate those bits even more because I realise how wrong they are. I thought religion was supposed to be this thing that made sense, that would flow through me and make the world a better place, but the more I learn about it and belong to it, the less sense it seems to make. Instead of giving me answers, it's given me more questions. I wanted to be like Charlotte, feel the same things she feels, see through the same eyes, but it's not that easy, is it?

I can't talk to my parents about it. Mum tries to help, but she doesn't know what she's talking about. How could she? She's a stay-at-home mum whose only problems in the world are washing clothes, cooking dinner, moaning about Dad, and going on about the fact she hasn't been on a 'proper' holiday in a few years. Big deal. There are people in the world with real problems. People are dying. People are fighting prejudice and injustice while she's off doing Yoga with that annoying woman Stella Blackwell.

Then there's Dad. He's an atheist, which would be fine if he was one of those cool ones who said things like, "live and let live", but he isn't. He has opinions on everything. Even things he knows nothing about. He could meet a world champion water skier and within minutes (and despite Dad never having water-skied in his life) he'd be giving them tips - yeah, he's that annoying. He thinks me going to church is a complete waste of time, which is fair enough because six months ago I would probably have thought the same, but he tells me about every two minutes. Boring. Why can't he accept me for the way I am?

I'm lying on my bed staring up at my ceiling. On the wall next to me is the 'One Direction' poster I got when I was sixteen. Sad. I was thinking about getting a big poster of Jesus to piss Dad off, but I decided against it. I'm not sure using Jesus to get back at Dad is a very Christian thing to do. Not that I'm the most religious person in the world. How can I be? You see the thing is, I'm in love. I have been for ages, but there's nothing I can do about it. How can I tell Charlotte how I feel? She's been my best friend for as long as I can remember, and we've been through so much together. How can I tell her I love her? That she's all I think about. That I want to be with her. I can't. I can't even tell those closest to me. I tried to tell Mum, but I couldn't do it. I have no one to talk to because the one person I talk to about everything is Charlotte. I thought about talking to Lucy, but she's just so perfect and makes me feel even more like a complete freak.

Charlotte and I used to be 'just friends'. I always thought we were closer than friends, and when we were younger and we'd share a bed, I used to love cuddling up with her. I don't know when I crossed the boundary between friends and whatever this is. You see, I don't even know what it means. Am I a lesbian? Is that it? Are the lines so black and white? It's not like I want to jump into bed with every girl at college.

I don't really fancy any other girls apart from Charlotte. I've also liked quite a few boys and have had crushes on a few. And then there was that weird moment with Dean Shankley from Drama. What does it all mean? Am I a lesbian, bisexual, or some sort of confused hybrid?

There's a knock and Lucy pops her head around the door.

'Dinner in five,' she says with a smile.

'Oh, right,' I say, trying to keep myself together, but she can see I'm in pieces. It's pretty obvious and the longer she stands looking at me the more I feel like I'm falling. That's it, I feel like I'm falling, and I don't know how or when I'm going to stop.

'What's the matter?' says Lucy, walking across and sitting next to me on the bed.

I don't know what to say. Can I tell her the truth? I know she wouldn't judge me. Lucy's brilliant and maybe she can help. I just don't know if I'm ready. We sit for a moment and I'm trying my best not to cry. I don't know whether I should tell her or not, but then I realise it can't be any worse than it already is. It's consuming me and if I don't tell someone soon it might eat me up completely.

'I'm in love,' I say tentatively.

'Trust me, that's something that doesn't get any easier the older you get,' says Lucy with a warm smile.

'Even for you?'

'Especially for me,' says Lucy, putting her arm around my shoulder. 'Love is complicated, Hols. We can never control who we fall in love with and it's not always the person we should.'

'Oh, thanks, I feel so much better,' I say, half-smiling and I feel like I'm not falling quite so fast anymore. I decide to tell her. It's Lucy. If anyone will understand it's her. Be brave. 'There's something else.'

'What?'

'I don't know, Luce, I'm really confused and it's embarrassing.'

'Trust me, nothing is as embarrassing as it is in your head. I bet if you told me, it wouldn't feel quite so huge and overwhelming.'

'You think so?'

'I know so.'

I take a deep breath and then look at my sister, hoping this isn't a huge mistake.

'It isn't a boy,' I say quietly.

'Oh, then what is it?'

'It's ... a girl.'

'A girl? I don't understand.'

'I'm in love with a girl. I'm in love with Charlotte, actually.'

'Oh. Right,' says Lucy, then she leaves a pause and takes a deep breath. I'm worried she's going to think less of me. That she's going to think I'm a freak after all, but then she says something I wasn't expecting. Something that changes everything between us. 'I'm in love too, Hols, with a married man and it's tearing me apart.'

And then she starts crying. And I start crying. And we're crying together. And it helps. It really helps.

'Fucking hell, Luce,' I eventually say.

'Sorry, I didn't mean to make this about me. It just felt nice to finally tell someone and I thought it might help. None of us are perfect, Hols, and it's like I said, we can't help who we fall in love with.'

'I know what you mean. I've been going crazy thinking about Charlotte. I don't want to be in love with her, it's the last thing I want, but I can't help it.'

'I know,' says Lucy, giving me a hug and squeezing me tight. 'I'm not supposed to be the other woman, but it just happened.'

It's funny because for my whole life I've always thought Lucy was perfect. Growing up, I always aspired to be like her, but I couldn't because I wasn't that clever, organised, or popular. I tried so hard, but she was always this untouchable person who could do no wrong. Now it turns out she's just as confused and vulnerable to making terrible decisions as me. We aren't as far away from each other as I thought, and it makes me feel closer to her.

We hug and talk for a while, before we go downstairs and eat. I tell her more about my feelings for Charlotte and she tells me about her and this bloke from her work, which really blows my mind. I can't believe Lucy would do something like that. She's always been so perfect. I do feel a little better, but it doesn't alter the fact that I'm in love with Charlotte and eventually it's going to change things between us. Maybe I can hold out, suppress my feelings until we go away to university, and then maybe it will be all right. I'm kidding myself though because I know it isn't going to end well. How can it?

Lucy and I walk into the dining room quite late so everyone is already sitting down and they're all looking suspicious. Dad is looking down quietly at his plate, Mum is as stiff as a board and cracking a strange smile, Matt looks like he's trying not to laugh, and only Lucy looks as bewildered as me.

'What's going on?' I say.

'What do you mean, darling?' says Mum.

'Something's going on.'

'Don't be silly,' says Mum. 'Nothing's going on.'

In the middle of the table there's some slightly burnt looking meat, some pathetic looking roast potatoes, and a pile of green mush I assume was once vegetables. This must be hard for Dad to stomach. He tends to go a bit over the top with the roast, but at least it's always delicious. This looks awful.

'What about you, Dad?' I say, looking across at Dad.

'What's that, darling?'

'What's going on? You might be the most annoying person in the family—'

'Thank you.'

'But at least you're always honest with me.'

'It wasn't my idea,' Dad starts, but then Mum kicks him

under the table. 'Ow, what was that for?'

'What was what for?' says Mum.

'I don't know what's going on, but this is super weird,' says Lucy.

'I told you we should have told Lucy,' says Matt.

'Oh, Matt, quiet,' says Mum.

'Told me what?' says Lucy.

'It's nothing,' says Mum, then the doorbell goes and a smile spreads across her face. 'Back in a mo.'

She gets up and skips off to answer the door, leaving us all sitting at the table, confused looks and knowing smiles clashing and making none of us sure what to say. It's then that I notice the extra place that's been set opposite me. Someone else is coming to Sunday dinner. We all sit and look at one another until eventually Mum walks backs in trailing a very nervous looking boy about my age behind her.

'Everyone,' says Mum. 'This is Gavin and Gavin, this is everyone. My husband, Greg, Matt, Lucy, Joan, and, of course, last but not least, this is Holly,' says Mum, and it's about as transparent as a pane of freshly cleaned glass. This is a set up. She's trying to set me up with Gavin. Gavin grins. Mum grins. Dad is looking down at his plate shaking his head. Matt is still trying not to laugh, Lucy looks dumbfounded, and I don't know what to say or where to look.

'Hellooo,' says Gavin in a mumbled Scottish accent. 'I'm Gavin. Oh, right, your mam already said that. Classic mistake.'

'Go on, sit down,' says Mum to Gavin, gesturing for him to sit opposite me. 'Let's eat everyone. Come on, tuck in,' says Mum over-enthusiastically.

And so we do. Us and the strange, invited-only-by-Mum visitor, Gavin. If only Mum knew about my recent conversion to lesbianism. I suppose this is her way of trying to help and Gavin isn't that bad looking. His hair is a bit curlier than I'd like, his nose is a bit big, his chin a bit soft, and his hands are quite hairy, but he's all right. The point is though, I didn't choose him. And he isn't Charlotte. Mum isn't to know that, but then she didn't have to invite a complete stranger over on the off chance we might hit it off, fall in love, get married, and produce lots of hairy handed grandchildren.

'This is nice,' says Mum, obviously trying to make a small dent in the thick layer of tension that's hovering over the table. 'Gavin just moved down from Scotland, didn't you Gavin?'

'Aye,' says Gavin.

'And you go to church, don't you Gavin?' says Mum.

'Aye,' says Gavin.

I wonder how Gavin got roped into this. Maybe he just says "aye" to every question he's asked. "Gavin, fancy going to a stranger's house for an unappealing roast dinner with a weirdly unstable family, with the slim chance of going on a date with a girl who you've never met and who's actually a 'in-the-closet' lesbian?". "Aye".

'Holly, tell Gavin about your church,' says Mum, looking across at me with an encouraging smile.

'What do you want me to say? It's church. It's a building, we go inside, sing hymns, and pray and outside there's dead people buried in the ground,' I say, and Gavin sniggers nervously.

'Classic,' says Gavin, and there's another strangely shaped silence, before Gavin breaks it. 'And this dinner, Mrs W, classic.'

This is apparently the last straw for Dad, who so far hasn't said a word. Dad puts his knife and fork down loudly, the fork crashing against the side of his plate, making a loud chinking noise, and then he looks across at Gavin.

'Gavin this is not a classic dinner. The meat is burnt to buggery, the roast potatoes are undercooked, the vegetables are mush, and don't get me started on the gravy. And no offence Gavin, but I don't know what Lizzy's playing at.'

'Maybe I should go,' says Gavin, but Mum's having none of it. Gavin starts to get up, but Mum puts her arm across his chest, a steely look of determination on her face.

'Sit down, Gavin. I invited Gavin here for dinner for no other reason than he's new to the area and I know his mother from Pilates, and I thought—'

'You thought you'd try and do a bit of matchmaking,' I say. 'But the thing is, Mum, and no offence Gavin, but you aren't exactly my type, and I don't need you to try and set me up with random strangers on the off chance we'll fall in love, get married, and live happily ever after.'

'Whose Gavin?' says Gran, suddenly perking up.

'This is Gavin,' says Mum, pointing at Gavin. 'Gavin's really bright, and funny, and I just thought it might help.'

'Is he Jimmy's boy?' says Gran.

'Whose Jimmy?' says Dad.

'Look,' I say, standing up, finally losing my patience with this whole pathetic mess. 'I'm sorry, but this isn't going to work out. I know you were just trying to help, but you're not. Gavin and I aren't going to fall in love just because you feel guilty. It doesn't work like that. I'm in love with someone else, someone I know and who's right for me. You can't interfere in my life like this. It isn't fair on me, and it isn't fair on Gavin.'

There's a silence around the table as no one really knows what to say, until eventually the silence is broken by Dad.

'Oh shit, it's coming again,' says Dad, grabbing his stomach, then rushing out of the room and upstairs towards the toilet.

I'm back in my bedroom. Dinner has been tidied away, poor Gavin was ushered off before dessert, and Gran is asleep in front of the TV. Lucy left to get the train back to Notting Hill and Dad and Matt are playing table tennis in the garage. I'm trying to listen to some music and not think about Charlotte, when Mum pokes her head around the door.

'Can I come in?'

'If you want,' I say, turning off my music.

Mum walks over and sits down next to me on the bed.

'I'm sorry about Gavin. I was just trying to help.'

'But did you think that was the best way, Mum, really?'

'Maybe it wasn't. I wanted to do something, and I felt helpless. After the whole business with the boy from church, I felt rotten, Hols. I wanted to make it up to you, and maybe I didn't go about it the right way, but my intentions were good. I want to be a part of your life. I want to help.'

'I know, but did it ever occur to you that maybe I don't need your help?'

'No. I'm your mum. I'm sorry, but I'm always going to try and help.'

'Then promise me you'll never try matchmaking again because that was horrible.'

'Fine, no more matchmaking,' says Mum with a smile.

With Mum sitting on my bed and being so nice, I think about telling her the truth. Lucy already knows and I know Mum won't really care, but it all comes back to the same thing. I don't know what this is yet. I'm confused so I don't want to drag anyone else into this until I know for sure. I don't want my parents to worry, and I don't want them interfering in my life, especially after today. And so I don't tell Mum. Not yet.

After Mum's gone, I start thinking about my earlier conversation with Lucy. Why is love so difficult? Why can't love be clear and defined? It's all so uncertain. I suppose it's why I've always had my moral crusades and why religion makes sense because it's so clearly defined. But love isn't like that. It leaps up and grabs you like a young puppy one day, excited, happy, eager, but then the next it's like a sickness that makes your heart heavy and the sky grey. I never know how I feel. How can anyone? It's all so fucking stupid when you think about it.

It's like Lucy said, you can't help who you fall in love with, but if that's true, if we have no say in it, why do we spend so much time trying to control it? Why are there endless TV show, books, films, agony columns, internet sites, and advice about it? When it comes to matters of the heart I feel completely lost. I suppose that's the good thing about family. They might drive me mental, annoy me, and in Dad's case piss me off most of the time, but at least I know they'll always love me, and I'll always love them. It's black and white and unlike the racist dog in Gran's film, I know exactly what it means.

February Roast

Matt

From the day we started working together, Saskia and I had a spark. I don't really know how to explain it, but when we're together it's like something inside of me changes. Imagine that one day someone invents teleportation, and you get teleported somewhere. Your whole body gets disassembled atom by atom and then put back together again, but when it is, it isn't exactly the same. A few of the atoms are put back in the wrong spot. It's nothing serious, all the main bits are present and correct, you haven't lost an arm or a leg, but somehow it's just different. This is how I feel around Saskia. Basically the same, but different.

When I started at the cafe, I knew she had a boyfriend, so I tried my best to play it cool. The longer we spent together though the more obvious it became that we were attracted to each other. I tried not to think about her like that and I attempted to avoid her but working so closely together made it virtually impossible. I tried to think of her as a man with disgusting body issues, without the gorgeous hair, beautiful eyes, and the perfume that drove me crazy. I desperately tried not to look at her bum because she has the most amazing bottom I've ever seen, and I tried to think of her in the least sexual way possible. I dreamed up scenarios where she would be talking about trains or doing something equally as dull like reading German poetry in a black bin bag. I tried so hard to stop myself falling for her. But I couldn't. Like the car crash on the motorway, try as I might, I couldn't help but look at it.

It happened late one night after we'd closed up. It had been a really good day at work. It was busy and hectic, and Saskia and I were both flirting with each other. The subtle touches, our in jokes that made us both laugh hysterically and the looks when we thought the other one wasn't watching. I almost didn't or couldn't believe it was happening and I kept second guessing myself. Was I imagining it? Maybe she was just one of those super friendly, tactile people or perhaps it was all in my head. However, once we closed up and we were the only two people left, all the built-up sexual tension spilled out in a passionate, heated, and inappropriate clinch in the kitchen.

We were working on the weekend rota when she accidently touched my arm, we both looked a bit surprised, and I knew it was my moment. I leaned in and kissed her. It was a gamble because if I'd gotten it wrong, it would have made working together unbearable, but luckily she didn't stop me. You know the big scene in the romantic comedy when the couple finally gets together? It's raining, they're standing on the pavement, some suitably heart-warming and yet uplifting music is playing in the background, and someone says something like, "I've wanted to do this from the moment I saw you," and then they kiss - that was us. We stopped after one kiss because she said she wanted to break up with her boyfriend before we went any further. Poor Phil was dumped, and it's been full steam ahead ever since.

Every spare moment away from work we're together and every second at work when we're alone we're kissing like naughty school kids behind the bike sheds. It almost seems impossible I can be this happy. I've been waiting for something to go wrong since it started. We both agreed to take things slowly, but it's hard. I fall in love quickly and I can't seem to help acting like an idiot, but I'm hoping it'll be different with Saskia because I like her a lot and to be honest, my track record of bringing girls home doesn't make for good reading.

Kelly Steadman, aged 11

Admittedly, it was her idea, and she only became my girlfriend after she sat on me in the school playground (Kelly was a lot bigger than me). Under duress (and threats of being sat on again) I invited her for dinner one night after school. Needless to say, Kelly ate us out of house and home and still sat on me after dinner. Luckily, Lucy spotted me gasping for air in the back garden and came to my rescue. Kelly was my introduction to the fairer sex, although I think it's safe to say that there was nothing remotely fair or sexy about Kelly Steadman.

Kelly McDonald, aged 15

Another Kelly, although whereas Kelly number one was the first person to sit on me, Kelly McDonald was the first girl I fell in love with. She was in my art class at school and from the moment I saw her across the room, cross hatch shading an apple, I knew she was the girl for me. We were too young for an official date, so I foolishly invited her over for dinner under the guise of 'just friends'. I thought I was bringing home the love of my life and she thought she was doing homework and having a cheese sandwich. I was so nervous I ended up locking myself in the toilet. Kelly was somewhat weirded out by this, and Dad drove her home before dessert was served. I was still in the toilet.

Lindsey Cork, aged 20

I'd been dating Lindsay for a few months when we both came home from university for the weekend. I thought it would be a good chance for her to meet my family. I was convinced she was the love of life and I'd told my parents all about her. They knew they were meeting someone special, but unfortunately Lindsey was having one of her bad days. It didn't go well. I ended up having an argument with Mum and Dad, before Lindsey and I stormed out and went to the pub.

Thinking about bringing Saskia home, I'll be happy if I

don't get sat on or end up crying in the toilet. Downstairs I hear the doorbell ring quickly followed by Mum's shrill cry.

'She's here!' squeals Mum excitedly. 'It's time! Positions everyone! Positions!'

I feel like I'm about to go on stage. I take one last look in the mirror and altogether it's not too bad. I wish I didn't have Dad's hair. It doesn't matter what I do to it, what haircut I get, it looks a mess. I tried shaving it once, hoping I wouldn't look like a complete thug, but having no hair just made my ears look enormous. And it wasn't until all the hair was gone that I realised I had an oddly shaped head. I knew it was bad because when the barber was done, instead of getting the mirror to show me the back, he just looked at it and said with a grimace, "I've never seen one like that before".

I don't know why I'm so nervous about this. It's just a casual dinner with my family, but for some reason it feels big. I haven't been this excited about life since Lindsey and I were still planning on travelling the world. I want this to go well. I need this to be perfect. I take a deep breath and start the walk downstairs, where my family are lined up like they're about to meet the Queen, and I can see Saskia's beautiful shadow through the glass in the door.

Greg

Lizzy always thinks the best of Matt and I try to do the same, but he blindly jumps into things like this all the time. It's like the time he wanted that exchange student from Belgium. He went on and on about it until we eventually caved, but when Arnaud showed up Matt wanted nothing to do with him. I spent a week trudging around London with Arnaud, showing him the sights, which wouldn't have been too bad except he kept wandering off. I lost him twice in Madame Tussauds, once in the British Museum, and then on the tube during rush hour. They had to put out a message for him and we eventually found him wandering around Tottenham Court Road like a strange, real-life version of 'Where's Wally?' in his striped, red jumper and bobble hat. After he returned to Belgium, 'Where's Arnoud?' became a family favourite whenever we popped into London.

I'm worried we're going to have a repeat of the Lindsey situation. It was obvious to everyone (except Matt) that he liked her a lot more than she liked him. Then she buggered off around the world without him and he was left heartbroken. He needs to learn to keep his emotions in check until he's been with them for a while before he goes completely gung-ho, guns blazing, engagement ring inside a small chocolate soufflé. I knew Lizzy for a while before I eventually asked her out. I was laying the groundwork, putting in the hours up front so I wouldn't be disappointed down the line. I tried to explain this to Matt, and he called me a "romantically impaired, emotionally illiterate, love snob", but as I explained to him, whether he agrees or not, I've been married for thirty-one years, and he hasn't. Love is like everything else in life, it requires work, dedication, and a bit of common sense. Matt just chucks the kitchen sink at it and hopes for the best.

'This is Dad,' says Matt.

'Call me Greg,' I say, shaking Saskia by the hand.

Saskia is very attractive and dressed in a beautiful green dress that sits snugly against her slim body. Matt might be my son and I love him dearly, but he's at best a bit of a slob. Saskia looks like she's a really together, successful young woman who's travelling the world and managing a cafe. Matt, on the other hand, can barely get out of bed on the weekend and last week he fell asleep on the bus and ended up in Barnet. I can see why he's so smitten by her though. She has a real spark. You know when you meet someone, and they just have an indefinable something. It's hard to put my finger on, but I know it when I see it and she definitely has it. Without wishing to sound like Simon Cowell, she definitely has the X Factor.

'Hi, Greg,' she says in a bouncy American accent, shaking my hand firmly. 'I have an uncle called Greg. He lives in Seattle.'

'Oh, is that right?'

'At least he was called Greg before the sex change. Now we call him Georgia.'

'I can assure you I'm definitely all man,' I say with a smile.

'Gross,' says Holly.

'Don't put the poor girl off before she's barely over the doorstep,' says Lizzy.

'And this is Mum,' says Matt, moving on quickly.

'Gosh, you're very pretty,' says Lizzy. 'Let me look at you.' Lizzy puts her hands on Saskia's face and drinks her in. Eventually she smiles and takes a deep breath. 'Absolutely gorgeous.'

'I'm not that pretty really,' says Saskia, blushing slightly. 'I really made an effort. This is as good as it gets. You should see me first thing in the morning without any makeup.'

This is going to be a difficult afternoon because there's something I have to tell Lizzy. I'm trying not to think about it, but I have to deal with it, and I have to deal with it today.

I promised her a holiday during the Easter break, but I've got to ask her if we can push it back until summer. I had a meeting with a literary agent, and she wants me to write another book. My first book 'Wilde on Wilde' did so well that she wants me to write a series of similar books. We've also started laying the foundations for the university tour, which we're hoping to start in the summer term. There's no way I can go away with all of this going on.

Unfortunately, Lizzy's already picked out a holiday to Turkey, bought a guidebook, a new bikini, and she's even got a special wax. I don't want to go into graphic detail, but it's pretty sparse down there. Apparently, Stella Blackwell is completely hairless, and Lizzy thought I might like it too. I can't get my head around it. Is it supposed to be sexy? Am I supposed to enjoy the smoothness or is it meant to make me feel like I'm having sex with an underage teen? I'm more confused than turned on. I know she's going to go ballistic about the holiday, and I don't know how to tell her without it turning into World War Three. She wants to book it tonight, so I have to tell her today and the longer I wait the more daunting it becomes.

'This is Gran,' says Matt, introducing Mum to Saskia. 'Gran, this is my girlfriend, Saskia.'

'It's a pleasure to meet you,' says Saskia sweetly.

Mum looks Saskia up and down and then says,

'I don't like Americans.'

'Gran!' says a mortified Matt.

'Oh, it's okay,' says Saskia, leaning in towards Mum. 'To be honest, neither do I.'

This seems to placate Mum, who gives Saskia a warm smile.

'I'm Holly,' says Holly with a wave.

'The actress?' says Saskia.

'I'm trying,' says Holly coyly.

'And I'm Lucy,' says Lucy, shaking hands with Saskia. 'The terrifying big sister. I'm sure Matt's told you how awful I am.'

'Actually, Matt's always telling me how incredible—'

'Okay, let's all move into the dining room, shall we? Tea?' says Matt quickly.

'I'd love a cup of tea,' says Saskia.

'You've already converted the American to tea? She's definitely a keeper,' says Lizzy, putting her arm around Saskia and we all walk off together towards the dining room.

Before we moved into this house, Lizzy and I lived in a little flat on the Caledonian Road and it was there that Lizzy wrote her play over a long warm summer. I'd only just started at the university. It was all very new, and we still weren't sure what was going to happen. Ever since we met, Lizzy had talked about being a writer. I'd thought about it too, but I've always had a practical side. A need to play it safe. So while Lizzy went about following her dream of literary stardom, I started working at the university. Even though I hadn't planned on becoming a lecturer, I soon started to love it and all my aspirations of becoming a writer were put to the side. Lizzy finished her play, and it got lots of positive feedback. She even met with a director, but then she fell pregnant with Lucy and all her dreams were put on hold. I'll always remember that summer fondly. Lizzy tapping away on her typewriter, the windows of our little flat open to London. Life seemed impossibly wonderful.

We talked about it a lot and I told her there was still plenty of time to write. She could do it in her spare time and as the children got older she'd have more freedom. She agreed and to be honest, I always assumed she'd pick it up again. I don't know what happened, but the spirit and energy she had for writing seemed to fade so now when she tells me she feels like she's putting her life on hold for me, I feel like telling her that I never asked her to stop pursuing her dreams.

I'm scared to bring up the holiday because I know it's going to cause a huge argument and I don't want that. I don't want to say it or even think it, but a part of her must be jealous of my success. She says she's happy for me, but if so why doesn't she understand that I need to pursue this with every ounce of my being? This is my moment and I have the opportunity to really change my life. To change our life. I've worked long and hard to get to where I am and looking back at the us who moved into this house, so full of hopes and dreams, I know things haven't exactly worked out how we thought, but this is where we are.

'This is delicious,' says Saskia. 'And these Yorkshire puddings are awesome. Possibly my new favourite thing.'

'You've never had them before?' says Holly.

'I've been in London for over a year, but for some reason I've never had a Yorkshire pudding. They're so good. It's like dessert for dinner.'

'What are your favourite English foods?' says Lizzy.

'I love a full English breakfast,' says Saskia.

'With that figure?' says Lucy. 'You can't eat them very often.'

'She's a real greedy guts. She eats more than me,' says Matt, gazing adoringly at Saskia.

'But unlike Matt, I run every day,' says Saskia with a smile.

'She's run three marathons,' says Matt proudly.

'Four, actually,' says Saskia with a smile.

'Matt won the three-legged race at school sports day,' I say and Saskia laughs.

'Only because Dad dragged me along with him,' says Matt. 'I crossed the finish line on my back.'

'Crying,' adds Lucy.

'Ah, bless,' says Saskia and I see her reach down below the table and squeeze his hand. 'Poor Matty.'

'So tell us, what attracted you to my little brother? It obviously wasn't for his dashing good looks, maturity, or vast wealth,' says Lucy.

'Thank you for that,' says Matt.

'It's okay,' says Saskia. 'And you're right, it wasn't any of those things, although he is gorgeous, obviously.'

'Obviously,' says Matt.

'He just has this unique quality,' says Saskia. 'A sort of youthful exuberance. He wears his heart on his sleeve and I admire that about him. He's kind, generous, creative, and funny. You have to have funny.'

'I think it's lovely,' says Lizzy, tearing up. 'Really, really, really lovely.'

'How much wine have you had, Mum?' says Lucy.

'Oh, stop it,' says Lizzy, rubbing her eyes. 'It makes me happy.'

Eventually, Lizzy and I get up to tidy away the plates before dessert. Saskia offers to help, but we tell her to sit down, and Lizzy and I walk into the kitchen, putting the plates down on the side.

'It's going great. Isn't it going great?' says Lizzy excitedly.

'It is,' I say.

'And Saskia, I love her. She's perfect for Matt. Just what he needs.'

'Lizzy,' I say suddenly, looking at her happy face and hoping it isn't about to change. Maybe the excitement and euphoria about me getting a literary agent might overshadow putting the holiday back a few months. 'There's something I need to tell you.'

'Sounds serious,' she says, turning to face me.

'I have a literary agent.'

'What? Wow! That's brilliant,' says Lizzy, putting her arms around me and then leaning up and giving me a kiss. 'How did this happen? Why didn't you tell me before?'

'I wanted to wait until everything was set in stone and all the paperwork was signed before I said anything. So you're happy for me?'

'Of course, Greg, why wouldn't I be? So how did it happen? Tell me everything.'

Her name's Andrea Schuman and she contacted me last month. She read 'Wilde on Wilde' and loved it. She thinks we can do a whole series of 'Wilde on' books. You know

'Wilde on Dickens', 'Wilde on Woolf' that sort of thing. She said it could even lead to a lecture series on television or radio. I tell Lizzy how exciting it is and that it could change our lives. I tell her my dream of working less, writing more, and I apologise for not saying anything before.

'It sounds perfect, but from the look on your face I'd say it's not all good news.'

'It is perfect, love, but it means we can't go to Turkey. Not right now anyway. I'm sorry, but we can definitely go in the summer. I promise,' I say and then I wait.

'I'm not with you.'

'Andrea wants to get started right away, the book tours starting soon, and with work too, I'll just have too much on my plate. I want to have a holiday with you. I do. I want to go away and enjoy ourselves, but at the moment I know I'd spend the whole time worrying about everything else. If we push it back just a few months I know it will be so much better.'

Lizzy looks at me and I can see her face changing – not so much changing as cracking - and the relaxed, smooth, happy face I've been seeing for the past month is replaced with the old, annoyed, pissed off one.

'I don't believe this.'

'It's just a few months, Lizzy.'

'A few months, Greg, really?'

'That's all, I promise.'

'So when you promised me under the stairs at Christmas that you were going to change, that was all a lie?'

'No, of course not.'

'Because you promised me things would be different. You promised you'd put us first.'

'I am putting us first.'

'And how exactly are you doing that?'

'Because if we go away now it won't be as good and I want it to be brilliant. Why can't you see that?'

'Because all I see these days, Greg, is lies and broken promises,' says Lizzy, and then I see a single tear slip out and slide down her face. 'Just be honest with me. This is nothing to do with books or work, you just don't want to go on holiday with me, do you?'

'Don't be silly, love.'

'Silly? You think that's all this is? Silliness. I'm tired, Greg. I try and support your work, I do, but it's always to the detriment of us. You keep putting off the holiday and I know it's only a few months, but you said that a few months ago, and you'll probably say it again in another few months.'

'I won't, Lizzy, I promise.'

'Promise? Do you even know what a promise is anymore, Greg? Your promises mean nothing because you keep breaking them.'

I look at Lizzy and she looks so angry, so disappointed, so unhappy and I hate to see her like this. Unfortunately, I see more of this face than the happy one. I forgot our wedding anniversary and now this. I don't know what to do anymore. I feel like whatever I do, however I approach a conversation with her, it ends up with us shouting at each other.

'How about a short break during Easter? We could go to Paris or Copenhagen, you've always wanted to go there,' I say, hoping to find some middle ground.

'I don't want a fucking mini-break, Greg, I want what you promised me!' shouts Lizzy.

The door to the kitchen opens and Matt pops his head in.

'Can you keep it down? We can hear you in there,' he says.

'Sorry,' I say, turning to the dishes on the side. The door closes and Lizzy is standing next to me. I can feel her anger crackling like a fire.

Matt

'That was interesting,' says Saskia.

We're sitting on my bed. Luckily, Mum changed my Tottenham Hotspurs duvet cover for some more grown-up stripes this morning and the Cheryl Cole poster is now rolled up awaiting further decommissioning orders. Downstairs the fallout continues from Mum and Dad's argument. I'm so annoyed with them. Why can't they think of someone else for once and by someone else I mean me? They could have waited until Saskia had gone. It's so embarrassing. I don't know what Dad's done, but Mum's been laying into him for the past half an hour, her annoyed shouts echoing up the stairs.

'I'm sorry, it isn't usually like this,' I say.

'Wait until you meet my family, they're much worse.'

'I'm going to meet your family, am I?'

'If you play your cards right,' says Saskia, leaning over and giving me a kiss.

This is the first time I've had a girl in my bedroom since Lindsey. I was heartbroken after she left, but now I'm with Saskia, it makes me appreciate what being with the right person feels like. It feels effortless.

'So this is where the magic happens,' says Saskia with a wry smile. 'If only this old bed could talk.'

'It wouldn't have much to say. Maybe some disappointing groans.'

'I don't believe that.'

'Honestly, just a lot of dull stories about me, alone, doing nothing very fun or sexy in my Power Rangers pyjamas.'

Saskia laughs, falling into me, and then putting her arms around me.

'So you're saying you haven't had lots of girls in this bed?'

'Define lots.'

'Oh, I don't know, twelve?' says Saskia, picking some fantastical number from her head. She makes a brilliantly cute face when she's thinking. She scrunches it up, so her forehead is wrinkled, and her mouth stretches into a parallelogram sort of shape.

'Definitely way less than twelve,' I say, slightly embarrassed by the real number.

'Okay, give me a rough number.'

'I can give you an exact figure. If we sleep together in this bed, you'll be lucky contestant number four.'

'Shut up, there's no way.'

'Truthfully. Hand on heart.'

'So you're telling me that you're sexy, cute, adorable, and nice?'

'I just think really bad at getting girls into bed,' I say and Saskia laughs.

I've been trying so hard not to fall in love with Saskia. She's everything I've ever wanted in a girlfriend and unlike dating Lindsey, it isn't a constant battle. I always gave so much more than I got back with Lindsey. At the time I didn't realise how one sided the relationship was, but it's different with Saskia. When you've been in a loveless relationship, you definitely know when you're in a good one. The only problem I have with Saskia is holding myself back. You can't tell someone after only a few weeks that you love them, can you? And even though things with Saskia are different, a part of me is still afraid of getting hurt again. Lindsey really messed me up emotionally and although I want to dive into my relationship with Saskia, swim among its pure, warm waters, I'm worried because what if I'm wrong again? What if I end up drowning? I don't think I could take it.

'You don't mind if I hang out in here, do you?' says Lucy, walking in and sitting down on the bed next to Saskia.

'My sister, the third wheel,' I say.

'Of course we don't mind,' says Saskia.

'Thank you, Saskia,' says Lucy, who gives me a little punch on the arm. 'I can't stand being around Mum and Dad when they're like this. They're driving me nuts. She's yelling at him and calling him a useless waste of space, and he's trying to ignore her and pretend nothing's wrong.'

'Sometimes it feels like we're the parents and they're the children,' I say.

'Lucy and I might be the parents,' says Holly, walking in and sitting down on the floor. 'But you're definitely "the children".'

'Hilarious coming from you, the youngest child,' I say, but she ignores me and starts playing on her phone.

Despite there being only a five-year difference between us, sometimes I feel like we're generations apart. I go on Facebook, Twitter, and sometimes I use Instagram, but Holly is online constantly. She can hold a whole conversation with me while texting someone else. She can Tweet, Facebook, Pin, Instagram, upload, Snapchat, and message all at the same time, while still having a conversation with someone on the phone. If I don't look a person directly in the eye when they're talking, I don't hear a word they say. Only twenty-three and I'm already starting to feel past it, while Holly and her iWorld are pulling away into the distance.

We all sit quietly, while downstairs we can hear Mum and Dad shouting at each other.

'Right, that's it, I've had enough,' I say.

'Enough of what?' says Lucy.

'Of Mum and Dad. Whatever's going on with them, we shouldn't have to be hidden away up here because they're behaving like a couple of kids. I'm putting a stop to this now.'

I start walking downstairs. I don't know what's happening with them. They were happy this morning, annoyingly so actually, but now they're embarrassing themselves and embarrassing me in front of Saskia. I don't care about Mum's holiday or Dad's career. I just want them to stop shouting at each other.

The trouble is that Dad's ridiculously stubborn and won't admit when he's in the wrong, and Mum is obviously having some sort of weird mum-life crisis. I blame it on Stella Blackwell. That woman is the devil. Even when we were kids she used to annoy me with her sharp fingernails, her powerful perfume, and the way she only talked about herself and her devil spawn Laura. Now there's a miserable girl. Every time I see Laura she looks like she's got a severe case of haemorrhoids. She tried kissing me once at a Christmas party. We were both drunk, but even so I couldn't do it. Even then I knew that doing a Blackwell is for life, not just for Christmas.

Mum and Dad are still going at it when I walk in. Dad is sitting at the dining table, head in hands, while Mum is prancing around and shouting something about that week in Wales. The holiday when Holly got the flu, Lucy had diarrhoea, and Dad went fishing, while I did the thing that's now only referred to as 'The Aberystwyth Incident'.

'You were useless in Wales, Greg, and you're useless now.'

'It wasn't my fault Matt did what he did,' says Dad. 'No one could have seen it coming.'

'But it wouldn't have happened if you'd been there instead of buggering off fishing. I was busy taking care of Lucy and Holly, I needed you to take care of Matt, and you didn't and that's why he did what he did.'

'I thought we weren't going to discuss what happened in Wales again?' I say.

'We weren't supposed to be,' says Dad, looking up at Mum.

'None of this is my fault. This is all your father's doing,' says Mum.

'I'm sorry,' I say. 'You know I am. I didn't mean for what happened in Wales to happen.'

'It's all right, Matt,' says Dad. 'You were young, you didn't know what you were doing.'

'But you should have been there. He needed you, Greg, we all did. You let him down.'

There's a silence as none of us knows what to say. We haven't talked about The Aberystwyth Incident for years.

'Mum. Dad. Saskia's here, can you please just stop?'

'I didn't start this,' says Dad.

'See,' shouts Mum. 'This is the petulant idiot I have to deal with.'

'I've had enough of this,' says Dad.

'So have I!' shouts Mum. 'I've had enough of you because the truth is, Greg, whenever we need you, you're never there for us.'

'Me never there?' says Dad, standing up, looking angrier than I've ever seen him before. 'That's rich coming from you.'

'What's that supposed to mean?' spits Mum.

For a second they just stand staring at each other, before Dad finally speaks.

'From the woman who abandoned her family and disappeared for two days. We thought you were dead, Lizzy. Your children were devastated, so let's not talk about people not being there because I've always been here, Lizzy. I never ran away when it got too tough.'

Dad stops and Mum is stood in disbelief, and I don't know if she's going to break down in tears or start shouting again. I don't know what to say because we've never discussed what happened with Mum. None of us has. She was gone and then she came back.

It's at this point, as Mum and Dad are at a standoff that I first hear the noise. It sounds like something from a ghost movie. It's haunting, suddenly loud, and then quiet. It's rough, harsh and then panic ridden, and it's coming from Gran.

'It's Gran,' I say, and we all run from the dining room towards the lounge, as Lucy, Holly, and Saskia come down the stairs.

'What's that noise?' says Lucy, her face as white as a

sheet.

I feel sick, my feet are suddenly heavy and my heart's beating heavily in my chest. I open the door and see Gran struggling for breath. Her head's back, and small strands of spit are leaking out and down her chin. It looks for all the world like she's dying.

Part Two

(March to July)

March Roast

Lizzy

The doctor called it a nervous breakdown. I'm not sure what it was to be honest, but whatever it was it started after Mum died. Mum and I never really got on, but for some reason when she died I felt this overwhelming sense of loss. Dad had only died a year before and suddenly I'd gone from having both of my parents to having none. It was funny because Mum was as healthy as could be, but as soon as Dad was gone she went downhill so fast. The official reason on her death certificate was a stroke, but I like to think she died of a broken heart. My parents didn't have a particularly romantic marriage, so thinking that at least feels like it all meant something. Like their marriage was important and not just a mistake that went on for too long.

Up until Dad died I'd been plodding along. I hadn't written anything in years. When the children were small I'd written bits and pieces, but slowly life took over and I just sort of stopped. It wasn't really a conscious decision not to write anymore, but something that happened without me even realising. It was always at the back of my mind and like so many other things, I always said, "one day". Only one day never came and then my parents died, and my world fell apart. I suppose the best way I can describe it is that it was a huge wake up call. I felt a sense of my own mortality.

The day I disappeared, I didn't really know what was going on. Have you ever started out on a walk and just kept on walking? That's sort of what happened. Only I ended up staying in a hotel in London for a couple of days without contacting anyone. I needed some time alone to process everything. I sat in cafes thinking about my life, imagining the future I wanted, and it all felt like a bit of a dream. It's why the doctor called it a nervous breakdown. Apparently, it's fairly common for people to want to disappear for a few days when life gets a bit much. A brief escape from reality.

I returned home to absolute chaos. Greg and the kids were all in a blind panic and after the relief came the anger and then finally the arguments. I told Greg everything. Where I'd been, what made me go, and what I wanted. I couldn't keep going along not doing anything for me because I'd spent so many years sacrificing all of my dreams and ambitions for the family, and I didn't mind because I love my kids, but I needed something to change. I wanted more. That was nearly five years ago, and it still feels like I'm waiting.

It's been different around the house since last month's trip to the hospital with Joan. It was terrifying when it happened. We all thought she was dying. Luckily, while we were all in shock and completely useless, Matt's girlfriend Saskia had the wherewithal to call for an ambulance and put Joan in the recovery position. It was one of the most difficult fifteen minutes of our lives until the ambulance came and Joan was taken away on a gurney, tubes and wires attached to her body, an oxygen mask over her gaunt face. Greg and I followed the ambulance in our car and waited anxiously at the hospital. I've never seen Greg so shaken up. He paced up and down while I got us coffee, hoping he wasn't going to lose his only parent, and my children weren't going to lose their last grandparent.

After everything that happened with his father, I thought he'd handle things better with Joan, but if anything he was worse. I didn't see him cry much when his father was dying. He broke down at the funeral, we all did, but during the disease he often had this stoic expression of acceptance plastered on his face. He didn't talk about it, but I knew it was hard for him because he was close with his father. George was larger than life and to see him wither and die in front of us was heart breaking, but Greg dealt with it so bravely. He hasn't always been so close to Joan, but I'll never forget the look on his face as we sat in the waiting room. It put all of our arguing into perspective, and we haven't discussed it since. Joan was fine. The doctor told us she'd had an "episode", but she was going to be all right. Relief washed through Greg and all the tension and problems between us have been put on hold.

I've been asking myself ever since if I was being selfish. Was Greg right? Am I asking too much of him? Maybe I should be supporting his dreams and ambitions more than I am. I want him to be happy. I want him to be a success, and if that means a bit more sacrifice from me then I don't think that's too much to ask. We're married and that means supporting each other, for better or worse, for richer or poorer, in sickness and in health. The vows we said thirty-one years ago still mean so much to me today. I explained to him that I wasn't really annoyed about the holiday. I was angry because I felt like he didn't care about me and whatever dreams I still had. I felt like he was putting everything else ahead of me. Ahead of us. He promised to do better, and I promised to be more supportive. He apologised for bringing up my disappearance and we both said sorry for some of the things we said. I still need something to change, but I've realised that maybe instead of waiting for Greg, perhaps it's time I did some changing myself.

We're in the living room and despite March being wonderfully warm, Joan is wrapped up like we're about to embark on a trek to Antarctica. Matt is slouched on the sofa watching television, Holly is sitting on the floor tapping away on her phone, and Lucy's running late.

The ovens on the blink and Greg thought he smelt gas so he's on the phone with the gas company. The roast is off, much to Greg's annoyance as he bought an expensive joint of Welsh lamb and was itching to try out a recipe from his new Hugh Fearnley-Whittingstall cookbook. I'm excited because it means we get to go out for lunch and there's a pub nearby that's supposed to do a lovely roast.

'We're just going to sit here and wait?' says Holly. 'Boring.'

'He shouldn't be much longer,' I say.

'Yes, no, I said yes. Yes!' shouts Greg from the hallway. 'Stupid bloody automated machine.'

'It might be a while. We should settle in for the long haul,' says Matt, who has the TV remote and is flicking through the channels at warp speed. 'Jamie Oliver, Jamie Oliver, Come Dine With We, Come Dine With Me, Come Dine With Me, Jamie Oliver, Don't Tell The Bride, cycling, who watches cycling? Jamie Oliver, Jamie Oliver—'

'Do you have to do that?' says Holly.

'What?' says Matt.

'Scroll through the channels with commentary. We can see what's on. We have eyes.'

'All right, just because you're in a bad mood.'

'I'm not in a bad mood,' says Holly, who quite clearly is in a monster of a mood.

I think she's worried because she's supposed to find out about her university choices soon. It's a tense time and she's been in quite a strop for the past few weeks. I'm sure she's going to be fine because she's doing well at sixth form, but she's worried because Charlotte has applied to Manchester too and they want to go together. I don't know all the details, but she's been unbearable. Although in her defence, it is annoying when Matt scrolls through the channels, especially when it's during the adverts of a show you're actually watching.

'It's all rubbish,' says Joan.

'What's that?' I say.

'Television. It's all cooking shows and reality this and that. It's not proper television.'

'What's proper television, Gran?' says Holly.

'I said yes!' shouts Greg from the hallway.

'Like they used to have,' says Joan. 'I used to watch Emmerdale Farm when it was a nice show about the countryside. Now it's all just sex and violence. I don't see the need for it, especially in the country.'

'QI, QI, QI, Jamie Oliver, Jamie Oliver, QI, cycling again,' says Matt.

'I'm going to my room. Call me when we're leaving,' says Holly.

'Don't go. Maybe we could play a game while we wait,' I say. 'Turn off the TV, Matt.'

'What sort of game?' says Holly suspiciously.

'Oh, I don't know, something,' I say optimistically.

'Ah, the classic family game of something,' says Matt.

'It will be fun,' I say, but all I get back from the room are blank stares. 'How about I Spy?'

'I Spy? In the lounge?' says Holly, as though I'd suggested skiing in the Sahara.

'It will really make you use your imaginations,' I say enthusiastically.

We used to play games like this all the time when they were little, and they'd jump at the chance. Lucy and Matt always competing and poor Holly trying to keep up. Greg and I would usually bow out first leaving the kids to battle it out until the inevitable arguments, tears, and then one or all of them storming off in annoyance. It sometimes felt like we were just passing time back then, trying to get through the day until bedtime, but now we have to beg them to do anything with us, I long for that old enthusiasm again. People say that kids grow up so fast and it's true, but what no one tells you is that once they're gone, once the world has them, they never completely come back. You spend eighteen years waiting for them to leave home and the rest of your life trying to get them to return.

'I Spy with my little eye, something beginning with G,' says Matt.

'Gran,' says Holly.

'Got it in one,' says Matt, pretend shooting Holly with his finger.

'We used to play I Spy in the car,' says Joan, her voice muffled by the scarf that's riding up and covering most of her mouth. 'Greg used to love I Spy. It helped pass the time on long drives. I Spy, jam sandwiches, and always a flask of tea.' Joan smiles and then drifts off into her own memories.

I had lunch with Stella Blackwell the other day and she told me about a women's retreat she's going on. It's in Oxfordshire and they stay in American Indian style tepees and do all sorts of "female activities". I'm not entirely sure what "female activities" are, but according to Stella, it's perfect for "women like me". When I asked her what she meant by "women like me" she said, "You know, slightly repressed". I don't think I'm repressed. I didn't tell her I got my vagina waxed. Although to be honest, it definitely wasn't worth it. For a start, it was excruciatingly painful. I can't believe women actually do it once a month. The girl at the place said you get used to the pain, but I'm not sure I want to and for what? So I can have a slightly scary looking vagina? I spent days applying moisturiser before I let Greg loose on it because it was so red. And that leads me onto what happened with him. I told him I had a surprise for him, but he obviously hadn't considered what it might be because when I told him to close his eyes and I put his hand down there, he leapt up like I'd grown a penis.

'Bloody hell, Lizzy, what happened?'

'I got it waxed. Do you like it?' I said coquettishly.

'It's weird.'

'It's naked.'

'I guess I'm used to it being dressed. To be honest, it's a little terrifying.'

'Terrifying?'

Not exactly the adjective I was hoping for.

'There's a certain mystery with the hair, Lizzy, but without that there's very little left for the imagination.'

'Do you want to look at it?'

'I suppose I should.'

We were in bed, and he moved down and had a look at it. He came back up a few moments later looking a bit shaken.

'What do you think?'

'I don't know, Lizzy. It's a little too—'

'A little too what, Greg?'

All the pain, the redness, the effort, and he just looked disgusted.

'A little too in your face.'

'Jesus, Greg, that's all you have to say? I'm trying to put some magic back in the bedroom and that's your reaction?'

'I'm sorry, it's just—'

'I know, Greg, "in your face", but don't you see that's part of the problem.'

'What is?'

'My vagina hasn't been "in your face" for a very long time!' I shouted.

And that was it. Not only did it cost me forty pounds, a great deal of pain, discomfort, and now itchiness as the hair is grows back, but Greg doesn't even like it. My experiment to spice things up in the bedroom has definitely backfired, but it goes to show that I'm not repressed. Maybe Greg is, but either way I'm going on the retreat. When I asked Stella what exactly happens, she said with a suggestive smile that things get "very real". It sounds like it might be an interesting weekend and maybe just what I need.

'Finally an actual person. I need to speak to someone about a potential gas leak,' says Greg from the hallway. 'You need to direct me to a different department. Can I hold? Well, actually, no I can't, wait, hello? Hello? You're kidding me. I can't believe you just did that, and this music again. Agh!'

I think Greg's going to explode before the oven does.

'Whose go is it?' I say, trying to get everyone back in the I Spy spirit. 'How about you Joan? Fancy a turn?'

'What's that?' says Joan.

'We're playing I Spy, fancy a turn?'

'Oh, I don't know.'

'Go on, Gran,' say Holly and Matt, and Joan smiles from beneath her scarf and agrees.

'I Spy with my little eye, something beginning with …' says Joan, before she has a look around the room. It takes her a moment, but eventually she settles on something. 'V.'

'V?' we all say in unison, looking around the room.

I can't think of anything in the living room beginning with V. Maybe Joan's mistaken. Matt, Holly, and I look around the room for a few minutes, none of us with a single guess.

'Come on,' says Joan.

'Are you sure it begins V?' I say.

'I'm old, not stupid,' says Joan.

'Seriously, Gran?' says Matt. 'There's nothing in here that starts with V.'

'We give up,' I say, after a few more minutes of silence.

'Varicose veins,' says Joan with a smile. 'My legs are covered with them.'

'But Gran, you're wearing trousers,' says Matt. 'And you have a blanket over your legs.'

'They're in the room, it's not my fault you can't see them,' says Joan.

'But,' says Holly, but before she can finish the front door opens and a moment later Lucy walks in and it's obvious something's wrong. Lucy's usually pretty good at hiding her feelings. Even when she was a child, while other children would have temper tantrums or complete breakdowns, Lucy would keep herself together. It used to scare me how much self-control she had. However, it's obvious something awful must have happened because she looks distraught. Her face is frozen and as white as a sheet. It's her eyes that give her away though. They look terrified.

'Is everything all right, love?' I say, but it's obvious it isn't.

Lucy

I've never been one for big public displays of affection. It makes me uncomfortable. Even on Valentine's Day when one of the girls at work gets a big bouquet of flowers, I'm not thinking, 'Oh lucky old her', I'm thinking how horribly gauche it is. People only send flowers to a public place so the whole world can see. They do it so all the other people look at the recipient and think, 'gosh they're so lucky, they must be with a totally brilliant person'. In a way it's selfish. The person sending the flowers is doing it as much for themselves as they are for their loved one. It's showy and I don't like showy love. I think love needs to be done and shown in private. It's between two people and it should stay that way. Then there's Richard and me. Of all the things I've done in my life, this is the only thing I'm deeply ashamed of. And that makes me despise myself because it's definitely not me. Suddenly I want to love someone and be able to shout it from the rooftops, to be able to get flowers at work, and most of all to tell my family. I want a public love because real love, proper, honest, and pure love, shouldn't be a secret.

Richard asked me to go away with him for a few days. Our relationship up until that point had always been about stolen moments. We'd had a few nights in hotels, but even they felt rushed and always left me with a slightly bitter taste in the morning. I loved the tender moments in the room, the cuddling after sex, talking late into the night like we were the only two people in the world, but then in the morning, during stilted conversation over an even more stilted hotel breakfast, I always felt numb. I suppose it was the guilt. I couldn't help but imagine his family back at their house eating breakfast, the kids asking where Daddy was, his wife trying to do it all by herself as Richard and I went about our affair. I never thought we'd get beyond a night away, and honestly, I thought we'd finish before anyone got hurt.

Now Richard wanted to take things to the next level, and I didn't know what to say. One of the advantages of our job is that we can go away for work if we need to. The lies are easily concealed behind the badge of the job. A night here, a night there, it's all possible without a full investigation. The blanket of media covers so many sins. This was a few weeks ago and I ended up saying yes. I wasn't sure about it, and I knew it was a bad idea, but I had to see. I wanted to know what it would feel like to be his proper girlfriend, rather than the awful secret that met him in distant pubs strategically far from work.

Early last week Richard and I were working late. Richard was a brilliant Script Editor with so much experience and knowledge that learning from him had been incredible for me. I felt like I'd progressed years in a matter of months. We were working in a bubble though and whether we knew it or not, people were starting to notice. Nothing was said and Richard didn't seem worried, but I always felt like people were talking about us. Richard told me I was being paranoid, but last week things changed dramatically.

We were in his office. It was nearly nine o'clock and we thought everyone had gone home for the night. We'd been working hard all day and once the rest of the team were gone, Richard asked if I wanted to stay on a bit longer. If I wasn't sleeping with him, I'd probably have gone home too, but work and Richard were all I ever thought about and the two were inseparable. Work was an excuse to spend time with Richard and spending time with Richard was an excuse to work. You see the thing is, I love what I do. My job has always been the biggest part of me. It's all I've ever wanted to do, and I was at the BBC doing it.

'Being around you all day is unbearably painful,' said Richard, looking across at me, his dark, sexy eyes piercing my skull and sending waves of adrenalin and excitement through my body. 'Just keeping my hands off you requires literally all of my will power.'

'Stop it,' I said playfully as he started running his hand up my back towards my neck. We were standing over his desk looking through a script. Most of the lights in the office were off, only a few remained, and along with the blue light from his computer screen, the room had a fluorescent glow. It was quiet except for the rumble of traffic from outside and the rain tip-tapping on the roof. 'What if someone comes in?'

'No one's here now. Hello? Hello? Hello?' said Richard, and all he got back was silence.

Richard continued rubbing my back and then he pulled me around and suddenly we were face to face and then we were kissing. We'd never done anything at work before and it was passionate and desperate, but then it stopped. It stopped because standing in the door was Melissa Brooks. I could never quite work out what Melissa had against me, but from our nervous first day together, she'd always been frosty around me, and since Richard and I started working together, her attitude towards me had deteriorated into open bitchiness. To be caught kissing by anyone at work would have been awful, but to be found by Melissa was possibly the worst thing that could have happened.

As I stood there, suddenly so aware we were the only three people in the office, I knew it was over. It was the moment in the heist film when the criminals realise they've been caught. It was a wild, crazy ride, right up until the end, but it was over. Nothing left to do but hand ourselves over, take the punishment, and roll the credits.

'So the rumours are true,' said Melissa, standing looking at us. 'I suppose it's one way to get ahead, eh, Lucy, to give it.'

'It's not what it looks like,' I tried to say, but she wasn't going to let me off the hook so easily and why should she?

'I think I know what it is,' said Melissa, a smile spreading across her face.

'Now look here,' said Richard. 'You didn't see this. It

never happened and if you tell anyone—'

Richard was trying to exert his authority, but he knew we were in real trouble. He knew what Melissa was like and he was trying to frighten her, but Melissa grew up in a rough east London suburb. She'd pulled herself up from the council estate where she was born to this. She knew how to handle herself and she wasn't afraid of us.

'You'll what?' said Melissa, knowing she had all the power and we both fell silent. 'Yeah, I didn't think so,' said Melissa, before she turned around and walked away with all the confidence in the world.

'Fuck,' said Richard as soon as she was gone. 'Do you think she'll tell anyone?'

'She hates me. Of course she's going to tell someone. What are we going to do?'

'I don't know, but it's going to be all right,' he said, but I knew it wasn't and I was sure he did too.

The next day I came into work and straight away I knew something wasn't right. Usually Richard comes over and we talk about what we have to get done, but he didn't. I desperately looked around the floor and I couldn't see him anywhere. Then I saw Melissa. She walked past me and smiled the same vindictive smile as the night before. Eventually, Richard appeared and called me into his office.

'What's going on?' I said as soon as he closed the door.

I was so nervous and stood in his office, I knew I didn't want to lose him. We couldn't last forever, but I wasn't ready for it to be over, and I suppose I thought we'd end on our own terms. He looked at me, his face for once showing the tremendous strain of a man on the edge. It was obvious something had changed. For the first time he looked scared too.

'She told Jones.'

'Fuck.'

Hugh Jones is our Department Manager and the only person at work who truly terrifies me. I wanted to cry, but I managed to hold myself together. We were stood in the room where I'd first met Richard, where we'd fallen in love, but now the office which held so many happy memories suddenly felt like a prison.

'He said we have to end it now. He doesn't care what we've done, but he wants it over. And he's moving you to another team.'

'No,' I said, and my voice wobbled towards tears. 'I don't want to move.'

'I told him I'd end it, but I can't. It's us. How can we end? I'd be lost without you.'

'But what if he finds out? What if other people find out? What if your wife—'

'We'll have to be more careful. I can't give you up. You're everything to me, Lucy.'

'But what about your wife and kids? Aren't they everything?'

'Well, yes, of course, but it's different, it's complicated.'

'But they should be, Richard. They should be everything to you,' I said, and now I was crying. 'You should be thinking about them.'

I don't know what came over me, but suddenly it was like a light came on and I realised what we were doing. Being found out by Melissa and now Hugh Jones knowing and being moved not because I was bad at my job, but because I was doing something bad. Suddenly it wasn't this exciting, dangerous affair anymore, but a life changing, terrible mistake that could cost me my career, his marriage, his kids, so many lives, and I knew we couldn't keep going because it was only a matter of time before more people found out. The scary thing though was that despite everything, Richard wanted to keep going. This was the point when he should be thinking about his marriage, his children, his career, but he wasn't. He was thinking about me and that was the last straw.

'What are you saying?'

'I'm saying we're over, Richard. We have to be over. We just have to be.'

'But I love you.'

'It doesn't matter, not anymore.'

And then I walked out of his office, grabbed my coat, and left the building. Back home I slumped down in bed and cried for hours. Richard tried calling me again and again, but I turned my phone off. I'd made a mess of everything. My career, my relationships, and for the first time in my life, I was faced with the prospect of complete failure. All the years of hard work, of playing by the rules, of having the ambition to match my intelligence, and all of it was going to waste because I'd been screwing my boss like a cheap slut.

'Is everything all right?' says Mum.

'I've really messed everything up, Mum.'

'What do you mean, love?' says Mum, her face wrapped in confusion. I know this is going to change everything between us, but what choice do I have? I have to tell her. I glance around the room at Matt, looking at me with worry, at Holly, the only one who knows about the affair, trying her best to give me a supportive smile, and Gran looking confused. Then Dad comes in and sees me, his face flipping like a coin.

'What's going on? What's happened, darling?' says Dad.

'I need to talk to you both. Maybe we can go into the other room,' I say.

Dad has the phone to his ear and immediately passes it to Matt.

'If you get someone, tell them we have a potential gas leak. Find out what we have to do and don't let them go until I've spoken with them,' says Dad.

I walk with Mum and Dad into the dining room, and we all sit down.

'Shall I make tea, or do you want something stronger?' says Mum.

'I'm fine.'

'I'll get some wine,' says Dad, who gets up and comes

back a few moments later with a big glass of wine and puts it down in front of me.

When I started the affair, I never thought about having to tell my parents. I suppose like Richard and I getting caught, I naively thought it wouldn't happen. I hate to do this to them. When I was a teenager I was such a good child and never caused my parents any heartache, except for one time I'd got in trouble at school, and I had to come home and confess. I was terrified. I remember the nauseating feeling in the pit of my stomach, the thin film of sweat on my hands, and the look of disappointment on my parent's faces when I told them what I'd done. I've never forgotten that feeling and it's the same one I have now. I take a deep breath and tell them everything. I tell them all about Richard and me from the beginning until this morning when he showed up at my flat. Mum and Dad sit quietly while I talk. My biggest fear is they're going to think less of me. That my own parents are going to think I'm a heartless bitch because why wouldn't they?

'Oh, Lucy,' says Dad, caught somewhere between disappointment and sympathy.

I look at Mum and she has a look I can't quite decipher. It isn't angry or sad, but she's quiet and her face is expressionless. Her eyes are glassy, and it looks as though tears aren't far away.

'Mum?' I say, but she still doesn't say anything and I'm beginning to get scared. 'Please say something.'

Dad looks across at Mum, but her expression stays the same.

'We're just in shock. It's hard to believe that you of all people could do this,' says Dad.

'You're angry with me, aren't you? Just tell me. I deserve it,' I say.

'Darling,' says Dad. 'We can't condone what you did, but we know you, and we know you already know what you did was wrong. We're disappointed, but you're our daughter.'

'And is that how you feel, Mum?'

Finally, after what feels like an eternity, Mum says something.

'Did you ever think about his wife? Did you ever stop for a moment and think about the marriage you were destroying?' Her voice is hard and cold and it's a side of her I've never seen before.

'Lizzy,' Dad says quietly.

'Of course I did,' I say.

'And yet it didn't stop you,' Mum says, and tears are suddenly blistering her eyes.

'I tried,' I say feebly, and then I see Mum look across at Dad.

'Lizzy, not now,' Dad says, his face changing, the colour replaced with a sickly white.

'What, Greg? Do you have something to say?' says Mum.

I look at Dad, who for once seems speechless. Mum stands up and looks at me.

'I'm disappointed because I thought we raised you better than that. I thought if you got nothing else from me, the least you got was a moral compass. I never thought you'd do something like this.'

'I'm sorry,' I say, feeling my own tears simmering just below the surface.

'What is it with people? You think you can do whatever you want, whenever you want, and there's some sort of rewind button when it all goes wrong, and people get hurt. Well there isn't a button. You can't go back. You can't change what you've done,' she says and then she walks out, and I'm left alone with Dad. A quiet, humble, sorry looking Dad.

'I'm sorry,' I say, finally crying and Dad wraps his arms around me, and I sink into him, feeling his warm, safe body envelope mine.

I was at home this morning getting ready to leave when Richard turned up out of the blue. I hadn't seen him or spoken to him since I left the BBC. I'd called in and requested a week or two off to get my head together, which given the circumstances they were more than happy to give me. Richard had tried to call and text, but I thought a complete break was best, so I ignored him. It was impossibly difficult because I wanted to see him, but I needed time to get over him and decide what to do next. I was hoping that with a few days to get his head together, Richard would realise where his priorities needed to be. I don't want to mess up my career or his, and I certainly don't want to break up his family.

He turned up this morning a complete mess. He'd told his wife everything, she'd kicked him out, and now he wanted to give us a go. I can't believe he's prepared to throw everything away for me. It's too much. It made me realise straight away that whatever I felt for him wasn't proper love like Gran and Grandad. It could have been if we'd met in a different way, if he hadn't been married or had kids, but I can't be the reason his marriage ends and the reason his children lose their dad.

Despite knowing how awful it is, I'm a little shocked by Mum's reaction. I didn't expect her to be so angry about it. I expected her to be disappointed in me, but she wasn't just disappointed she was angry. My mind starts wondering why and without having to journey too far, it soon stops, and the obvious answer is waiting for me. She's speaking from personal experience. I have no idea what sort of experience because it's Mum and Dad, and despite them having problems, I can't imagine either of them having an affair. Before I have the chance to talk to Dad about it, Matt suddenly pokes his head around the door.

'I have someone on the phone,' he says.

'Do you mind?' says Dad to me. 'I've been on hold all morning.'

'Of course not.'

Dad gets up, smiles, takes the phone from Matt and disappears into the hallway. Matt looks a bit awkward, but then he comes over and puts his arms around me. Then he does something he hasn't done in a very long time, he kisses me on the head and says,

'Love you, Lucy-poosey-polly-wally.'

It's the name he called me when we were kids, and it makes me smile, and it's a million times better than all the tears I've been crying since Richard and I broke up.

It's a short while later and Dad's still on the phone, shouting at someone who apparently "doesn't know his arse from his elbow" and the rest of us are in the lounge waiting to leave for the pub. Mum came down a short while ago, her ruddy cheeks a giveaway she'd been crying, and she hasn't looked at me or said anything since. There's a quiet tension in the room and all because of me.

'What were you doing before I turned up and ruined everything?' I say, breaking the silence and trying to lighten the mood. "Own the drama" I'd once read in Cosmopolitan.

'We were playing I Spy,' says Holly.

'Correction, we were playing I Spy, but Gran was playing Spot What's Under Her Trousers,' says Matt.

'What? What's that?' says Gran.

'Her I Spy was something beginning with V,' says Matt. 'Have a guess, Lucy.'

'V? I have no idea,' I say, looking quickly around the room.

'Varicose veins,' says Matt and I laugh, followed by Holly, and then Matt, while Mum sits stoically on the end of the sofa.

'They're sending someone out,' says Dad.

'But I'm starving. My stomach is literally eating itself,' says Matt.

'We need to eat. How long's it going to be?' says Mum.

'An hour or so,' says Dad.

'Then we'll see you at the pub,' says Mum briskly. 'Come on kids, Joan, let's go.'

Mum helps Joan up, while Holly heads out of the door

into the sunshine.

'Do you want to walk with me?' I say to Matt.

'Love to.'

And so I walk with Matt, out of the front door and towards the pub, with Holly walking ahead with Mum and Gran. I can't tell Matt about Richard yet. I want to, but most of all, I want to spend some time with my little brother without thinking about the mess I've made of my life because despite what people might think, Matt and I get each other.

'I know why you're crying,' says Matt.

'Why's that, little brother?'

'Because after twenty-eight years, you finally realised I'm better than you,' says Matt, looking at me with a smile.

'That's definitely it,' I say, putting my arm through his and walking into the sunshine towards the pub.

April Roast

Holly

It happened and there's no going back. Charlotte and I kissed, which should be completely brilliant news (right?), but it isn't. It's the worst because everything is weird between us, and I don't know what to do to fix it. I think she hates me, and she won't return any of my messages. I've ruined everything. I'm not even sure how it happened. I definitely didn't plan it. If anything I was trying not to kiss her. As much as I've wanted to for ages, the thought of it making me pathetically weak at the knees, I knew I couldn't because she didn't feel the same way. She didn't fancy me, wasn't a lesbian, and definitely wasn't in love with me. But then it just sort of happened.

It was the day we got our acceptance letters from university. Charlotte and I both applied to Manchester, and we were worried that only one of us would get in and the other would be forced to go to their second choice. Then we got our letters and we'd both got in. We couldn't believe it. We were so excited, so happy, and so we decided to celebrate.

We ended up going to a student pub that's always packed with kids from college. It's a bit of a dive, with perpetually wet and blocked toilets and they always have some rubbish student band playing loud guitars with incomprehensible lyrics. It was fun though because we started drinking early and there were lots of people we knew from college, including Charlotte's boyfriend Josh. It's always a bit weird when Josh is around. He's always got his hands all over Charlotte, trying to cuddle her, hold her hand, and play with her ears (I'm sure he has an ear fetish). Even Charlotte seems a bit annoyed by his constant need for attention.

We drank all afternoon and into the evening until we were both wasted. Charlotte finally lost her patience and told Josh to leave her and her "fucking ears" alone. Josh got all moody and started sulking so that's when we ditched him, giggling and laughing, left the pub and headed back to her place.

I've slept at Charlotte's so many times over the years. We've known each other for so long that I don't even have to ask. We got back, and after making some very messy toasted cheese sandwiches, we went to bed. We always share her bed, which isn't that big, so there isn't much extra room. We were both still drunk and we fell into bed in just our underwear and immediately started cuddling up to each other. Usually we'd just fall asleep, but we were still buzzing from the news and from being out all day. We talked for a bit, but then suddenly we were kissing. I honestly don't remember if I started it or if she did, but I didn't want it to end. I thought that finally Charlotte and I might be together. It all seemed so easy. We'd go away to university as a couple. Together. In love. I couldn't have been any happier until Charlotte pulled away, her face suddenly sober and full to the brim with shock and terror.

'What are we doing?' she said.

'It's okay, I've wanted to do this for ages.'

'But we can't, Hols, it's wrong.'

'It doesn't feel wrong,' I said, and I tried to kiss her again.

'No, stop it. We shouldn't be doing this.'

'But I thought you wanted this?'

'I don't. I'm not a lesbian.'

'But—'

'I think you'd better go,' said Charlotte, pulling the duvet away from me and over herself, as though covering her semi-naked body might somehow cover up the memory of what we did. 'Just get out!'

I stumbled in the darkness and found my clothes, all of the alcohol draining from my body. I got dressed, left, and walked home in the dark, crying. From being so happy, so excited for the next three years, I was plunged into the terror of losing my best friend forever.

I put my headphones on and turn up the volume. As I'm lying here, I start thinking about God. It's been strange going to church because I didn't really believe before and to be honest, it was always about spending time with Charlotte. However, being a part of it has really opened my eyes. For my whole life I've always felt like the odd one out. I know I was a mistake. Mum and Dad have never told me, and they probably never will, but it doesn't mean I don't know. Maybe it's why I don't feel as close to them and why I'm so confused but going to church for the first time I felt like I belonged somewhere. I don't know if there's a God or not, and some of the Bible is a bit weird, and definitely sexist, but I like the feeling of being a part of something bigger than myself. When I'm there, I feel like an important member of the family, which is more than I feel here sometimes.

As I'm looking up at the ceiling, a face appears above me with a smile. I take off my headphones and smile back at Lucy.

'You all right, Sis?' says Lucy.

'Fine.'

'You don't sound fine and you're listening to Damien Rice.'

'What's wrong with Damien Rice?'

'He's pretty depressing, Hols.'

'You like James Blunt. He's not exactly upbeat.'

'True, but nothing compared to Slit Your Wrists Rice. Do you want to talk about it? Is it to do with Charlotte?'

Just the mention of her name and I can feel my face immediately change. It's hot and red and my mouth refuses to stay still, and before I can help it tears are leaking out and down my face.

Growing up, Lucy and I weren't very close. I adored and aspired to be her, but I think to her I was just her annoying little sister. She had her group of friends; the in crowd at school, full of prefects, the brainy ones, the popular ones, whilst I had Charlotte. For quite a few years I resented Lucy for being so perfect. How could I possibly follow in her footsteps? Then I realised I didn't have to be like her. The thing was though, I didn't know who I was. That's the problem when you spend years idolising someone else and wanting to be like them; when you stop, you realise all the time you spent wanting to be different was time you weren't getting to know you.

'Charlotte and I kissed.'

'Oh, wow,' says Lucy. 'How was it?'

'Awful. I think she hates me.'

'I'm sure she doesn't hate you.'

'She won't talk to me, message me, or anything.'

'It doesn't mean she hates you. She's probably confused. She kissed her best friend, who also happens to be a girl. It's not something you can do without questioning yourself a lot. It's a big deal.'

'I suppose because I know how I feel, I assumed she felt the same,' I say, and Lucy looks at me with a smile. 'What?'

'Do you remember the time I took you into London? You were about ten.'

'The first time Mum and Dad let me go in without them.'

'You were so excited. Dad spent about an hour before we left going over the rules. Do you remember that?'

'He wouldn't let me leave until I repeated them back to him. Number one: stay by Lucy the whole time, never leave her side, and hold her hand crossing the road. Number two: don't talk to any strangers, except Policemen or Beefeaters. Number three: don't have any fun whatsoever, blah, blah, blah. Typical Dad.'

'We did have fun though, didn't we?'

'I just remember I got to spend the whole day with my big sister. It was the first time I felt properly grown up.'

'And it was brilliant until you went missing.'

'I don't remember that.'

'You don't remember me freaking out in Harrods

because I told you to stay exactly where you were and not to move a muscle for five seconds, and then when I came back and you'd gone? You don't remember me having to run around Harrods until I found someone in Security to start an all-out search for you?'

'Not really.'

'And this is exactly why you don't understand why Charlotte might be a bit confused. You've always been the same, Hols, and I don't mean this in a bad way, but sometimes you live in a bubble. A little Holly bubble. It didn't matter that Dad spent an hour telling you the rules and that I told you not to move. Even at ten you had this thing that makes you so singular of thought, so focused on you that you exclude what anyone else tells you.'

'So you think I'm selfish?'

'No, it's not that. You aren't selfish at all, it's just, you don't always think about other people. You have this thing where it's like you shut out the world and only hear what's in your head. It's why you've always driven Dad around the bend.'

'And why's that?'

'Because he's like that too. He lives in his own little world, only thinking about what he needs instead of what Mum needs, and again, it isn't so much him being selfish as him not knowing how to include everyone else in his thought processes.'

'But Dad's really annoying. You really think we're alike?'

'More so than either one of you would ever admit,' says Lucy with a warm smile.

'Jesus, Luce, it's worse than I thought.'

'Dad's not that bad.'

'To you, his favourite. I don't think he sees me in quite the same way.'

'He loves you, Hols.'

'It doesn't feel that way sometimes.'

'Then make more of an effort. I'm not always interested in what Dad's waffling on about, but I still listen.'

'You want me to listen to Dad?' I say incredulously.

'I'm just saying. It's a two-way thing.'

'Yeah, Dad's way or the highway.'

'Just give him a chance.'

Then right on cue, Dad pokes his head around the door, looking very pleased with himself.

'It's ready,' says Dad.

I have no idea what Dad's doing in the shed. All I know is that for the first time in forever we're not having a proper roast dinner on Sunday roast day. Dad went out yesterday and got all the ingredients for a Ploughman's lunch because apparently he doesn't have time to cook. Who has a Ploughman's lunch for Sunday dinner? I'm seriously disappointed.

Lucy and I get up and go downstairs. Matt, Mum, and Gran are already trundling outside into the garden. It's a warm day and sunshine is shimmering through cracks in the branches of the tree next to the shed. It wasn't so nice when I got up to go to church this morning in the hope Charlotte would be there. I wanted to explain, to apologise, because I can't handle this. Her parents said she wasn't feeling well and had stayed at home. I thought about going over and seeing her, but I didn't want to be needy like Josh, so I left church, came home, and spent the morning in my room feeling sorry for myself.

We all stand around the shed and Dad's in front of it with a big smile on his face.

'Thank you all for coming to the grand opening of my new shed,' says Dad.

'Shouldn't you have red tape or something?' says Matt.

'It's fine, we don't need red tape,' says Dad.

'I don't understand what's going on,' says Gran. 'Is it different?'

'Sort of,' says Dad.

'It looks the same to me,' says Gran.

'On the outside, yes, but on the inside it's unrecognisable. So, without further ado, I give you my brand-new writing shack.'

Dad steps aside, opens the door, and lets us all in. I'm not really in the best of moods for this, but I follow everyone inside. It's quite a tight squeeze with us all in there, but eventually we get in and Dad starts telling us about it.

I haven't been in the shed for years. When I was younger I used to help Dad with the gardening. Lucy and Matt wouldn't do it, but I liked gardening with Dad. It was the only thing we ever did together. Just the two of us. Even now the shed has the same smell of freshly cut grass and oil. I remember one time being in here with Dad. It was a warm spring day, and he was sitting down at the bench fiddling with the hedge trimmer that was always breaking. I was sitting watching him. He was showing me how to fix it, but Dad's never been very good at fixing things, and he was getting more and more frustrated. In the end he gave up with the hedge trimmer and instead we sat talking. I was twelve, just sitting in the shed talking to my dad. It's the best memory I have of us. When Lucy and Matt are around I feel like he forgets about me, but in here I felt like he was just my dad and I loved it.

'This is my writing desk. I found it at an antiques shop in Finchley. Here's the wood burning fire to keep me warm in the winter months. Over there's a table and two chairs, just in case I have visitors and I have a camp stove to make tea so I can keep writing without having to go indoors. What do you all think?' says Dad, obviously proud of his handy work.

'Yeah, great, but I'm starving, when's lunch?' says Matt.

'I don't understand, where's the lawn mower?' says Gran.

'Very nice,' says Lucy.

'Yes,' says Mum, with a pensive smile.

Dad looks crestfallen as everyone filters out. Matt walks out grumbling about his empty stomach. Lucy, Mum, and Gran walk out with Gran still asking about the lawn mower, until it's just Dad and I standing together.

'What do you think, Hols?' says Dad eagerly.

I look around and it is very impressive. He's totally transformed the old shed into a warm and comfortable writing cave. I look at the desk and there in a small wooden frame is a photo of me. It's one of my old school photos. I look about twelve and I'm smiling a forced school photo smile with my crooked teeth and slightly askew ponytail, but seeing it there makes me happy.

'I love it, Dad.'

'Really?'

'It's warm, cosy, and it still has that smell.'

'The shed smell.'

'Exactly, the shed smell.'

'Thanks, love. I guess we should probably head back indoors.'

'Do you mind if I stay in here for a while?'

Dad looks a little surprised, but then he smiles and sits down at his desk.

'I'm not that hungry either. Do you mind if I join you?'

'Not at all,' I say, sitting down at the table. 'You can tell me about your book.'

'You're interested?'

'Not really, but you know, it's better than small talk.'

'Where to start,' says Dad with a smile.

Suddenly all thoughts of Charlotte, and the complete and utter mess that's my life, are put aside as I listen and pretend I'm twelve again, just a girl, in a shed, talking with her dad.

Lizzy

The retreat was amazing. Before we left Stella said it was going to, "blow my world wide open" and it definitely has. I didn't realise this sort of thing went on. I've seen television shows about things like it, but to be in the heart of it, in the eye of the storm, was incredible.

Stella picked me up on a Friday morning in her Range Rover. The retreat started in the afternoon and went through until Sunday morning. She told me to wear something loose and comfortable. I was in an old grey tracksuit, my hair tied back in a ponytail, with no makeup. Makeup is strictly forbidden at the retreat because apparently it masks our true self. It was the first time I'd ever seen Stella without it. Even at Pilates, when most of us are a bit rough around the edges, she looks as though she's off to attend a film premier. Stella doesn't do 'just out of bed'. She still looked amazing. Her lithe, hairless body was tucked tightly into a shimmering silver tracksuit, her supple face moisturised and elegantly pale against her dark hair which although tied back, still looked a million dollars.

We arrived at the retreat and at first glance, it seemed to be a lot of the same sort of women. Middle and upper middle-class, middle-aged women, all in tracksuits. The retreat was set against the backdrop of a very salubrious estate in Oxfordshire and despite the closeness of the main house, which looked like something lifted straight from a Jane Austen novel, we were going to spend the weekend in native American tepees. There was going to be no luxury for us. No four poster beds or cavernous bathrooms where we could soak for hours in giant rolled baths and the only luxury we were allowed to bring was a single roll of toilet paper. I went with Andrex Touch of Luxury with added aloe.

I was sharing a tepee with Stella, Penny from Buckinghamshire, Sally from Gloucester, Eleanor from 'the Wolds' - annoyingly she refused to say Cotswolds the whole weekend - and Linda from London. The six of us would share the tepee, which only had blankets on the floor, no beds, no sleeping bags, and no pillows. I suppose this is what Stella meant by "very real" - uncomfortable. Still, and despite being a bit put off by the conditions, once we started on the actual activities all of that seemed to go by the wayside.

The first evening we all sat down in a big circle. We began innocently with each of us sharing a story about our lives, but with the added ingredient of a native American herb called Peyote. It's supposed to help bring us from ourselves to ourselves and be ourselves. It's basically a drug that gets you high and you feel like you're floating above yourself while being deep within yourself. I realise that doesn't make any sense, but it did at the time.

Before long women were getting naked, howling like crazed wolves, crying, laughing, hugging each other, supporting each other, and loving each other because despite our differences, we were all the same. The leader (Algonquin or mother), sat in the centre of the circle and helped things along. We were all soon naked and embracing womanhood through the spirits of our female ancestors. It didn't matter about the shape of our bodies, or the amount of hair we had on our private bits, we were all lost together on the same magical journey. We went back to our tepees naked and full of love. I don't even remember falling asleep that night.

The next morning I was surprisingly lucid considering the night we'd had. Across the tent there was a tangle of limbs, bodies strewn together. We'd gone from strangers to a small family in the course of one night. After we'd all woken up, we had a native American style breakfast, and then we began the day's activities. First off we had Yoga and meditation, followed by arts and crafts, then after lunch we had group bonding exercises. It reminded me of the school camping trip I took back in 1973, only with a lot less orienteering and no pervy Mr Norris.

The main event on the last night was the physical bonding circle. Again we had the Peyote and we sat in a circle discussing various aspects of our lives; more specifically, our sex lives. The last night was all about discovering our hidden sexual self. Apparently most women fail to fully grasp the power of their own orgasm. I was starting to feel a bit uncomfortable and English about it, but slowly and with the help of the Peyote, I started to loosen up and share details of my own sex life. Compared to most, mine felt very depressing and provincial. Some of them did things like bondage, role playing, watching pornography, swinging, and even anal sex – not something I've ever entertained, and Greg's never attempted to venture off the beaten track.

Some of the group were first timers like me and some had been countless times before like Stella, and it soon became clear who was who. I honestly wasn't expecting what happened next to happen. Like the first night we all got naked, and there were tears, there was howling, and people hugging and laughing, but this time things were taken to the next level. I don't consider myself a prude at all, but even I was shocked when some of the women started masturbating and having orgasms right in front of me. It suddenly got all very late-night Channel Four.

"Let it go," said Algonquin. "The orgasm is the most beautiful thing a woman can give herself. The ultimate pleasure". I looked across and Stella had already started. She was groaning, moaning, and then she kicked her legs out and started screaming in pleasure. I didn't know where to look. I'd never done that sort of thing before. I noticed a few of the other 'newbies' looking as shocked as me, but gradually one by one we all joined in.

I'm not sure how to explain what happened next, but it was like something took over my body and mind. I was an animal. I don't want to get too graphic, but I joined in with the group and before long I had my first orgasm in two years. I have to admit it was a bit strange, but the power of the orgasm surprised me, and I cried when it was over. All the women eventually climaxed, and we fell into a messy, sweaty heap, and then we watched as Algonquin masturbated and appeared to have the strongest orgasm yet. At one point she had both legs behind her head and was screaming something in Italian. She finished with a flourish on all fours, barking like a dog. Apparently, according to Stella, she draws all of the group's orgasms together and channels that energy into one super orgasm.

The drive home the following day was a lot different to the drive there. It was a sunny day, so we turned the music up and sped along the M40 back towards London singing our lungs out to Shania Twain. I felt liberated and for the first time in years, I had an energy and a freedom that almost made me start crying again. Instead I yelled and howled along to the radio with Stella, until we were back in suburban Muswell Hill.

'Has it changed you?' said Stella, as we sat in her Range Rover outside my house.

'Definitely. Not in the ways I thought it might, but it's opened my eyes.'

'You know they have a couples retreat too.'

'And what do you do there, have sex in front of everyone?' I said with an incredulous laugh.

'Actually, yes. It's very liberating.'

'I can't imagine Greg being up for that.'

'Paul loves it. He embraces sex in front of strangers.'

'Greg barely wants to have sex in private. I can't imagine him becoming Don Juan with an audience.'

'You never know,' said Stella with a grin.

When I got home, I felt a bit strange, but as the days went on life got back to normal, although I haven't been able to completely shake the impact of the retreat. I haven't told Greg what happened because despite his pretence that he's an enlightened intellectual, Greg's actually quite English and stuffy about anything a bit different. At least I finally had an orgasm, although I didn't imagine it would be with a group of middle-aged, middle-class women, in a field in Oxfordshire.

'It's just not right,' says Matt indignantly.

'I don't mind it,' says Lucy.

'But it's not a roast. It's just cheese and stuff,' says Matt, prodding a pork pie.

'Stop complaining and eat up,' I say.

'Someone's in a huff. Is it about the shed?' says Matt.

'I'm not in a huff,' I say.

'She's definitely in a huff,' says Matt to Lucy. 'And I bet it's about the shed.'

'Then leave her alone and eat the pork pie you've touched about fifty times,' says Lucy, giving me a conciliatory smile.

I'm annoyed about so many things I don't know where to start. It started last month with Lucy's confession about her cheating with that man from work. I was so disappointed she could do something like that. How could my little girl be so thoughtless and cold hearted? I've always been so proud of my kids, and not because of their achievements, but because I always thought they knew the right thing to do. Then she tells me that and all the business with Greg came shooting back in a moment. The same, familiar pain I felt back then returning and racing through my body. "Just one night". "It meant nothing". "A stupid mistake". Greg's words filling my mind with an anger that hasn't completely gone away.

Then there's Greg's shed. Why is it that Greg can spend a fortune, and a considerable number of hours, making himself the perfect writing shed, but he can't take the same amount of time to work on our relationship? When I wanted to spend time together he was too busy, and I gave him the benefit of the doubt, but he's spent the last two weeks either in the shed or getting things for the shed. The shed has become the most important thing in Greg's life. He even bought a magazine called 'Inside Shed'. When he showed it to me, I joked he needed a magazine called 'Inside Lizzy' instead, but he didn't laugh and to be honest, neither did I.

After my weekend at the retreat, I felt energised and empowered, and as though anything was possible, but now I feel small and meek again. I want to share myself with Greg, change the course of our life, but instead he's moved himself into the shed and I'm back where I started.

'Is this it?' says Joan.

'Greg thought a change would be nice. Something lighter,' I say.

'But I can't eat cheese, it gives me gas,' says Joan.

'You can eat the ham, the salad, some bread?' I say.

'I can get ham and bread at the home. This isn't a roast. I came for a roast.'

'I'm with Gran,' says Matt. 'I say we make a formal complaint.'

'About what?' says Greg, walking back in with Holly just behind him.

'A formal complaint about this meal. It isn't a roast,' says Matt.

'Obviously, but I didn't have time. I was too busy with the shed,' says Greg.

'There you go, too busy with the shed,' I say.

'Even Mum's in a huff about it,' says Matt.

'I'm not in a huff, Matt. Just leave it will you,' I say, trying to keep myself together.

'Are you in a huff about the shed?' says Greg. 'I thought you liked the shed.'

'It's fine, Greg, I'm not bothered about the shed.'

I hate the shed. I despise the shed. I'm jealous of the fucking shed!

'See, she's not bothered about the shed,' says Greg. 'Let's tuck in and eat, shall we?'

'I suppose I'll eat some bread. Is there any wine?' says Joan.

'You aren't supposed to drink alcohol with your medication, Mum,' says Greg.

'If this is dinner, the least you can do is pour me a glass of wine,' says Joan.

'Go on, Dad, give Gran some wine,' says Matt encouragingly.

'Just one,' says Greg, who goes off and comes back with a small glass of red wine.

As we're eating, I start thinking about my predicament and I decide something. Last month I realised I needed to do something just for me. I need my own life outside of my family, so I went to the retreat and that was all about pleasuring ourselves, admittedly in the most literal sense of the word, but it was about putting ourselves first. Everything that's happened to me recently has been leading me towards greater independence and now it's time to exert myself. If Greg is going to have his shed, then I need something that's only for me. I'm going to start writing again. I remember sitting in my old bedroom as a teenager, writing as though nothing else in the world mattered. It was always my saviour. My saviour from the boredom of growing up where I did, where everything fun, exciting, and interesting felt so far away. Writing let me feel nearer to the world I so desperately wanted to be a part of. It's saved me so many times in my life. Maybe it can save me again.

The doorbell rings unexpectedly. It's Sunday and we're all here. Maybe it's Jehovah's Witnesses. Greg starts to get up, but I gesture for him to sit down because the last time he talked to the Jehovah's Witnesses, he forced them to come in, sit down, and he wouldn't let them leave until they conceded that there's a possibility God doesn't exist – which took two hours. I walk into the hallway, open the front door, and stood there is Holly's friend Charlotte.

'Hello, Mrs Wilde, is Holly in?'

'Sorry, love, we just sat down for dinner. Is it important?'

'Sort of,' says Charlotte, a little self-consciously.

'Then you'd better come in,' I say, standing aside. Charlotte has been Holly's friend for years and she used to come over all the time, but recently they've tended to spend more time at her house. I wonder if it's because of the religious thing. Her parents go to church every week. Maybe Holly feels more comfortable around them. 'Come on through.'

Charlotte follows me into the dining room where Joan is topping up her wine and Greg's going on about the bloody shed. As soon as we walk in Holly's face changes.

'Charlotte,' says Holly, standing up.

'Sorry to interrupt,' says Charlotte.

'No problem,' says Greg. 'Please join us. I'll grab an extra chair from the garage.'

'Who's this?' says Joan.

'This is my friend Charlotte,' says Holly.

'Hello,' says Charlotte.

'Enormous breasts,' says Joan, and Charlotte goes bright red.

'We'll be upstairs,' says Holly, and Charlotte smiles politely then follows Holly upstairs to her bedroom.

'That was weird,' says Matt after a moment.

'What was weird?' says Greg.

'Those two. Did you feel the tension?'

'Says Mr Observant,' says Lucy.

'Exactly. If I noticed it then something is definitely going on.'

'Don't be ridiculous,' says Lucy.

'I once knew a girl with enormous breasts,' says Joan. 'Samantha Simcock. She used to jump over the pummel horse in PE and they'd knock her in the face.'

'I think you've had enough wine,' says Greg, trying to move her glass away, but Joan's having none of it.

'Quiet,' says Matt. 'I'm trying to hear what they're saying up there.'

We all go quiet, but we can only hear muffled voices. I

hope Holly is all right. I felt so awful about the whole Gavin debacle. I want to be present in her life. I want to know what's going on and I want to help her. Eventually it all goes quiet and then we hear footsteps coming down the stairs. The door opens and in walk Holly and Charlotte, and they're holding hands, which is a bit odd, I suppose. Although after my weekend retreat with Stella, nothing should surprise me anymore.

'I have something to tell you,' says Holly with a tentative smile. 'Charlotte and I are dating. She's my girlfriend.'

The room stays quiet, and I have no idea what to say. I look across at Greg and he looks just as shocked as me. Holly is gay? How did I not know this? I thought she liked that boy at church. She told me all about it. I'm so confused. I don't mind that she's gay. It's fine, but why didn't she tell me? I thought we'd bonded. I thought she needed me.

'Is anyone going to say anything?' says Holly after a moment. 'Surprise? Devastating disappointment?'

'You're a lesbian?' says Matt.

'Yes, Matt, I'm a lesbian.'

'A lezzie? A carpet muncher? A girl with comfortable shoes?' continues Matt.

'Yes, Matt, we're gay.'

'I'm glad you finally told everyone,' says Lucy with a smile.

'You knew about this?' I say to Lucy.

'I needed someone to talk to,' says Holly.

'And you couldn't come to me?' I say, my voice wobbling.

'Sorry,' says Holly. 'But Lucy was there, and she was really helpful. Thanks, Luce.'

'I'm shocked,' says Greg. 'I had no idea, but if it makes you happy then I'm happy.'

'Thanks, Dad,' says Holly with a smile.

Am I the only one who's a bit put out by this? I'm her mother. I should have known. The whole conversation I had with her about the boy she was in love with, when I thought we were bonding, and it was all a lie. Trying to help her by inviting Gavin for dinner and all the time she was gay. Why couldn't she talk to me? What's so wrong with me? I thought I knew my children, my husband, but now it seems I don't know any of them.

'Now I think about it,' says Joan. 'I think Samantha Simcock might have been a gay. Oh, I'm confused.'

'So am I,' I say getting up, my emotions getting the better of me.

'Mum?' says Holly, looking bewildered. 'What's the matter?'

I don't know what to say, but I'm angry and confused, so I rush out of the room and head straight upstairs and fall down on the bed.

Am I such an awful mother? I've always tried so hard to have a good relationship with all my children. All the dreams I had of cosy chats with my kids over coffee, talking about our lives, our feelings, and being the sort of mother who was as much a friend as a parent. I don't care whether she's gay, straight, or swings both ways, but what hurts is that she couldn't confide in me. Holly's going off to university soon and then I'll know even less of her. I'll be less to her. I feel like I'm becoming the one thing I feared more than anything else in the world: my own mother.

May Roast

Lucy

'Jim's still crying,' says Dad. 'He's gone into the foetal position next to the dishwasher.'

'Who cares?' says Matt. 'I think I've ruined everything with Saskia.'

'I'm sure you haven't,' says Mum. 'She's probably just a bit peeved.'

'A bit peeved? After what you said, I'll be surprised if she ever talks to you again,' I say to Matt.

'What do I do about Jim?' says Dad. 'I don't know what to say to him. The old Jim was outgoing, gregarious, the life and soul of the party, but now it's like he's broken.'

'I'm broken,' says Matt.

'Stop being so melodramatic,' says Holly.

'I'm not being melo anything,' says Matt. 'I'm distraught.'

'I don't think much of this trifle,' says Gran.

'That's because it isn't trifle,' says Mum. 'It's an Eton mess.'

'Is anything what it's supposed to be today?' says Gran in disgust. 'The gravy wasn't gravy; the trifle isn't trifle.'

'I love it,' says Charlotte.

'Thank you, Charlotte,' Mum gushes, still over-compensating for how she took their news last month.

'This probably isn't the best time, but I have an announcement,' I say, before taking a deep breath.

'Is it about the trifle?' says Gran. 'Because if it is, I wouldn't bother.'

'No, Gran, it's about my job at the BBC.'

'I should go after Saskia. Do you think I should go after her?' says Matt interrupting me.

'Hello, talking here,' I say to Matt.

'Sorry my life isn't as important as yours.'

'As I was saying. It's about my job at the BBC. I quit,' I say, and there is a sudden silence around the table. Mum and Dad are looking at me with incredulous expressions on their faces, Matt is speechless for once, and no one says a word.

I've wanted to work for the BBC for as long as I can remember. It's always been my one big burning ambition in life. It's such an institution and since my first day there, fresh out of university, I felt like I belonged. However, since the affair with Richard, everything I've worked towards has been tarnished and it isn't the same anymore. Something's changed and I can't keep going along pretending it's going to get better when it quite clearly isn't. The only solution was to quit. Actually, it was a mutual decision so I get a small compensation package, which should keep me going for six months or so while I put my life back together.

'Well?' I say after a moment when no one says anything. 'Any thoughts?'

It's at this moment that there's a loud crash in the kitchen. We all get up and rush into the kitchen to find Jim lying on the floor, surrounded by broken glass and a pool of red wine. He has a gash on his head and is bleeding onto the floor, the blood and wine joining together into a stream and seeping between the cracks in the kitchen floor.

Three hours earlier

'Jim Whitby,' says Dad proudly. 'So glad you could make it.'

'I wouldn't miss it for the world,' says Jim, in a big, booming public school voice.

He's standing on the front step, and we've all been summoned to come and meet the great Jim Whitby. Dad seems to have a bit of a man-crush on Jim. He's been talking about him all morning as though he's some sort of God, dragging out every last university anecdote and drunken Jim tale to anyone that who'll listen. Despite being the same age as Dad, he's very handsome, and has aged much better, like a vintage wine to Dad's mouldy cheese. He definitely has an aura about him. He's tall, still has a suave head of well-groomed greying hair and is dressed impeccably in obviously expensive clothes. From what Dad said this morning, it seems that when he started teaching after university, Jim got a job in the financial sector and has made an absolute fortune. After years in Hong Kong and New York, he now lives in a large house in Cambridge with his wife and daughter. Jim Whitby is Dad's hero and by the end of the day, Dad assures us, we'll all love Jim just as much as he does.

I'm actually more worried about fixing things with Mum than falling in love with an old friend of Dad's. Mum and I are talking, but the tension that's been there since the day I told her about Richard is still loitering with intent. I never got to the bottom of why it made her react the way it did. I understand she's disappointed in me, but it felt so out of character for her to react that way. I'm convinced it has something to do with Dad. I haven't had the chance to bring it up yet and I'm a little scared what I might discover when I do.

'Come in. Right, introductions. Obviously you know Lizzy,' says Dad, a little flustered.

'A pleasure as always,' says Jim, before he holds her hand and gives it a kiss. Mum lets out an embarrassingly high-pitched squeak. 'You haven't changed a bit, Lizzy.'

'This is my eldest, Lucy. The one who works at the BBC,' says Dad proudly. 'You met her when she was really small.'

'You definitely got your mother's good looks,' says Jim, which makes me blush slightly.

'And this is Matt.'

'Ah, yes, the budding photographer, it's a real pleasure,' says Jim, shaking Matt's hand to within an inch of its life - and there's the Type A testosterone.

'Hello,' says Matt, slightly shaken by the brutal handshake. Poor old Type B Matt. 'I didn't know Dad talked about my photography.'

'You'd be surprised what your dad talks about,' says Jim.

'And moving on quickly, this is Matt's girlfriend, Saskia. She's American.'

'Hi,' says Saskia.

Jim leans in and gives her a kiss on both cheeks.

'Bloody love the Yanks,' barks Jim. 'I spent a few years in New York. Brilliant place. Best food in the world.'

'And this is my youngest, Holly.'

'You saved the best for last,' says Jim, and even the usually glib Holly seems a bit gushy in front of him. He leans in and gives her a kiss on both cheeks too.

'And this is Holly's friend, sorry, girlfriend, Charlotte,' says Dad, embarrassingly so.

'Do you have to say it like that?' says Holly.

'Like what?'

'Like we're the headliners in the family freak show.'

'But we're hugely supportive of your ... "situation",' says Dad. 'Aren't we, Lizzy?'

'Hugely,' says Mum, putting her arm around Charlotte.

'I think it's great. Come one, come all. It's a pleasure to meet you,' says Jim.

Dad's been going absolutely crazy about the whole Holly and Charlotte business since they announced it last month. He's seeing it as a sort of atheist victory over the old fashioned, narrow minded and judgemental hypocrisy of religion. Charlotte's religious parents didn't take the news so well, which is why she's been spending most of her time here. It's become like a sort of atheist Jihad for Dad.

'There's one more person to meet. Remember my mum? She's in the living room. Come through, she'll be so happy to see you.'

Jim goes through into the living room, and we all follow him like we're on a tour. The great Jim Whitby meets the Wilde family with Dad the tour guide leading him through the generations and the new additions to our family tree.

'Mum, remember Jim from university?' says Dad.

Gran looks up at Jim from her chair, squints her eyes slightly, and then a wrinkly smile spreads across her face.

'Of course I do,' says Gran, who doesn't usually know what day of the week it is. 'Still as handsome as always.'

'And you haven't aged a bit,' says Jim, leaning down and kissing her on the hand.

'Oh, Jim, really,' says Gran in a silly hitch pitched tone, similar to Mum's squeak.

'Right, time for drinks, methinks,' says Jim. 'You know at university, your father could drink anyone under the table,' Jim says to Holly, putting his arm casually across her shoulders.

'Everyone except you,' says Dad, and they start walking off towards the kitchen.

'Remember Edinburgh?' says Jim, laughing loudly. 'Absolute carnage.'

I watch as the whole family continues the grand tour, while I sit opposite Gran. She has a magazine on her lap, but she isn't reading it, which is probably a good thing because it belongs to Matt. It's one of those men's magazines with a half-naked girl on the front cover and advice on how to pleasure your girlfriend while still having time for your mates. I have no idea why it's on her lap because I'm fairly sure she doesn't need to know where her G spot is.

I have some really big news to tell the family, but I don't know if today's the day or not. Dad's so happy with Jim being here, Saskia's here with Matt, and I don't know how Mum and Dad are going to take it. I feel like Mum's still on the edge after everything that's happened recently, and I don't want to be the one who pushes her over. I have to tell them though. It's such a big deal and they're my family. They deserve to know what's going on and if I don't tell them soon I'm going to explode.

I had to leave the BBC. I couldn't carry on with Richard still being there. Every day I felt like I was being pushed further and further into the hole we'd created. I was being buried alive by the guilt, the embarrassment, and the shame of what we'd done. The only way out seemed to be to leave.

I talked to my boss and together we came to a solution that suited everyone and so I'm done. My last day is next Friday and then I'm unemployed. I know how proud Dad is of me working there and no matter what he says, I know he's going to think less of me. Even the way he introduced me to Jim, it's like working for the BBC has become a part of who I am. I suppose I'm afraid of what's going to happen when I don't work there anymore. Will there still be enough of me left?

The next hour goes by in a whirl of laughter, wine, and tales of when Jim and Dad met at university. Jim's a real storyteller and has us all in hysterics and Dad goes into great and lengthy detail about his tour for 'Wilde on Wilde'. It's fun listening to Jim, but I can't help feeling a bit sad because Matt's here with Saskia, Holly's here with Charlotte, and I'm the only one without a partner. Since I was sixteen I've always had a boyfriend. I like being in a relationship. I like the security of having someone in my life I can rely on, go to bed with, or spend the evening watching TV with. Matt's love life has always been up and down like a bad hot air balloonist, and this is Holly's first love, but what's happened to me? I'm happy for them, but while they're both in the flush of new love, I'm still yearning for the married man I can't have and that makes me feel even more pathetically sad. I feel like the loser at the awards ceremony, trying to put a brave face on as the camera pans in front of me. Do your best congratulatory smile. Pretend you're happy for the winners. Clap like you really mean it.

Eventually Dad gets back to the kitchen to finish cooking dinner. As usual he's gone all out so we have free range, rare breed Cornish game hens, roasted with assorted vegetables and a fancy sounding au jus. Mums fished out the good china and everything is looking and smelling fantastic. Mum is laying the table, Holly and Charlotte are upstairs in her room, and Saskia is making a phone call, and so it's just Matt, Jim, and me in the living room. Gran's still not reading the magazine and is staring off into space with a weird sort of half-smile on her face. Jim, who's been drinking like a fish since he arrived, is already pretty drunk, and Matt's had a few as well. I'm taking it steady because the last thing I want to be when I give Mum and Dad my news is completely sloshed.

'So what's a beautiful, young, successful woman like you doing without a boyfriend?' says Jim. 'They must be queuing up.'

'Hardly,' I say, laughing a trill little laugh, while trying to hide the sadness and embarrassment on my face. Matt sees it though and gives me a supportive smile.

'Lucy's too busy working on her career,' says Matt. 'She's doing really well at the BBC.'

'Well, I …' I start to say, but then I stop because I don't know what else to say about it. The truth will soon be out. 'What about you, Jim, Dad said you have a daughter?'

'That's right,' says Jim a little uncomfortably. 'But I don't see much of her these days, what with one thing and another. Modern life, eh? We're always too busy. I'm lucky if she sends me the occasional text to tell me she's still alive.'

'Right,' I say, as party animal Jim starts to look a little sombre.

'And what about you and the Yank? It seems pretty serious,' says Jim to Matt, his face suddenly changing, the momentary uncertainty of being asked about his own life now replaced with his previous cocksureness.

'It's early days,' says Matt coyly.

'But it seems like you like her a lot,' says Jim, his drunken words falling into each other. 'I mean, it's obvious you're more into her than she is into you … so to speak,' says Jim, and I think both Matt and I are a bit shocked. Jim's swaying slightly on the sofa and Matt is starting to look very uneasy. It's obvious that Jim has unwittingly touched a nerve.

'I don't think so,' says Matt.

'Really?' says Jim. 'Listen Matt, it's fine, really, nothing to be ashamed about old boy. It happens to the best of us. It happened to me with my wife. You meet an attractive woman, you're in over your head—'

'But it's not like that,' says Matt, now serious and verging on angry; a side to Matt I've only seen a few times before. Matt usually goes out of his way to avoid any sort of confrontation. 'If anything, she's definitely way more into me.'

'If you say so,' says Jim, with an antagonising laugh.

I'm going to say something. I'm going to intervene and move the conversation away from Matt and Saskia, but before I can Matt jumps in again.

'I do say so. She's all over me, actually Jim, but to me it's just casual. I'm just good at looking interested, keeping them happy.'

'Really?' says Saskia, standing at the door, arms folded across her chest. 'I had no idea I was such a bad judge of character.'

Saskia finishes, tears washing around her eyes as she turns around and walks out, the front door slamming shortly after.

'Oh dear, someone's in the doghouse,' says Jim with a chuckle, before he gets up from the sofa, almost falling over in the process. 'More wine, methinks.' And then he walks out leaving Matt a complete and utter mess.

By the time we're all sitting down to eat, Matt is beside himself because Saskia won't take his calls or return his texts. Jim's even more drunk than he already was and it's obvious to everyone (except Dad) that he isn't altogether all right.

'How's the Cornish game hen?' says Dad to Jim.

'Incredible,' says Jim and Dad smiles proudly. 'Incredible that the man who lived off beans on toast and fried egg sandwiches for three years at university could make this. Lizzy obviously trained you well.'

'This has got nothing to do with me,' says Mum.

'I think it's just lovely you all sit around the table

together, the whole family with partners, gay, straight or otherwise. I wish we'd done more of that,' says Jim.

'You and Arabella have a different life though, don't you? High-fliers, always off somewhere exotic. Living the dream,' says Dad.

'More of a bloody nightmare these days,' says Jim, his voice etched with sadness, and we all look across at Dad, on whom it's beginning to dawn that Jim Whitby, life and soul of the party, is actually a depressing drunk with a crumbling marriage, whose only solace is at the bottom of a bottle.

'Still,' says Dad, trying his best to keep things together. 'How's the food, Mum?'

'Gravy's too runny,' says Gran.

'That's because it's an au jus,' says Dad.

'The gravy's not gravy?' says Gran in a huff. 'And I suppose these aren't roast potatoes?'

'I haven't eaten a meal with Arabella in six months,' says Jim from nowhere. 'No, make that eight months, and that was a bloody disaster. The counsellor said we should make the effort. Oh, yes, Greg old boy, we're seeing a marriage counsellor. Correction, we were seeing a marriage counsellor before that bitch stopped showing up because apparently the thought of sitting in the same room as me makes her feel physically sick.'

Then Jim starts crying. He's falling apart in front of us and it's horrible – and somewhat uncomfortable - to watch. I look across at Dad, who seems completely shocked by all of this. He obviously had no idea that Jim's marriage was in trouble. Jim's shoulders sink forward, and his head drops, and he starts vibrating as the tears continue to come. We all look at Dad, waiting for him to do something.

'Hey, mate,' says Dad eventually, reaching across and placing a hand on Jim's shoulder.

'She's gone,' says Jim, head in hands. 'They've both gone and today's our wedding anniversary. Would have been twenty years. Twenty years down the drain.'

'Maybe we should talk about this somewhere else,' says

Dad, slowly getting up. 'Let's pop out to the shed.'

'I don't want to go to the fucking shed! I want my wife back, my daughter back. I want my life back,' says Jim, a mess of drunken words and tears.

'Come on, Jim, it can't be that bad,' says Mum, as she walks over to Jim and puts her arm around him. 'Let's go into the kitchen, shall we? I'll make some coffee.'

Jim slowly gets up, and Mum walks him into the kitchen, still whimpering like a scolded puppy and leaving us all shell shocked.

'That was super weird,' says Holly.

'He's obviously going through something very difficult. He needs our support and understanding,' says Dad.

'He's the one who ruined things with Saskia. I need your support and understanding. I'm going to call her,' says Matt, before he disappears into the hallway.

'I'm going to see how he's doing,' says Dad.

It makes you think, doesn't it? Jim was obviously a hot shot at university. From what Dad's told me, Jim was by far the most intelligent, charismatic, and outgoing person he knew. Unlike Dad, Jim was raised in an upper middle-class family, went to private school, and seemed destined for greatness. Maybe professionally he's achieved that, but personally he's a mess. I don't want to end up like Jim Whitby, pissed, ranting about my soon to be ex-partner at the family roast of an old friend. It's embarrassing, but more importantly, it's sad. I'm sure Jim never thought this would be his life. He probably imagined himself in his fifties, a man at his peak, successful, loved, happy, with years left to enjoy his money and family. It's what I imagine too. And yet here he is, drunk, unhappy, his life falling apart around him, crying in our kitchen. I can't let that happen to me. I can't be Jim Whitby, next generation.

'Voicemail,' says Matt, sitting down with a thump. 'I'm going to have to go and see her.'

'At least stay for dessert,' says Mum, walking back in with a big glass bowl filled with a delicious looking red and white mess.

'Jim's still crying,' says Dad. 'He's gone into the foetal position next to the dishwasher.'

'Who cares?' says Matt. 'I think I've ruined everything with Saskia.'

'I'm sure you haven't,' says Mum. 'She's probably just a bit peeved.'

'A bit peeved? After what you said, I'll be surprised if she ever talks to you again,' I say to Matt.

Greg

Three hours later

I'm just back from the hospital. I left Jim lying in bed nursing what's going to be one hell of a hangover. I rang Arabella and she was on her way to see him. I mentioned he'd told me about their marriage problems, and she said it had been over for a long time, which took me by surprise because I've seen Jim twice in the last year, and not once did he say anything about it. That's Jim though. He's always been the same.

Jim's always been my yardstick. We were the best of friends at university, and I know we haven't seen much of each other over the last twenty years, but I've always considered him one of the most important people in my life.

It all started with a rivalry. We met Lizzy around the same time and we both fell for her. I didn't think I had much of a chance. Jim was better looking, taller, from a far more well-to-do family, and he had that untouchable charisma and charm. And yet somehow Lizzy chose me. From that moment on we competed for everything, and over the years he's always been the one making more money, living in Hong Kong and then New York, and then he married Arabella, the young, attractive wife. Every time we caught up for drinks, usually at a bar in the city, where Jim could put everything on his company account, I always left feeling slightly inferior. Slightly less successful, less happy, less perfect, but now he's changed so much from the person I once knew. Whereas once the alcohol helped him to be the life and soul of the party, I can see now it makes him miserable and glib. I suppose all of these years I was wrong. I thought he had everything; the jet set lifestyle, the glamorous job, the model wife, and I felt like my own life was a bit drab in comparison, but the truth is, I've always been happier than Jim. My job might not pay as much or fly me across the globe in first class luxury, but I love what I do, and I know my marriage and family has had its blobs of disappointment, but we're still together, still sitting around the table on Sunday roast day.

'How is he?' says Lizzy.

'He's more embarrassed than anything. The nurse said the gash on his head isn't serious, but they're keeping him in overnight to be on the safe side.'

'What a relief. I'm glad he's all right,' says Matt sarcastically. 'While my life's falling apart in front of your eyes.'

'Did you manage to talk to Saskia?' I ask.

'Briefly.'

'And?'

'She's really mad at me and thinks that I'm, in her words, "an immature little boy with trust issues".'

'She'll come around,' says Lizzy supportively. 'Maybe I should talk to her. Do you want me to talk to her?'

'Ah, no thanks, Mum,' says Matt.

As my mind drifts off from Jim and back towards my own family, I start thinking about Lucy. I can't believe she quit the BBC. After all she's done to get to where she is and how hard she's worked, she's throwing it away because of some man. For years I've been so proud of Lucy and now she's disappointed me twice in such a short space of time. I was upset over her affair, Lizzy and I both were, but this is just ridiculous. Why compound one bad mistake with another?

'Lucy let's talk about the BBC,' I say when there's a lull in conversation.

Matt, Holly, and Charlotte get up and leave, probably sensing what's coming. Mums already positioned herself in the living room in front of the television. Mum likes to watch 'Songs of Praise' before I take her home and because she's going deaf, it's on really loud and it sounds like we're having a religious house party.

'Before we start,' says Lucy. 'I know I've let you down. First with Richard and now this and I'm sorry.'

Lizzy reaches across and holds Lucy's hand. 'This is your life, love. You need to be happy for you. I know I didn't react well when you told me about the affair and I'm sorry about that, but I think this is a positive decision and we support you. Isn't that right, Greg?'

I can't believe Lizzy is supporting this. I look across at her, trying to convey my complete and utter incredulousness, but she doesn't seem to fully comprehend my annoyance and just gives me a wrinkled frown in return.

'That's not exactly what I had in mind,' I say.

'And what do you want to say, Dad?' says Lucy.

'Look, darling, I'm sure you had a good reason to quit, and I know it must have been tough after what happened, but you can't throw away your career because of one mistake. You can't run away.'

'I'm not running away, Dad, and I'm not throwing my career away. There will be other companies, other jobs.'

'But they're not the BBC, darling, and that was the dream, remember?' I say, and Lizzy gives me a look across the table. 'What, Lizzy? You think this is okay?'

'No, but it's her life. It isn't fair to put our feelings, our regrets, our issues onto her.'

'I just think that leaving the BBC isn't the answer. It was your dream since you were a teenager and you're throwing it away, and for what? For some man?'

'Not just because of Richard. It's everything. The whole business. I feel so guilty about what we did and seeing him every day was making me miserable. The BBC isn't the be-all-and-end-all, Dad. It was brilliant, but I'm good at what I do.'

'Then stay and fight for it. I think you're giving up too easily,' I say.

'Sorry for once not doing exactly what you want of me. I'm such a let-down, aren't I?'

'Don't be ridiculous. I supported you when you told us

about Richard, but I don't support this, Lucy. You've wanted this your whole life, but you've hit a rough patch and you've quit. Just think about it because otherwise I know you'll regret it.'

'And how do you know, Dad? Maybe this will be the making of me. Maybe this will be the best decision of my life.'

'Because you can't just quit when things get difficult. Life doesn't work like that. You can't run away when the going gets tough,' I say, and I look across at Lizzy, realising what I've said. Lizzy looks bereft. I wasn't talking about her disappearing, but obviously she thinks I am.

'I'm sorry, but I'm not you, Dad. I can't be like you.'

'But no one's saying you need to be.'

'Really?' says Lucy. 'Then why do I feel like my whole life you've treated me that way? You've always been harder on me than Matt or Holly. You let them get away with murder. Jesus, Matt was living at home unemployed for the last year and nothing was said. Holly does whatever she likes, and it's supported all the way, but with me it's ... it's like I'm meant to be this perfect daughter, but don't you see? I'm not perfect.'

'Oh, darling,' says Lizzy, getting up and giving her a hug. Lucy is crying and I don't know what to say. I never meant for her to feel that kind of pressure. I always felt like we were supporting her, but the drive, the ambition, that all came from her. I didn't realise it came from us or because of us. 'It's all right, love. You don't have to be perfect. You just have to be happy with who you are. Isn't that right, Greg?'

Lizzy and Lucy look at me expectantly and I don't know what they want me to say. Am I supposed to just agree and nod? Is that what being a good father is? Like one of those nodding toy cows I had as a child? Just keep bobbing my head and everything will be all right.

'I need a drink,' I say, getting up and walking into the kitchen. I pour myself a big glass of wine, I take a gulp, and feel the warmth kick the back of my throat.

The last thing I want to do is push Lucy away, but how can I be happy about her making a mistake like this? It was the same with Holly being a born-again Christian. It caused problems between us, but I'd rather she knew how I felt than pretending I didn't care when I did. I was fine with her coming out as a lesbian because I don't see a problem with it. Unlike religion, it makes sense. What Lucy's doing doesn't and no amount of emotional blackmail, shouting, or talking is going to change that.

'What the hell's wrong with you?' says Lizzy, storming into the kitchen. 'That poor girl's pouring her heart out, looking for our support and all you can do is tell her she's making a mistake and then leave to get a drink? Jesus, Greg, even for you that's pretty shit.'

'I'm sorry, Lizzy, but I don't agree with it. It's ridiculous and telling her it's fine to throw away her career because of one stupid bloody man, who definitely isn't going to lose his job over her, isn't something that's in her best interests. It makes me angry just thinking about it. She doesn't need us to be her best mates right now, she needs us to be her parents.'

'And so what? I'm not being her parent?'

'That's not what I said, Lizzy.'

'And I suppose you weren't referring to me when you said, "you can't run away when the going gets tough"?'

'It's not always about you, Lizzy.'

'I know that, but guess what, Greg, it's not all about you either!' she yells. 'And by the way, I'm not the one who just walked out on a difficult conversation with their daughter.'

I take a long sip of wine, trying to cool down. Trying to keep myself together.

'You were happy to yell at her when it was something you didn't agree with,' I say after a moment. 'How is this any different?'

'It's completely different and you know it. Jesus Greg, can't you see, even with your limited emotional capacity, can't you see what we've done? This isn't about her job or the affair, did you hear what she said? She said she feels like she needs to be perfect, and we've done that to her. We've made her afraid to make mistakes.'

'That's nonsense.'

'Sometimes,' says Lizzy, her face wide with incredulity and anger. 'Your insensitivity amazes me.'

'I just think that decisions define us, Lizzy, and I don't think this is a good one. Every decision we make changes our life.'

'And you would know about that, wouldn't you?'

'What's that supposed to mean?'

'You've made some terrible decisions, Greg, and they've certainly changed our life.'

I know what she's referring to and it hits me hard. I can almost feel the impact and it knocks me back. I look at Lizzy and she doesn't flinch.

'This isn't about me and what I did,' I say eventually. 'This is about Lucy.'

'Exactly, and right now she needs our support and just because you can't be there for her, it doesn't mean I can't,' says Lizzy, and she turns around and walks out.

From the living room I hear 'Abide with Me' blaring out from the television. Holly and Charlotte are watching it with Mum, and I'm not entirely sure, but they might be singing along with it. I can hear Lizzy and Lucy talking in the dining room and Lucy is still sniffing up tears. Jim is in hospital with a gash on his head and his estranged wife and daughter are on the way to see him. Matt is out, presumably trying to plead his case with Saskia, and I'm alone in the kitchen drinking a large glass of Cabernet Sauvignon.

Today wasn't supposed to be like this. Today was going to be about old friends and family. I bought some expensive rare breed Cornish game hens, and I wanted it to be perfect. I suppose the thing is though, things aren't perfect, are they? I thought Jim had the perfect life and it turned out that none of it was true. I thought Lucy was perfect, and even though

I didn't and don't expect her not to make mistakes, she has and there's nothing I can do about it. I suppose perfection doesn't really exist, except in our minds and in our plans because when we imagine something, it's always the best version of it. Whenever I think of Dad, it's only ever the good bits. When I think of Lucy, she's still a child, mistake free and innocent, full of hopes and dreams, and maybe that's the only time when things really are perfect. But then again, maybe I'm just remembering the best version of it.

The front door opens, closes, and a moment later Matt walks into the kitchen. I can tell straight away that whatever happened with Saskia didn't go well. He stands for a moment looking at me and I don't know what he's going to say, and then completely out of the blue, he starts crying.

'It's happened again. I've lost her, Dad. I've lost Saskia.'

For a moment I don't know what to do. It's Matt. He's a grown man, but then I look at him and he's just my son. My little boy. Of course I know what to do. I walk over and wrap my arms around him, he leans into me, and I hug him as tight as I can.

'It's going to be all right,' I say, feeling his body shudder against mine.

As I hug Matt, I can't shake the feeling I had when Lizzy mentioned the one-night stand that nearly ended our marriage, and despite what I say to Matt, I wonder if it is going to be all right. If in the end, things are going to work themselves out.

June Roast

Greg

You know when something in your life feels so perfect that the only way it makes sense is to mark it down in the 'it was just meant to be' box? That was Lizzy and me. From the moment we started going out together it felt so natural. We wanted the same and felt the same about so many things, and most importantly, we got on so easily. Life together has always been so full of laughter, happiness, and love. Then we had the kids, and it was even better. Our love was multiplied. I have so many wonderful memories of when the children were small. The house was always full of noise and life, and it felt like it was never going to end. Maybe it was naive, but I didn't think for a moment that we wouldn't always be that happy.

When Lizzy disappeared, it changed so much between us because I didn't see it coming. She didn't even leave a note to let me know she was all right. I left for work on a Wednesday, and I didn't see her again until Saturday morning. Not a single phone call, text, or message. Nothing. I thought I knew her. All of her. Lizzy and I were happy, we were for life, and I never imagined for a moment that she could leave us like that. I was devastated and trying to explain to the children that their mother was missing was the hardest thing I've ever had to do. Lying in bed unable to sleep, wondering where she was, terrified I was never going to see her again, and afraid that my life, the life I loved so much, was gone. She came back, walking in through the front door, and I wanted to hold her, never let her go, but she wasn't herself. I asked her again and again why she'd done it, but she didn't say much and what she did say didn't make much sense.

The doctor said she'd had a breakdown. The stress of losing both her parents was too much, but all I could see was that she felt something and couldn't talk to me about it. Over the weeks and months after her disappearance I wanted to be there for her. I tried to talk to her, listen to her, but she was distant. We were always so close, so in-sync, and here she was, almost a complete stranger and gradually our relationship began to unravel. I didn't mean for what happened next to happen. It wasn't Lizzy's fault, but I was lost, and I felt alone, and Ruth was there for me. I just needed someone to talk to.

I'd known Ruth for a few years. She'd done her degree with me and then her master's and she was working on her PhD. She'd always been flirtatious, but I never thought anything of it. Why would I? I was a happily married man and the thought of cheating on Lizzy had never entered my head. However, as Lizzy and I started to fall apart and as things between us got even more desperate, I started to spend more and more time at work, and that's when it happened. Instead of going home one Friday afternoon, I decided to go for a drink instead. A few drinks turned into many and when Ruth showed up, flirting with me as always, it got out of hand. She was attractive and much younger than me and I didn't have the willpower to turn her down. I needed to feel something other than sadness and Ruth was it for a few hours. She was a moment away from my own life. It isn't an excuse, but I wasn't happy, and we ended up sleeping together. For one night I forgot about everything else and made a terrible mistake that's haunted me ever since.

It was a few weeks later when I decided to confess everything to Lizzy. The guilt of it was tearing me apart and I knew I had to tell her. We'd never kept secrets from each other, but the look on her face when I said the actual words, made me wish I had. It took us a long time to get past it. Lizzy was so angry with me, and I felt ashamed, but I think she felt the same as me; we couldn't throw away our marriage for one stupid mistake, and so we put everything behind us. Lizzy's breakdown and my affair. We agreed to fix our marriage and forget about the past. At least that was until last month when Lizzy brought it up again, and suddenly we're back in the same place, both wondering if we can mend our marriage again.

The only good thing that's happened recently is that because of Matt's situation with Saskia, he and I have become a lot closer. We're talking, bonding, and for the first time in a long time, I feel like his father.

'How's things at work?' I say.

Matt and I are in the kitchen preparing the roast. I'm slicing potatoes, Matt is peeling carrots, and we're both drinking from a nice bottle of red wine.

'Not great,' says Matt. 'Saskia and I talk, but it's all very professional and when I try and make a joke or say something nice, she generally ignores me or says she has to go and do something else. It's driving me crazy.'

Since Saskia and Matt broke up, he's been so down, and it reminds me of the time just after Lindsey left. I know he felt like Saskia was The One. Matt tends to get excited about these things and throws himself into it completely but when it doesn't work out, he's always the one left devastated. I suppose a part of me admires him for being so open and ready for love. It's a quality I don't share and it's something I saw in my own father. I've tried to protect Matt, and in doing so, perhaps I've not given him enough credit. At least he's still working at the cafe. Seeing Saskia every day must be so difficult, but he's sticking it out and I'm proud of him for that.

'It will get better. Maybe she'll come around in time.'

'I don't know. I really hurt her. She says she can't trust me and that I need to grow up.'

'I'm not going to argue with that.'

'Thanks.'

'You know what I mean. You're only twenty-three, Matt. Maybe you need some time to just be you, earn some money, find out what you want to do with the rest of your life. There's no rush to settle down, get married. Perhaps this is a blessing in disguise.'

'I wish I could see it like that, Dad, but I can't. I love her.'

'I know, son,' I say, seeing the flicker of pain that's so clearly written across his face.

The girls are in the living room watching TV. There's a real male/female divide in the house today. I almost didn't do a roast this month because things with Lizzy and I are so tense. I have the feeling it's all coming to a head, but the truth is, I'm not ready for it. I'm not ready to have the big talk. All of our lives are changing, the world we've known for so long is moving on, and I'm not ready for any of it. It's the reason I decided to have the roast in the end, because I know there's not many left. Holly will be leaving for university soon and I don't know what's going to happen with Lucy and Matt, but there's a definite feeling that we're coming to the end of an era.

'How did you know with Mum?' says Matt.

'Know what?'

'That she was, you know, The One?'

'I just did, I suppose. When I first met your mother she wasn't that keen on me to be honest. I think she thought I was a bit boring. She'd been seeing all these other interesting, creative types and I was the safe choice. But the thing is, we always had a connection. It was there from the moment we met, and I don't know whether that's love at first sight, but we always felt right together. I know it's horribly cliché, but it did feel like it was meant to be. Your mother and I had magic, that's the only way I can describe it. Like magic.'

'That's how I feel about Saskia.'

'Then don't give up on her. If you really believe she's it, then you have to keep fighting.'

'I just wish I knew what she was thinking,' says Matt and I laugh. 'What?'

'The day you know what Saskia's thinking, please let me know because it will be a first for men everywhere.'

'But I thought you were the relationship expert. "I've been married for thirty-one years, son, I know what I'm talking about",' says Matt, doing what I hope is an awful impression of me.

'That doesn't mean I understand women. It just means I know how to survive in a marriage. Take the business with the holiday. Yes, it was a hard decision to delay it until the summer, but I did it for us. I'm working hard for the both of us, but your mum still got mad about it and as usual it wasn't about the holiday. It's about what the holiday represents.'

'Lindsey used to do that all the time,' says Matt. 'Arguments were never about what I thought they were about.'

'And that's how they work, son. They're always one step ahead.'

'So how do we win?' says Matt, looking at me expectantly.

'There's no winners in marriage, Matt, only survivors.'

I know this isn't true because of my own parents who loved each other completely until the very end. Dad used to buy Mum flowers every Friday after work and not because he was in her bad books, but just to remind her how much he loved her. Every weekend the flowers would sit, pride of place, at the dining table as a symbol of their love. They were always there, almost until the very end when Dad started to forget. The flowers took on a whole new meaning because they weren't just flowers, they were them. Always happy, bright, and cheerful. My parents both won at marriage, and I used to feel the same about Lizzy and me.

'I don't think that,' says Matt, taking a sip of wine. 'Even though Saskia and I aren't together, every second we were I felt like I'd won. You should feel the same, Dad.'

'I used to feel like that,' I say, feeling the unfamiliar creep of emotions beginning to overtake me.

'Then don't give up. Someone very wise once told me, "If she's The One you have to keep fighting".'

I look at Matt and smile and he smiles back. He continues peeling the carrots and I'm slicing potatoes and there's a quiet togetherness between us that hasn't been there for a long time. At least if nothing else in my life feels right at the moment, this does.

Lizzy

I'm so angry with Greg and maybe I shouldn't have brought up the past (the past we both agreed to move on from) but why should I move on when he so obviously can't? "We're defined by our decisions," he said about Lucy, but it was obvious he was talking about me. I made a bad decision, but guess what? So did he. I don't agree with him because I don't think decisions define us. What defines us isn't the decisions we make, but how we react afterwards. Our actions define us, not our words. Greg likes to talk a lot and promise me so much, but he never comes through. His actions never match his words, so when I heard him berating poor Lucy over her decision to quit the BBC, I couldn't help but lose it.

It's always been Greg's problem. He tries to control everything and everyone. He has an idea how life should be and when things don't go as he thinks they should, he can't handle it. It's why we're in the position we are now, because he can't change. Because he can't adapt. Life is changing and as parents, as husband and wife, and as people, we need to change too. Going on the retreat with Stella opened my eyes to a new world, to new possibilities, and to maybe a life without Greg.

'What's it like?' says Lucy to Holly.

'What's what like?' says Holly.

The boys are in the kitchen cooking the roast and us girls are in the living room. Holly is lying on the sofa with her legs over Lucy, and Joan is sitting in her chair in the corner.

'Being with a girl. What's it like?' says Lucy with a tantalising smile.

'Do you mean compared with a boy because I haven't been with one,' says Holly.

'Let's keep this PG, shall we?' I say, nodding across at

Joan.

'Well, obviously not compared to a boy, but you've done stuff, what's it like?' says Lucy.

'Why? Are you interested in joining the lesbian movement?' says Holly with a smile.

'God no, I like my men,' says Lucy. 'Just interested.'

'Do you want to hear this?' Holly says to me.

'Why because I'm so old and conservative?' I reply.

'No, because you're my mum,' says Holly.

'I could tell you stories that would blow your mind,' I say, and Holly and Lucy pull disgusted faces at each other.

'I think we'd rather keep our minds un-blown, thanks Mum,' says Lucy.

'It's nice,' says Holly after a moment. 'It feels right. We're both exploring ourselves, and each other and it's exciting. It feels for the first time in my life like I know who I am.'

This is the first time we've really talked about Holly being gay and it's nice to hear her side of it. It is incredible that I never had an inkling she might be gay. I realise it's not always so black and white and if she didn't really know, how in the world was I supposed to? I do feel bad I wasn't there for her or that she felt like she couldn't talk to me about it. I feel like I let her down. I suppose all that matters now is that she's happy.

'I'm thrilled for you,' I say.

'Me too,' says Lucy with a smile.

'And the best part is that I don't have to deal with disgusting, sweaty men and their ugly penises flopping about all over the place,' says Holly, and Lucy and I both laugh. Joan looks across for a moment with a raised eyebrow then she laughs too.

I've started writing. It's such a relief to finally be writing again after all these years. It's the first thing I've done in a long time that's just for me. I've spent so long taking care of everyone else that at first it felt a bit selfish to say bugger the housework, the washing, and cooking dinner, I'm writing. I've started on a novel and it's slow going, but it feels good to be using my brain again. I think it was a bit shocked at first, but gradually it started to catch on to what it was meant to be doing. I was worried that I'd have nothing to say, but once I opened the floodgates, it all started pouring and it hasn't stopped since.

'It's sad, I know, but I still miss Richard,' says Lucy. 'I know I shouldn't, but I miss not being in a relationship.'

'The trick is to remember all the things about him that really annoyed you,' I say. 'That really pissed you off. That will help you move on.'

'You mean like how he used to grind his teeth in his sleep and always squeezed the toothpaste from the middle. God, that was so annoying,' says Lucy. 'Seriously, how hard is it to squeeze from the bottom?'

'I have to say that there's nothing about Charlotte that annoys me,' says Holly with a self-gratifying smirk. 'She's perfect.'

'Okay, you can shut up,' says Lucy with a smile, hitting her sister on the leg.

'Anything else about Dad that annoys you?' says Lucy. 'Apart from the obvious.'

'How long have you got?' I say.

The truth is, Greg does so many things that annoy me, it would take hours to write the full list. I could start with the way he doesn't properly listen to me. We can be sitting together, and I'll be telling him a story about my day or something that he has to do, and he's looking right at me, and it looks for all the world like he's listening, but he isn't. And I can't watch the news with him because he talks over every report with his opinions, as though they're somehow more important than actual experts. And the way he insists I iron his underwear because that's what his own mother did, and when there's something to be done around the house, perhaps there's a mess or the washing pile is getting a bit high, instead of doing it himself, he'll make a sarcastic comment about it. As if I'm the only one who's capable of doing housework.

Just after we were married and before we had kids, Greg and I used to share everything. We assigned household duties according to our strengths and weaknesses. Greg took out the rubbish, washed the dishes, and took care of the garden, while I cooked, cleaned, and washed and ironed the clothes. Greg took care of security and would make sure the windows and doors were locked every night before bed. He was in complete charge of the car, taking it for its MOTs, making sure the tires had the right about of pressure, and I was in charge of finances and paying bills. I suppose we were a pretty standard male/female couple, but it worked, and we both pitched in and helped the other. Sometimes when I was tired or wanted to write, Greg would cook and wash, and I would take out the rubbish if it got too much. We were a team, but gradually it stopped. Having the kids turned me into a proper housewife. Greg suddenly saw our roles as clearly defined and I was stuck, labelled as the person in charge of the house and kids, while Greg was the breadwinner, who expected his dinner on the table at the end of a long day. We'd gone from two intelligent, creative, modern thinking young people with the world at our feet, to a hackneyed, stereotypical married couple. Despite our literary pretensions and all the talk of us being different, part of a new generation, we were no better than our parents and grandparents.

Greg

'Go and hide,' said Dad excitedly, pointing to a clump of trees nearby. 'And I'll start counting.'

I ran off towards the trees, looking around eagerly for a good hiding spot. I was seven years old and playing with my father on a bright Saturday morning at the park near our house. Mum was sitting on a bench watching her two men with a smile on her face. I was an only child, so I spent a lot of time playing with Dad when I was little. I know my parents wanted more children, but there was some sort of complication when I was born, and Mum couldn't have any more children. I was it. Their only hope.

I scampered off into the woods and found a hiding place. It was a really good one, at the base of a tree, covered by a bush, and in a small hole. I was almost invisible, or so I thought at the time. I remember hearing Dad's voice in the distance.

'Coming ready or not,' shouted Dad, and I felt that rush of excitement you only feel when you're a kid. When playing games mattered more than anything else in the world.

I loved playing with Dad. He was always that little bit louder than other dads and more fun. He didn't mind if other parents thought he was a bit crazy, which he undoubtedly looked sometimes. I think he always felt bad that I was an only child because he came from a big family, so he acted like a big brother rather than a father sometimes. He'd be climbing trees, running around the playground flapping his arms around like a giant bird, or playing football with all the enthusiasm of a child. He'd dress up for my birthday parties and be a clown or a cowboy. As fathers go, he was just about perfect.

I sat hiding, arms wrapped around my knees, listening to my father's footsteps on the ground. I sat for a while, smiling, shaking with excitement as Dad searched for me. Sometimes I'd hear him talking to himself.

'Oh, where could he be?' Dad would say. 'In here?' Then I'd hear him jumping out at a spot he thought I was hiding in. 'Ah ha!' Dad would shout, followed by, 'Not in there'. I sat waiting and waiting, and then it went quiet. Even at seven I knew Dad would pretend he couldn't find me and then after a few minutes he would. I knew I had a good spot, but it was taking longer than usual. A knot grew in the bottom of my tummy; I was worried that Mum and Dad had forgotten about me, and I was alone. Eventually I heard footsteps and excitement replaced the worry. I sat in my spot, waiting to see Dad's face, but it wasn't him. Mum appeared instead and straight away I could see something on her face and in her eyes.

'Found you,' said Mum.

'Where's Dad?'

'Oh, your silly old father's just having a little sit down. Come on, quick, out you come,' said Mum. Her eyes still looked funny. She was smiling, but I could tell it wasn't a proper smile. 'We're going on an adventure.'

'What sort of adventure?' I asked, plodding across the grass with Mum, who was holding my hand and walking quickly. She kept me close to her side, squeezing my body against hers.

'Fancy going to Aunt Hilary's house for a special lunch?'

Hilary (not really my aunt) lived a few houses down from ours. She had two boys and a girl, and we'd often go over and play. I liked going there because she always had the best biscuits and would serve us pretend tea, which was really milk, but still in proper cups.

'Yes, yes, yes!' I said, and so we walked off to Aunt Hilary's house.

As I walked past the bench where Mum had been sitting, I saw Dad. He was leaning over and had his hand on his chest. He didn't look across at me and I couldn't work out why he wasn't playing hide and seek anymore.

I was ushered off to play and I remember the looks on the adult's faces, the something different in Mum's eyes, but as soon as I got there I started playing and forgot all about it. It's the beauty of being a child. The innocence of the world around you and being able to focus entirely on the moment. Once I was playing, I didn't think about Dad or Mum, but only what we were doing. Once home so late that night, tired and puffy eyed, I went straight to bed. My eyes were closed, and I was in a heavy sleep before I even had the chance to ask for a goodnight kiss from Dad.

At seven, I didn't know what was going on because my parents protected me from it and now I'm a parent, I know why. It's our job, isn't it? My parents protected me because they could and I'm so glad and thankful they did.

It wasn't until years later I learnt what had happened that day. While looking for me in the woods, Dad had felt dizzy and faint and then he'd had a heart attack. It was only a minor one, but Mum called for an ambulance, and he spent a couple of days in hospital. When he returned home nothing was said about it. Dad joked, laughed, and made up a story about where he'd been, and I believed every word. As I sat in my hiding place beneath that tree, waiting excitedly for my father to find me, he almost died, and that terror scares me more now than it did then because now I have nothing to protect me. Now I'm open against the world and it's scary and there are times when I wish I was a boy again because then I had my parents who protected me from everything. Who shielded my little life from everything bad and dangerous.

I'm washing up when Lizzy walks in. Neither of us say anything and she picks up the tea towel and starts drying. The kids and Mum are in the living room. Dinner was a tense affair with Lizzy and I not really talking. Even the kids weren't particularly talkative. Matt's reeling from his problems with Saskia, Lucy's still unemployed, and Holly was miles away, tapping away on her phone. It wasn't a great Sunday roast. Now Lizzy and I are in the kitchen, washing up together and I don't know what to say to her and what she wants to say to me.

'Thank you,' I eventually say, while she puts plates away in the cupboard, rattling them against each other noisily.

'You're welcome,' says Lizzy.

Another silence. I think of my father and decide that I need to face this head on.

'Is this it?' I say.

'Is this what?'

'Is this going to be the talk?' I say, looking across at Lizzy. 'I know you're angry with me, and I'm sure it's about a lot more than just what happened with Lucy. I want to fix it and I know I'm a big part of the problem, but Lizzy, whatever it is, surely we can discuss it like grownups. I don't want a shouting match. I can't face another argument.'

I look at Lizzy and she looks at me and we both look a bit beaten up and tired. Maybe it's just the day because it's not particularly pleasant out there. It's blustery, wet, and dark. Maybe it's the culmination of all the arguing, the tension, and the problems with the kids. I don't know what it is, but neither of us looks anywhere near ready for a big talk or an argument. I know I'm not. As Lizzy's always keen to remind me, I have opinions on everything, and I'll argue until I'm blue in the face to prove a point. I'm usually so concerned with being right and having things my way that I'm blinded to anything else. I know this is one of my big flaws. I'm aware of my own limitations, but today I just can't do it. Today I want to be like my mum when Dad had a heart attack. I want to protect my family. I want to make sure Matt, Lucy, and Holly are happy. I want to look after Mum because who knows how much longer she has left, and most of all, I want Lizzy to be okay because she's my wife and I love her. I want to pull all of my family close to me and squeeze them into my body where they'll be safe from all the dangers in the world.

'Let's just clean up, shall we?' says Lizzy in a sombre, monotone voice.

And that's exactly what we do. Today isn't the day and we both live to fight on because although my parents were winners, and hopefully one day Lizzy and I will be too, at the moment it's all about survival. It's about getting through another day together in the hope it gets better.

Lizzy

'You're too emotional, Lizzy,' Mum used to say to me, and I could never understand why. What was so bad about being emotional? And how could I be "too emotional"? I had emotions. They were a part of me, and I had as much control over them as I did the hair that had suddenly started sprouting up all over my body. My teenage years were a very confusing time. I felt so many emotions and I couldn't talk to my mother, so I had to deal with it on my own. This was in the days before sex and health education in schools, so I literally had to learn everything myself.

The only good thing about having a mother like mine was that I became independent very early on in my life. By fifteen I could take care of myself completely and by university I was entirely self-sufficient. I read books on sex, reproduction, periods, unwanted body hair, and anything else my mother didn't or wouldn't tell me. The only thing I still couldn't control was my emotions. I had a lot of them and still do.

However, standing next to Greg in the kitchen, washing the dishes, I feel numb. I'm tired. I feel like we've wasted so much time arguing and where has it got us? I had a really good talk with Stella Blackwell after Pilates on Friday. We went for a coffee, and I told her everything.

'It sounds like you need a holiday,' said Stella.

'If Greg ever finds the time,' I said, sipping my flat white.

'Why wait for Greg? You don't need him to have a holiday.'

'What? Go away on my own? I'm not sure I could.'

'Or with me. How about a girl's holiday? Oh yes, that's a brilliant idea,' said Stella clapping her hands excitedly. 'Wherever you want. Thailand? South of France? Dubai? I could do with a week away. Peter's been so busy at work, and I've been feeling a bit flappy and useless.'

I started thinking about it and it made sense. If Greg didn't have the time for a holiday, then I'd just go away with Stella instead. We'd probably have more fun anyway. Then she went on to tell me about a new women's retreat that was coming up, and we idled away the afternoon daydreaming about a girl's holiday somewhere hot and tropical. Maybe it's why I can't be bothered to argue with Greg anymore because I don't need him the way I used to.

For so long I relied on Greg for everything. He was my whole world so when he let me down I was heartbroken. But after the retreat with Stella, I realised I was still me. The girl Greg met at university. The girl who was so self-sufficient and independent was inside me and I realised that marriage isn't about needing someone, it's about wanting someone. When I met Greg, I didn't need him, I just wanted him. The same when we got married, but somewhere along the way, I stopped just wanting him and started needing him. That's when I became unhappy and when it all started to go so wrong.

Stella and I agreed to meet up this week and go through holiday brochures and decide on something. It's already June and despite Greg agreeing to a holiday, we still haven't sat down and booked anything. Greg's summer holidays start in a few weeks and who knows what's going to happen. I'm sure he'll have an excuse as to why he can't go away. He'll be writing his new book, he won't have the time, the weather won't be right, or his star sign will say something about not flying. Whatever the reason, it doesn't matter anymore.

Greg eventually leaves to take Joan home, Matt's upstairs in his room, Holly's left to go and see Charlotte, so it's just Lucy and I in the lounge having a cup of tea. Since she quit working at the BBC something's changed in her and I'm worried.

'How's everything with you?' I say.

'Oh, you know, fine,' says Lucy unconvincingly.

'Are you sure, love, because you don't sound fine,' I say, and Lucy looks at me, her face etched with insecurity.

'I suppose the thing is, I thought I'd enjoy some time off. I've worked hard for so long that I thought a break would do me the power of good. Relaxing, thinking, reading books instead of scripts, catching up with friends, a bit of travel, and even watching some rubbish daytime television. I thought it would help me figure out what to do next, but if anything it's made me feel lost. I don't know what I'm doing and I'm starting to think that maybe Dad was right and quitting the BBC was a mistake.'

'You can't think like that, love,' I say. 'This is good for you and sometimes it's not bad to feel a bit lost. What's that old saying? "Not all who wander are lost".'

'That's all very well, Mum, but I'm not like you and Matt, floating where the wind takes you. I need to work. I need to belong somewhere. I need the comfort of a regular pay cheque.'

'Just like your father,' I say with a wry smile.

'Unfortunately,' says Holly. 'How are things with you two by the way?'

How are things with Greg? Not good would be the correct answer, but this is Lucy. I can't tell my own daughter the truth because I don't want to frighten her. I don't want her to think for a moment that her parents could possibly break up.

'We're fine,' I say.

'Just promise me you aren't going to be one of those sad couples who break up the minute the last kid's out of the door.'

'I promise.'

'Good because that would be the worst thing in the world,' says Lucy, and she adds for emphasis, 'The worst.'

I smile and tell her that of course it isn't going to happen, and I agree that it definitely would be the worst. The thing is though, it's possible. I'm not saying that I've given up on my marriage because I haven't. I'm not saying that I don't love Greg because I do. All I know at the moment is that we're not okay and if it doesn't get better, if Greg and I don't change, then sooner or later, the idea of us breaking up won't just be an idea.

It seems ludicrous to me because I always wondered how couples reach the point when divorce is the only answer. At what point is being apart better than being together? When do you call time on a marriage? I really don't know what the answer is. I do know this though, maybe for the first time in my life, I'm not being too emotional about it. I'm thinking clearly, rationally, and perhaps if my mum were still alive, she'd finally be proud of me.

July Roast

Joan

People today. Things aren't what they used to be. It's not like the good old days. This is all I hear at the home. Whining old people. It's all they do. Eat. Complain. Sleep. And die, of course. Roger Mungford died last week. He was eighty-two. He'd been poorly for a while and had been on death watch for weeks. Every morning Nellie and I would wait for them to wheel him in for breakfast, hoping he'd make it down for one last meal. You see that's what happens. People are there one day and then gone the next and we're all waiting for our turn. It's the world's most depressing queue.

It was Wednesday morning and Nellie and I were at breakfast. Soft boiled eggs and soldiers on Wednesday. We always wait for Roger, but on that morning he didn't come down. We talked to the supervisor, and she said he'd passed away during the night. At least he went quietly in his sleep because that's the thing when you get to our age, it's not when but how.

Since I moved in ten people have died. You'd think it would be more depressing, but it's why we're there, isn't it? It's like I always say to Nellie, just because we have board games and a ping pong table, it doesn't mean it's a holiday camp. Although Ted Maplin who does 'Sing Along with Ted' did used to work at Butlins.

I do enjoy Sundays with my family. It gets me out of the home. On Tuesdays they run a bus to the big Tesco's, and they have a Costa Coffee. In the summer we get days out to the seaside, which is lovely, although it takes ages to do anything because of all the old people dithering about and the ones in the wheelchairs don't help much. Len the driver is a nice man, and he likes to whistle while he drives, which reminds me of George.

When Greg was a boy we'd pack up the car and head off on holiday and all the way George would whistle. Greg would sit in the back with his head in a book. It's no surprise he's ended up doing what he's doing. I'm so proud of him. I'm proud of all of them. Thinking about watching the kids grow up is one thing that makes me sad because I know I'm not going to be around for all of it. I'd love to watch Lucy and Holly walk down the aisle and I'd give anything to hold a great grandchild in my arms. George loved his family, and it made me so sad when he got Alzheimer's. He just wanted to see his family and know who they were, but the disease took that away from him. It's like I was saying, it doesn't matter when we go, but how. At least I have my mind. When I say goodbye, I'll know who I'm saying goodbye to.

'You all right, Gran? Do you need anything?' says Lucy.

'I'm fine thanks, love.'

Lucy smiles at me and walks out of the living room. She's been going through something at work. I don't know what exactly because no one ever tells me anything. All I know is she used to work at the BBC and now she doesn't and it's something to do with a man. I pick up bits and pieces. They don't think I'm listening, but I am. It's a surprise because Lucy's always been so sensible, but no one's immune to love, are they? I know Greg's not happy with her leaving the BBC. I've heard them arguing about it and it's still a bit tense between them. He'll get over it though. Greg's always been like that. He holds onto things. I've told him before that he needs to let them make their own choices. It's something you realise more and more as you get older. You can't control everything. Life is what it is, and we just have to hang on and enjoy the ride. I did while George was here. I never wanted it to end, but without him it's harder to see the point.

'8 Out Of 10 Cats, Would I Lie To You, Would I Lie To You, 8 Out Of 10 Cats, show jumping, seriously, who watches show jumping?' Matt's talking to himself on the sofa.

Poor Matt's been so down after that business with his girlfriend. The American one. I know he really liked her. He liked the other one too. I can't remember her name, the one who left to go off around the world, but she wasn't right for him. This one was different though. She was special. I could tell. I saw the look in his eyes when she'd walk into the room.

'Why do you do that? I say.

'What's that, Gran?' says Matt.

'Flick through the channels complaining nothing's on?'

'I don't know, I'm bored.'

'Then do something.'

'Like what?'

'Why don't you fix things with that girl?' I say, and he looks across at me.

'I can't.'

'Why not?'

'Because I've ruined it.'

'Oh tosh. Nothing is ruined. You just need to get off your bottom and talk to her.'

'She doesn't want to know. She said I'm not the person she thought I was.'

'And what do you think?'

'I love her, Gran.'

'Then you need to do something. You can't sit here complaining when she's out there.'

'But Gran,' says Matt hopelessly.

'No buts,' I say, and then it comes to me. What Matt needs is to believe in love again. He needs to hear the story of me and George. 'I think it's time I told you how your grandfather ended up proposing to me, but first pop the kettle on and make me a cup of tea. Then I'll tell you everything.'

Matt smiles reluctantly then gets up and wanders off towards the kitchen. I hear the kettle click on and I settle in to tell Matt how his grandfather and I got engaged. It's a story I love to think about, but rarely get to tell. At least to people who are completely with it. I tell the same stories again and again at the home to the same people, mainly to Gordon Hubbard, although to be fair he does have dementia.

'Here you go, Gran,' says Matt, setting my tea down on the coffee table.

Matt sits cross legged on the sofa and I take a sip of my tea before I pop it back down on the table.

'Ooh, that's a nice cup. Ready?'

'Ready.'

'I met your grandfather at the pictures,' I start, but before I've finished my first sentence, Holly and Lucy come in and sit down too.

'Gran's telling me how Grandad proposed to her,' says Matt.

'I've never heard this before. I'm in,' says Lucy.

'Me too,' says Holly excitedly.

I have my three grandchildren all sitting in front of me. This is a lot better than sitting down with the old people at the home, starting a story while they drift off and stare into space. I take another sip of tea before I start again.

'I met George at the pictures. I'd gone along with my friend Elsie Booker. She'd met a man she liked the look of. I can't remember his name now, Jack or John something, I think. She didn't want to meet him alone, so she brought me along for company and her fella brought along George. I was nineteen and I hadn't been out with many men before. George was so handsome. I remember he was dressed in a grey suit that was a little too big for him and he kept pulling up the sleeves. I learnt later that he'd borrowed it from his father without asking. He got into a lot of trouble for that. Typical George.

'After that first night, I saw George again and we got along so well. He was so kind and gentle, and he also had this amazing happiness about him. He was such a jolly person and so he made me happy too. It was just after the war and a lot of people were still reeling from it. There wasn't much joy around in those days so when it came along you knew it.

'Before long we were courting, but he hadn't met my family. You see the thing is George came from a real working-class family. His father worked down the markets and so did your grandfather. My family were middle class and the idea of me marrying beneath us, and especially a barrow boy from the East End, was out of the question. My father had high aspirations for me so I kept George from my parents as long as I could, but I knew they'd have to meet eventually.

'I was terrified my father would stop me from seeing him. I was young, but even so I knew I was falling in love with George. Eventually he came for dinner. I even remember what we had to eat. Mum made a joint of beef, which was a big deal back then. Rationing had only ended the year or so before and meat was still very expensive. George told me afterwards that he'd never had a joint of beef like that before. He came, dressed smartly and bless him, he did his best. He tried so hard to impress my father, but it was obvious from the moment he walked in that my father didn't approve. "Not good enough for my daughter", he told me afterwards. Dad could tell from the way he talked and the clothes he wore that George was, "as common as muck". My father did his best during dinner to pretend everything was all right, but as soon as George was gone he forbade me from seeing him again.'

'What? That's terrible,' says Holly. 'I hope you told him where to stick it.'

'It was a different time back then, Holly. You couldn't talk to your parents like that.'

'Even at nineteen?' says Lucy.

'It didn't matter. I was living under his roof. What he said was the law and that was it.'

'I would have moved out,' says Holly.

'I didn't have a choice. I had a job, but it didn't pay much. I was a young girl.'

'That's terrible,' says Holly.

'Awful,' says Lucy.

'Okay, feminist front, let Gran finish her story,' says Matt.

'In the end, I arranged to meet George to break the news. I was so sad. He was everything to me, but what other choice did I have? I met him at the park. We sat on a bench, and I told him everything. I cried my eyes out, but George didn't say anything. He didn't waver, he didn't get angry, and instead he grabbed me by the hand, and we started walking back to my house. I was so nervous because I didn't know what George was going to do and I knew my father would kill me if he found out I'd seen him again.'

'What did he do?' says Lucy.

'We got back to my house and George knocked on the door before I even had the chance to get my key out. He still hadn't said a word and I was too afraid to ask what he was going to do.'

'Did he punch your father?' says Holly.

'No, Holly, he didn't punch my father.'

'Did your father punch Grandad?' says Holly.

'No one punched anyone,' I say with a laugh. 'When my father opened the door, surprised to see us stood there, George asked very politely if he could come in. My father, strict, but always one for keeping up appearances, didn't want a scene on the front doorstep. Heaven forbid. Once inside my father demanded to know what was going on. He shouted at me and warned George he wasn't the sort he wanted his daughter spending time with. George still hadn't said anything at this point. I was starting to get worried. Eventually, my father stopped shouting and that's when your grandfather started talking.'

'What did he say?' says Lucy, on the edge of her seat.

'He explained ever so eloquently how much he loved me, how much he respected me, and that he'd do anything and everything within his power to make me as happy as possible. Then he asked my father for my hand in marriage.'

'What? Seriously?' says Holly.

'I was completely shocked and so was my father. I didn't know what my father was going to say, and to be honest, I think he was probably going to reject the notion completely out of hand, but George had one last card to play.

'He looked at my father with an expression I hadn't seen on his face before or since, and then he said, and I'll never forget this as long as I live, "I love Joan more than life itself. She's the only girl for me and if you can't see your way clear to accepting our love today, Mr Thurbald, then I'll go away, but I'll keep coming back every day, every week, every month, and I'll ask for her hand in marriage again and again until you say yes. I'd do anything for your daughter and I'm not going to let her go just because we were born in different parts of the same city". I was speechless.'

I can see tears glistening in both Holly and Lucy's eyes.

'What did your father say?' says Matt.

'He didn't have much of a choice and begrudgingly gave his blessing, but not before he gave George the lecture of his life. He told him that if he didn't take care of me then he'd have him to answer to and when he finished George got down on one knee and asked me to be his wife. With everything that had happened, I hadn't really thought whether I'd say yes or not, but it didn't take long for me to decide. I loved him then just as much as I do now.'

'It's like one of those old black and white films,' says Lucy.

'So romantic,' says Holly.

'So you see, Matt. If you really love someone, you don't give up when it gets tough, you fight harder because that's what love is. It's not giving up.'

'So what, I should ask her to marry me?' says Matt.

'If you think she's The One, then why not?'

'Because it's crazy, it's ridiculous, it's—'

'It's what you do when you know you can't live without someone,' I say, and I look at Matt, my grandson, and he smiles at me, and it reminds me of the smile George gave me when I agreed to be his wife.

There's a woman at the home called Veronica Stapleton. She's a sort of therapist counsellor and we're encouraged to see her at least once a week. She has a little office near the recreation room that smells like potpourri and cigarettes. She's always talking about living in the moment. She says it's important to have a positive mindset at our time of life. The past is in the past and although it's fine to remember it fondly, we should live in the present because it keeps us alive longer. I think she's talking absolute rubbish. She's in her thirties, what does she know about getting old? What does she know about watching the love of your life dying in front of you? It's all a load of claptrap if you ask me. How can we possibly live in the moment when this is the worst part of our lives? It's all very well pretending we're lucky to be alive, but what's the point when all we do all day is pass the time until it's time to eat, then pass more time until it's time to go to bed. It's not exactly the high life, is it?

I miss George and I feel comforted in knowing that when I die I'll be with him again. I know Greg doesn't believe in God and to be honest, I've never been a regular church goer, but these last few years I've started to think about it. I have to believe I'll see George again. That I'll hold his hand. Give him a kiss. He made life worth living and despite what Veronica Stapleton says, without him the only thing keeping me going is the past.

'What did you say to Matt?' says Greg, walking into the living room a short while later.

'What's that?'

'Matt. You said something to him and now he's going to do something reckless.'

'I was telling him the story of how your father proposed to me.'

'And did you say anything else?'

'Just that if he really loves this girl he shouldn't give up so easily.'

'Oh God,' says Greg.

'What's he going to do?'

'I don't know, but he's managed to persuade her to come for dinner. He's in his room getting ready, but before he went upstairs the last thing he said was, "It's time to go big or go home."'

'But that doesn't make any sense, he's already home.'

'No Mum, it means he's going to do something spontaneous and knowing Matt, probably a bit stupid.'

'Maybe it's just what he needs. After all, you can't go through life always being sensible. You know what your father always said, don't you?'

'What's that?'

'The only thing that matters is happiness. That's it, Greg. You can't make Matt happy. You can't decide what's best for him. You need to trust he'll make the right choices that will make him happy.'

'But what if he makes the wrong choices, Mum? What then? Because you know Matt, he doesn't have the best track record for making good decisions. Remember Hamster World? It took us weeks to find those hamsters. We never did find the third one with the dodgy leg.'

'Well, yes.'

'And there was the school trip to France. The school had been going to the same hotel for fifteen years, Mum. Matt goes once and they're banned for life. Admittedly, it wasn't entirely his fault, but it's like I said at the time, you don't point a baguette at someone in the dark. And whether he was practising his French or not, he certainly shouldn't have told them to put their hands up.'

'He's always been impetuous, but if it goes wrong you'll be there to pick up the pieces. Just like we did with you, remember? You weren't always so sensible when you were a boy.'

Greg looks at me and smiles.

'Maybe you're right, Mum.'

'Mums usually are. He's a grown man. Let him live his life.'

'Love you,' says Greg, before he leans in and kisses me softly on the cheek.

'Love you too and before I forget, and while I'm giving out advice, make sure you apologise to Lizzy.'

'What for?' says Greg, suddenly looking defensive.

'I'm sure you'll think of something.'

The last time I saw George was the day before he died. I'd been sitting by his bedside for weeks, but I hadn't seen George, just the hollow shell of a body he'd become. It was just after ten o'clock in the morning when he turned and looked at me and right away I knew my George was there. I could tell from his eyes. I reached across and held his hand. It was all withered and bony, but I still loved holding it.

'You all right, love?' I said.

'My Joan,' he said. 'My beautiful Joan.'

I didn't want to, but I couldn't help myself. I cried. I always tried to keep myself together, but on that morning I couldn't help it. It had been so long since he'd recognised me. Since he'd said my name out loud.

'My handsome, George. You're still in there then? Still with me?'

He smiled the last smile he would ever smile.

'Always,' he said, and then he closed his eyes and I never saw him again, but I'll always be thankful for that one last moment. For our last goodbye. It's what keeps me going. The thought of his smile, the feeling of holding his hand in mine, and seeing the love in his eyes.

Matt

I'm in my bedroom trying to compose myself. I can't believe I'm about to do this, but it's like Gran said, if you love someone and know you can't live without them, you have to jump in feet first. If Grandad hadn't taken the risk with Gran I wouldn't be here. I love Saskia. She's the girl I want to spend the rest of my life with and so here I am, laying it on the line for love.

'Can I come in?' says Dad, poking his head around the door.

'Dad, if you're here to try and talk some sense into me and stop me from doing what I'm about to do then don't bother.'

'I just want to talk.'

'No, Dad, this is my life and whether you approve of what I'm doing or not, I don't care.'

'Matt,' says Dad, ever so calmly.

'What?'

'I'm not here to change your mind.'

'Oh.'

'I mean I was, I thought about it, but then I was talking with your gran, and she made me realise that this is your life. I can't tell you what to do and even when I do you ignore me anyway. I can't make you happy, son. You need to do that yourself. So whatever you're going to do, I want you to know that I support it. I just want you to be happy.'

I'm stunned. It's Dad. The man who's about as emotional as a plank of wood. I've always known my parents love me, but Dad's just not very good at showing it. We've been better recently, but it's still Dad. The nearest he ever got to actually 'opening up' was the time he hurt his back and was on those strong painkillers that made him go doolally. He was talking in tongues and at one point was dancing around the living room, flinging his legs in the air and claiming he was "Michael fucking Flatley", which really didn't help his back. But even then the best he could do was tell me that actually, and despite everything, he quite liked me. Quite liked me was the best he could do off his head on drugs. Now he's telling me he supports me and wants me to be happy. If ever there was a good sign, a reason to believe that what I'm about to do isn't the worst idea in the world, surely this is it.

'So whatever I'm doing, you're going to support me?'

'Yes.'

'However crazy you think it is?'

'However crazy it is,' says Dad.

'I'm going to ask Saskia to marry me,' I say, and I watch as Dad's face changes. The calm certainty is replaced with a sudden disbelieving horror.

'You're going to ask her to marry you?!' says Dad, horrified.

'Yes.'

'Are you crazy? That's the single worst idea I've ever heard. You can't get married. You're too young. You don't have any money. You don't have anywhere to live. It's. It's—'

'It's what I want.'

'But you've only been dating for a few months.'

'So?'

'It's completely irresponsible, Matt. It's ridiculous.'

'And this is you supporting me?'

'Matt, I'm just … I don't know what to say.'

'Why don't you start with, "This is your decision and even though what you're doing isn't something I would do, I realise it's your life and so best of luck with it".'

'But?'

'But what, Dad? I love her. I know it's only been a few months and technically we're not going out at the moment because I was an idiot, but I know she's The One.'

'You said the same about Lindsey and look how that

turned out.'

'But this is different, Dad.'

'Why? Why is it different?'

It's different because from the moment I met Saskia I had this feeling I've never had before. I felt like I needed to be with her, near her, in her life, and once I was, I've never been happier. There's no way of knowing or explaining what true love is or why you need to be with someone, you just know. Dad would probably like a better explanation than that and preferably one that involves some sort of chart with empirical evidence, but I don't have a chart and how can you prove what love is?

'Because it just is, Dad. You must have felt the same with Mum. You just knew, right?'

'But we'd been together longer, we had things in place.'

'I don't want to wait, Dad. Sometimes in life you need to do something. Carpe diem. Seize the day. I'm going to do it, whether you agree or not. I have to do this.'

I look at Dad and I don't know what he's going to say. I expect him to tell me that he thinks this is an awful idea and he can't support me. I assume he's going to disapprove because that's what he's always done.

'It doesn't seem like I have much of a choice, does it?' says Dad eventually, a smile spreading across his face.

'So you're with me?'

'I'm your father,' says Dad, and it almost looks as though he has tears in his eyes. 'Whether I agree with you or not, I'll always be with you.'

'Thanks,' I say, slightly awkwardly.

'Although no more Hamster World because that really was a terrible idea,' Dad says and we both laugh, and for some reason having Dad on board makes me feel a lot more confident about doing this. It's like when you're lost and you're with someone else, it doesn't feel quite so bad because even if you do end up taking a wrong turning, at least you aren't doing it alone. Also you have someone else to blame when it goes horribly wrong, and you end up being airlifted shivering and malnourished out of a crevasse and taken to hospital.

'Right, big talk out of the way, I need a favour,' I say.

And so I tell Dad my hastily put together plan. I would have liked more time to organise it and I never imagined I'd be proposing in my house, in front of my family, but this is it. I need to do this today and it might be the most embarrassing moment of my life if she says no (which is highly likely considering our current situation), but I have to do it because I'll never be able to live with myself if I don't at least give it my best shot.

After the whole Jim Whitby disaster, I tried talking to Saskia, but she wasn't interested. Apparently, it all goes back to her ex-boyfriend Hank.

She met Hank at university, and they fell madly in love. She thought Hank was her big love story. Hank was everything she needed. He was intelligent, handsome, funny, and destined for a successful career in medicine. After university, they moved in together and she started her slow rise up the corporate ladder. The families were friends, Hank and Saskia went on holiday together, and it only seemed like a matter of time until he popped the question. There had even been talk of a trip to Paris. Then she found out that her Hank was cheating on her with numerous women and that he was actually a lying, cheating bastard.

Hank broke her heart and that's when she decided to leave her life behind and come to England. "Distance helps the heart mend," she told me one night at the pub. So when she heard me talking to Jim, all she saw was Hank. Bloody Hank ruined everything. The way I see it, the only way to deal with the Hank factor is to go big. I need to show her how much I love her and that I'm not Hank. I'm the anti-Hank and I'm sending an anti-Hank missile her way.

'Hi,' says Saskia a little uncertainly.

She's standing uncomfortably at the front door, quickly

moving from one foot to the other. The move I've seen before, but only at the restaurant in front of really difficult customers. I guess that's how she sees me now; difficult. She looks perfect. Slightly pissed off, definitely wishing she was somewhere else, but perfect, nonetheless.

'You look beautiful, and that's just your face, I haven't even looked down at the rest of you,' I say, gabbling nervously. 'Although I'm sure that's lovely too.'

'Matt, why am I here? And why are you dressed like you're going to a funeral?'

'This old thing,' I say, looking down at my black suit. 'I wanted to look nice.'

'Why?'

'You'll see.' Saskia stands on the doorstep for a moment looking confused. The rest of my family are waiting in the living room. Since I made my decision, I've been thinking about what to say. The words seemed so important, but now she's here all I can think about is Gran's story and I suppose all that matters is that I tell her how I feel. 'Please, come in.'

I decided to do it in front of my family because I wanted to show everyone how much I've grown up. That this isn't another typical, Matt jumping into things too quickly, disaster. I'm not a kid anymore and I want everyone to see it. It's a gamble, but one I'm prepared to take if it means Saskia realises how much I love her and how serious I am about this. Saskia walks in and I gesture for her to go into the living room. I close the front door behind me and take another deep breath.

'You know you're acting really weird,' says Saskia, stopping when she walks into the living room where all my family are sitting down. 'Oh, hello all of Matt's family.'

'Hello,' everyone says as I walk in behind Saskia.

'Can you please sit down on the sofa,' I say to Saskia.

'Is this some sort of weird English intervention?' says Saskia.

'Trust me,' I say.

It's the only free seat in the room, so Saskia sits down

somewhat awkwardly in between Mum and Dad on the sofa. Grans in her chair and Lucy and Holly are on the floor. I look across at Dad and he gives me a supportive smile. It's show time.

'Can I say before you start that I'm not comfortable with this,' says Holly.

'Me too,' says Saskia.

'I know this is a little unconventional, but I needed to do something unconventional. The way things ended with us, Saskia, I let you down and today I was talking with Gran, and she made me realise I couldn't leave things like that. The truth is everything I said to Jim was because I was scared. I was scared that what happened with Lindsey was going to happen again. I was scared because I knew how I felt about you and for the first time in my life, I knew what I wanted. If I could travel in time just once my whole life, I'd go back to that moment and do it differently because hurting you is the worst thing I've ever done.

'As I'm sure you already know, we Wildes aren't very good at expressing our feelings. We're English, you see. You didn't know my Grandad, but he knew how to open up. He knew how important it was to say bugger it and let it all out. He chased his dreams and I want to do the same. I don't want to look back with regrets Saskia, and so here I am, in my best suit, which I know makes me look like I'm going to a funeral, in front of my family, who probably think I've lost my mind, but I'm ready to tell you everything.'

I take another very deep breath.

'Before you I was lost. I didn't have a job, any prospects. I'd spent the last year feeling sorry for myself, but for some reason, on that day when I walked past the cafe, I knew I had to go in. Something was making me, and it wasn't until today I knew what it was. I was meant to meet you. You and I are meant to be together, and I don't know if I believe in destiny or fate, but I believe we were meant to meet that day.

'I know it's soon and we're not even going out at the

moment because I was a monumental idiot the last time you were here, but in the words of Hugh Grant in your favourite film, Four Weddings and a Funeral, "In the words of David Cassidy, in fact, while he was still with the Partridge Family, I think I love you,". Actually, Saskia, I know I love you. I do. I love you so much. I love everything about you and most importantly, I love how you make me feel. You make me so happy, Saskia. You make me believe in myself. You make me a better person and everything I aspire to be is because of you. I know you think I'm not the person you thought I was. That I'm stupid and immature, but you're wrong. I'm ready for this and I want it more than anything in the world. So, bearing all that in mind, I have something to ask you.'

I look at Saskia sitting on the sofa, and she looks beautiful. Terrified, confused, but beautiful nonetheless, and despite not being able to feel my feet, and my heart racing at a million miles an hour, I know this is the right thing to do. I slowly get down on one knee.

'Saskia, I know this is going to seem like the craziest thing in the world, especially considering everything that's happened, but would you do me the greatest honour in the world and be my wife? Will you marry me?'

I stop and listen to the silence in the room, but my eyes are completely focused on Saskia. She has tears in her eyes, and she looks about as shocked as everyone else probably is. You see the thing is, when I was listening to Gran's story today, I just knew. I want to spend the rest of my life with Saskia. I'm done thinking about it, talking about it, and not doing anything about it. I'm tired of being alone without the one person who makes me happy. The silence seems to last forever, until eventually Saskia looks at me with the biggest smile I've ever seen.

'It is crazy,' she says between tears. 'But, and maybe I'm crazy too, but yes. Yes!'

'What?! Really?!' I say in disbelief. 'Fuck right off! No wait, sorry, I didn't mean like fuck right off, I meant—'

'It's okay, you stupid, English idiot. I'll marry you,' says Saskia.

Then it goes crazy. Mum's crying, Gran's crying, Saskia's crying, I'm crying, Lucy's crying, Holly's crying, and even Dad's wiping his eyes with the sleeve of his shirt.

'Give her the ring then,' says Holly, and it's then I realise I don't have a ring. In all the commotion and planning what I was going to say, the one thing I hadn't thought about was having an engagement ring.

'I don't have one,' I say, looking across at Saskia. 'I don't have a ring.'

'You can have mine,' says Gran suddenly. I turn around and Gran is taking off her engagement ring. 'It's what your Grandad would have wanted, and I've been waiting for one of you to get engaged so I can pass it on before I go.'

I walk across and get the ring from Gran. I give her a kiss, and I walk back over and get down on one knee again. Saskia starts crying even more and then I slip the ring on her finger and incredibly it fits and looks absolutely perfect. I get up and Saskia and I hug and kiss and from behind me I hear cheers. Then Dad is patting me on the back and Mum is kissing Saskia on the cheek.

'This calls for champagne,' says Dad, and he rushes off to the kitchen.

'You definitely did go big,' says Lucy giving me a hug. 'Congratulations.'

'Nice work,' says Holly, then I look across at Gran who has tears streaming down her face but is smiling more than I've seen her smile in a very long time.

'Can we have a moment alone?' says Saskia in my ear.

I grab her hand and we go upstairs to my room. I close the door and then I walk across and hold her hands and stare into her eyes. We stand like this for what seems like forever until eventually she says,

'I love you, Matt, and I can't wait to spend the rest of my life with you.'

'Me too.'

'There's just one thing.'

'What's that?'

'I have to go back to California at the end of year. What then? What are we going to do? I couldn't handle being apart from you.'

'I guess I'll come with you.'

'And live there?'

'Why not?'

Saskia smiles and then laughs, and then she kisses me again.

'You know my family are going to think I've gone completely mental. I was only supposed to come here for a year, travel, and then go home. I wasn't meant to bring back a husband.'

'And when I woke up this morning, I didn't know I'd be getting engaged. The world works in mysterious ways.'

'Are you coming down for champagne?' says Dad, poking his head around the door.

I look at Saskia and she looks at me and we both smile. I've never been happier and when I look down at the ring on her finger, I think of Grandad putting it on Gran's finger all those years ago, and that really is the cherry on the cake.

Part Three

(August to October)

August Roast

Greg

'He's coming,' says Lizzy excitedly.

It's Matt's birthday. He's turning twenty-four and we've got him quite the present. He's wanted a car for ages and because I got the extra money from my book we decided to splash out. It's only an old Volkswagen with ninety thousand miles on the clock, but it's a car and definitely better than my first car which blew up on the M1. We've been hiding it up the street for the past few days, so Lizzy went out this morning, moved it outside the house and put a big red ribbon on top.

'Happy birthday!' we yell as Matt comes ambling down the stairs looking very much the worse for wear. Lizzy starts clicking away with her camera like she's a member of the paparazzi and Matt unwittingly plays along by covering his face with his hands. Matt went out last night and didn't get in until almost three o'clock this morning. I heard him stumbling up the stairs and falling over in the bathroom, before finally going to sleep fully dressed on the landing, forcing me to get up and move him into his bed.

'I need coffee. Lots of coffee,' says Matt, his voice croaky and hoarse.

'I'll make you coffee, but first,' says Lizzy, 'we have a surprise.'

'Can it wait?' says Matt, scratching his head. 'I really don't feel well.'

'Come on loser,' says Lucy, pushing him out of the front door.

We walk outside into the front garden with Matt groaning and moaning. Holly, Lucy, Lizzy, Matt, and me bringing up the rear. As soon as we step onto the pavement, with Matt still looking bewildered, he sees the green Volkswagen with the giant red bow on top.

'Surprise!' says Lizzy, snapping away with the camera again.

'What? This? A car? For me?' says Matt dubiously.

Matt seems genuinely touched. His hangover seems to quickly dissipate and when I hang the keys in front of him, a huge grin appears on his face.

'Get dressed. You can take us out for a spin,' I say. 'Although only a short one because from the stench of alcohol emanating from your body, you're horrendously over the limit.'

Matt turns around and sprints back indoors, making us all start laughing. I look at Lizzy and smile and she smiles back, but the happiness is tinged with the same expression of sadness she's had since the morning we got the news about Mum.

I'd seen Mum the night before. I had my usual visit. I sat drinking tea, she was listening to Fred Strang and his Festival of the Fifties, a blanket over her legs, slowly tapping her feet. I gave her a kiss on the cheek, said I'd see her soon, and left her talking to another old lady. I drove home as usual without knowing that was the last time I'd see my mum. The last time I'd look her in the eyes, see her smile, hold her hand, and kiss her on the cheek. The last time I'd smell her perfume when I gave her a hug goodbye. The next morning the home rang and told me she'd passed away in the night. She'd gone to bed as usual and hadn't woken up. I was in shock, but at least she'd gone peacefully in her sleep. Unlike Dad, who'd gradually slipped away from us, slowly dying so that when his body eventually gave in we'd already grieved for him, Mum went suddenly and without warning. I went into autopilot over the next few days making the funeral arrangements and we buried her on a warm Friday morning.

The funeral felt surreal. It passed me by if I'm honest, as though I wasn't really there but watching it on television.

The church was half-full of family and friends, people were talking about her, telling stories, laughing and crying, but all the while I felt numb. Is it possible to feel ambivalent about death? It's funny because when I thought she was dying a few months ago, the idea of losing her terrified me, but now she's gone I'm not sure how I feel. This is probably why Lizzy wants to talk about it. I'm not allowed to feel nothing. I have to feel something. Lizzy doesn't understand why I didn't cry at the funeral, but Mum was old and ready to go, and I don't see as much sadness in that as everyone else. Tragedy is when a person dies in their prime or when they get Alzheimer's and gradually disappear in front of you. Mum lived her life. It was her time to go, and she went quietly, peacefully, and without years of pain and disease. I know since Dad died she hasn't been happy, so why should I be devastated she's gone? Why mourn her loss when the timing was obviously right?

Am I fine? Of course not. Mum died, and its heart breaking to imagine that I'll never see her again, but does it mean I have to pour my heart out? Grief is personal and private, and despite the nauseating Americans and their desire to make everyone talk about everything, I'll deal with it myself. This is the problem though. Lizzy wants to talk. She wants to talk about Mum, us, the future, the past, the kids, the house, and everything else in the world. She wants to talk because she thinks we need to talk, but right now I'm just not in the mood. Why do we have to talk about everything in an attempt to make us both happy because that's the problem with talking, it doesn't make us happier. It makes us sadder. What good will it do talking about her disappearance, my one-night stand, Mum dying, or any of the other problems we've been having?

The truth is I'd rather bury myself in work. If I could I'd lock myself away in my shed and write, but I can't. I'm struggling terribly with my book. I sit in the shed every morning staring at my computer but nothing's coming. My agent's expecting me to give her something at the end of this month, but at this rate all I'm going to have is a title. I thought this would be much easier the second time around, but my mind is blank, only filled with thoughts of things that have nothing to do with the book. I've been on summer holidays for a few weeks and I'm still staring at the same blank screen, making hundreds of notes, reading furiously, but getting nothing down on the page. I panicked the other day and wrote about ten pages, but when I read it back the next day it was awful. So I'm back staring at the blank screen with the annoying little cursor daring me to do something. "Go on, write something, I dare you. Yeah that's what I thought. No talent. None. Zero. Zilch". I've started to resent the cursor to the point where I keep it hidden at the side of the screen so I can't see it.

The worst part is I keep telling everyone it's going so well. According to the last email to my agent, I've already written the first few chapters and now she can't wait to see it. No one knows the truth which is that it couldn't be going any worse. I'm supposed to be writing 'Wilde on Woolf', the ultimate book about the life and work of Virginia Woolf, but instead I'm sitting in my shed dreaming about a faraway point in the distance that doesn't actually exist. It's easier to imagine book signings, publication parties, and glowing reviews in Sunday supplements than it is to write the book that will make it happen.

After a few minutes, Matt comes racing out of the house fully dressed, the hangover gone, and we all pile into the car. I get in the front with Matt and the girls squeeze in the back.

'Okay, birthday boy, start her up,' says Lucy.

Matt puts the key in the ignition and turns it. When we bought the car it started first time and even this morning, when Lizzy moved it outside the house, it was fine. However, for some reason it doesn't start. Matt tries a few times and nothing.

'Great, you bought me an old banger,' says Matt.

'Let me try,' I say.

'Because it must be the way I'm turning the key,' says Matt.

'A loser even on your birthday,' says Lucy.

I get out and go around to Matt's side of the car and he slides across into the passenger seat. I check everything's okay with the car then I turn the key. Still nothing.

'What a massive surprise. Dad couldn't start the car with his brilliant new method of key turning,' says Holly.

'Let me try again,' I say.

'Be careful not to flood the engine,' says Lizzy.

'I know about cars, thank you, Lizzy,' I say. I turn the key again and this time it seems to be trying a bit harder, so I keep the key in and keep turning it. 'Come on, come on.'

'You're going to flood the engine,' says Lizzy again.

'Lizzy, please, I'm not,' I start to say, but then the engine makes a strange spluttering noise, and it dies. I've obviously flooded the engine.

'I told you,' says Lizzy.

'Someone should have warned him,' says Holly.

'It must be the way he's turning the key,' scoffs Matt.

'For fuck's sake, will everyone just shut up!' I say, finally losing my temper. There's a silence in the car as everyone seems to be stunned by my sudden outburst. I'm holding onto the wheel, my grip getting tighter and tighter. I can feel the tension in the car, but no one wants to say anything, or maybe they just don't know what to say. It stays quiet for a minute before Lizzy starts to speak.

'Remember that time we drove with your parents to Southend?' she says. I check the mirror and she's looking at me. 'We went in our car and your parents drove ahead in theirs. When we set off it was lovely and sunny, but by the time we parked at Southend the clouds were coming in and before we even got out of the car the most torrential rain was coming down. We were next to them in the car park, you'd already unpacked lunch, and we were waiting for the rain to stop, but Joan had other ideas. While we were tucking into sandwiches, Joan was out of the car, umbrella up, and she and George went for a walk along the front.'

'We sat in the car for twenty minutes watching them fight that umbrella against the wind. They were drenched by the time they got back,' I say with a thin smile.

'"We came here for a walk", she said stubbornly, "and a bit of rain isn't going to stop us",' says Lizzy laughing. 'Typical Joan.'

'She was soaked through to her underwear,' I say, and we all laugh before settling back into silence.

'When are you two off?' says Lucy to Lizzy.

'Tuesday afternoon,' says Lizzy. 'I can't wait. Two weeks in Turkey. Sun, sand, sea—'

'Wrinkly old people sex?' says Matt.

'Gross,' says Holly.

'I've been waiting for this holiday for a long time and I'm,' says Lizzy, then stops herself and looks at me in the mirror again. 'We're going to enjoy ourselves, aren't we, Greg?'

'Of course, can't wait,' I say.

Last month Lizzy told me she and Stella Blackwell were planning a holiday together. I couldn't believe it. Lizzy told me it was fine and that I didn't have to worry about it anymore, but despite what she thinks, I wanted us to have a holiday together. Lizzy didn't seem keen at first, but I suddenly felt as though it was really important. I've been promising her a holiday for such a long time, and I know it's my fault we haven't gone away, but I realise I need this too. We need this. We talked about it, and I eventually managed to persuade her to cancel her plans with Stella and go away with me instead. I don't know why I feel like it's important, but I just know if we don't do this, or if it doesn't work out for some reason, it might be the beginning of the end for us. That might sound a bit dramatic, but it's how I feel at the moment. I owe Lizzy this. I've got a lot wrong this year, for the past few years, but I'm not going to get this wrong. I need this holiday to fix us.

'How's the job hunt going?' I eventually say to Lucy.

Tellingly Lucy looks out of the window and not at me.

'I haven't really started,' she says.

'Just don't take too long, darling, it's brutal out there.'

I don't know what's happened to Lucy since she lost her job at the BBC. She's always had the drive, enthusiasm, and a bloody mindedness to succeed, but now it seems to be gone. She doesn't seem to care anymore and I'm worried because she isn't the same girl I've always known and admired. If anything she's like the old pre-Saskia Matt, who would laze around at home watching 'Cash in the Attic', avoiding work with an almost adamantine belligerence, while his bedroom slowly acquired a smell that I can only describe as toxic. I hope she snaps out of it soon because I'd hate to see her lose everything she's worked so hard to achieve.

'I did get this though,' she says, lifting up the sleeve of her shirt and showing us a tattoo on her upper arm. It looks like a black mess to me. 'It's Chinese for courage.'

'I love it,' gushes Lizzy.

'It's probably Chinese for Kung Po Chicken,' says Matt. 'I'm sure I've seen that symbol on a menu.'

'Very funny,' says Lucy. 'I checked online fool.'

'Charlotte and I are thinking about getting matching tattoos,' says Holly.

'You'll be doing no such thing,' I say, finally having enough of all this tattoo nonsense. Why does everyone under thirty nowadays think that getting a bloody tattoo makes them somehow deeper and more interesting?

'I don't think it's up to you, actually,' says Holly.

'It is if I'm paying for it.'

'So you don't like mine?' says Lucy to me.

'I just think it's reckless getting that when you don't have a job, that's all.'

'It was half-price, actually. I know someone who works in the shop,' snaps Lucy.

'But still, darling. Get a job first and then get one of

those ugly things.'

'I have the money, Dad, and I don't think it's any of your business what I do with it,' snaps Lucy.

'It is when you're wasting it on that rubbish.'

'Anyone for I Spy?' says Lizzy, trying to put a dent in the tension between me and Lucy.

Silence fills the car like an invisible gas that makes my head light and dizzy. My hands are sweating, and I can feel everyone's eyes drilling into my head. I know what they're all thinking. This is probably about Mum, but it isn't. I'm just stressed about the book, and the holiday, and Lucy not having a job, and I'm worried about Holly going off to university, and Matt getting married. Everything seems to happening all at once. Life is moving too fast, and I don't know how to slow it down. I feel like I'm on one of those travelators at the airport and I just need to get off and take a breather. It's probably why I can't write because I can't clear my mind of all the other things that are weighing me down. My mind needs to be focused solely on the book instead of all this other stuff. I wish I could go back to when everything was easier. When the kids were young, and Lizzy and I were happy.

'I Spy with my little eye, something beginning with T,' says Matt.

'Tyre?' says Lucy.

'No.'

'Tree?' says Holly.

'Nope.'

After a few more guesses and some silence everyone gives up.

'Turd,' says Matt. 'Right there on the pavement. A big festering turd.'

'It's been a while, maybe we should try the car again,' I say.

'Start her up,' says Matt. This time I turn the key and she starts first time. The engine's humming like its brand new and everyone claps and cheers. 'Get out old man. It's time for me to take you all for a drive.'

I get out and Matt slides across and I get in next to him.

'Where are you going to take us?' says Lizzy.

'How about my new house?' says Matt, as he looks across at me, probably hoping to catch the surprise on my face.

'I don't understand,' says Lizzy.

'I'm moving in with Saskia. I'm finally out of your hair.'

And then from behind me Lizzy starts crying and I don't know what to say.

Lizzy

I can't believe my little boy is moving out. I know he isn't little anymore (or a boy for that matter), but he'll always be that to me, no matter how old he is. Things are changing so fast. First the engagement and now this. I didn't mean to start crying when he told us, but I couldn't help myself. I realise it was going to happen eventually, but with Holly going off to university and Lucy in Notting Hill, that's it. It's just going to be Greg and me. Me and Greg. Us. Greg in his writing shed and me inside doing what, exactly? It's selfish, I know, but I'm worried. I know the kids are going to be all right, and Greg's got his writing and his career, but what about me? What's my thing? I suppose I'm worried that without the kids to look after, I won't know what to do with myself. It's as if I've forgotten how to just be me or maybe it's that I'm terrified of what I'll discover when it is.

When you have a house full of young kids driving you to the point of insanity on a daily basis, you dream about the day when you finally have some time to yourself. I remember imagining a life when the kids were all gone. I thought about spending more time with Greg, learning a new language, and finally reading all the books I never had the time for. What I didn't think about is that now Doomsday is finally here, I'm much older than I was when the kids were driving me bonkers, and there's more hours in the day than I need to do everything I want.

I'm also upset about Joan, especially because Greg isn't talking about it. He's pretending everything's fine, but I know it isn't. How can it be? When Joan had that funny turn and we thought she was dying, he was in pieces, but now he's all right? I don't know if it's shock or denial, but he's holding it all in and I know it's going to come out eventually. Maybe a holiday's just what he needs. Away from the day-to-day normality of life, perhaps Greg will actually open up and talk.

'When did you decide to move out?' I eventually say to Matt.

'We've been talking about it since the engagement, but last night we finally decided,' says Matt. 'I thought you'd be happy.'

'I am. I'm just going to miss you, that's all,' I say.

'And what about me?' says Holly. 'Will you miss me when I leave for uni?'

'Oh, Holly, of course. All my kids gone, I can't believe it,' I say, and start crying again.

'Right, shall we get going?' says Greg sharply, cutting into my tears.

'I have to get to church. I'll get out now,' says Holly.

'Just five minutes around the block, Hols?' says Matt. 'Then I'll drop you off at whatever church is this week's religion du jour. Catholic church, the synagogue, that Indian temple?'

'My regular church will be fine. Let me just message Charlotte,' says Holly.

I was all ready to go away with Stella Blackwell when Greg begged me to go on holiday with him. I honestly didn't think he'd be bothered and at first I said no because I'd already arranged everything with Stella, but eventually I agreed. I'm hoping it's going to be the start of something new between us. We're staying in a small villa right on the beach. It's going to be hot, relaxing, and if this doesn't put the spark back in our marriage, nothing will. I'm trying not to think about it like that though and I haven't said anything to Greg, because I'm worried that if this is a disaster, it could be the end of us. That might sound a bit melodramatic, but things have been so difficult between us that I fear another major setback might be too much for us to come back from. I hope I'm wrong.

'Right, let's crack on, shall we?' says Lucy impatiently.

Matt's checking the mirrors and making sure everything

is right before we set off.

'Because you have so much to do?' says Matt.

'What's that supposed to mean?' says Lucy indignantly.

'Keep your hat on, loser, just because your life's going down the drain,' says Matt.

'Excuse me?' says Lucy. 'My life is not going down the drain.'

'Then what would you call it?' says Matt.

'I'm just taking time off to figure things out. Like you've been doing for the past year.'

'Right, after I had that affair with my boss, oh no wait, that was you,' says Matt.

'Please stop arguing,' I say.

'We're not arguing, Mum, we're bantering. She gives me crap. I give her crap. It's just the nature of us,' says Matt, but then he stops because Lucy starts crying and the car goes deadly quiet.

Lucy is just like her father and hardly ever cries. Even at Joan's funeral, while Holly and Matt were in floods, Lucy kept herself to a gentle, respectable sob, gently wiping the corners of her eyes with a tissue. She'd do well as a member of the royal family. I thought she was fine being unemployed. She's told me on more than one occasion how much she's enjoying the freedom. Matt turns the engine off.

'Sorry, Luce, I thought we were mucking about,' says Matt.

'It's not that, it's that you're right,' says Lucy. 'My life is going down the drain and I don't know what to do about it. I've been kidding myself that I'm just taking some time off, pretending everything's fine when it isn't. It isn't fine.' I reach across and put my hand on her leg and give it a gentle squeeze. 'I don't know what I'm doing anymore.'

She leans into me, and I put my arm around her.

'It's going to be fine, love,' I say. 'It's only been a short while since the BBC, you're young, you have the all the time in the world.'

'But don't you see, Mum, I don't. Even now the clock's

ticking on my career. The longer I'm out of it, the more graduates will be getting ahead, and I'll be forced to get a job in telesales, or something equally as shit and then before I know it I'll be forty, in a crap job, a complete and utter failure because I once had an affair with my boss. So no, Mum, it's not going to be fine. I've really fucked everything up.'

'For Christ's sake, Lucy, get a grip,' says Greg suddenly. 'Stop being so defeatist about it. You just need to stop moping about and get a job.'

We all sit stunned. The air in the car is suddenly changed and I don't know what to say. I look across at Lucy and she's looking at Greg, her face red and puffy from the tears.

'That's a bit rough, Dad,' says Holly. 'Just because you think every problem in the world can be solved by getting a grip, it doesn't mean you're right. Sometimes we need to break down, cry, let our emotions out before we can get better.'

'I just meant,' says Greg, suddenly looking a bit uncertain. 'You know what I mean, don't you, Lucy?' I look across at Lucy and she's still crying and then I look in the mirror at Greg and his face is getting redder. 'Lucy?'

'Why do you always do that?' says Lucy, through the sniff of fading tears. 'Why do you always have to play the stiff upper lip card? Would it kill you to cry about Gran? We all cried. Everyone except you. You know she's gone right? Your mum's gone and she's not coming back. You do realise?'

'Of course I realise. I know she's gone and I'm not ever going to see her again.'

'No,' continues Lucy, her voice getting louder until she's almost shouting. 'She's gone, Dad. She's dead. Your mum is dead! She's dead! She's dead!'

I'm about to jump in, say something, stop Lucy because she's going too far, but then something happens. Greg's head drops in front of me.

'I'm not ever going to see her again,' Greg says quietly.

'I'm not ever going to see Mum again.'

For a moment I'm not sure what to do. None of us are. I lean forward and rub his back with my hand. Greg sniffs and then takes a deep breath and it's obvious he's trying not to cry. He's trying to keep himself together, but he needs this. We all need this.

'Mum's dead,' says Greg.

The tears finally come and wash over the car.

The whole family as one reaches out and we put our hands on him. I'm rubbing his back, Matt's squeezing his arm, Lucy's holding his shoulder, even Holly is reaching out and has her hand on his other shoulder. This is what we're here for. This is what we do on the rare occasion Greg lets us in. Eventually the crying stops and Greg sits up, wiping his face, trying to regain his composure.

'Sorry,' he says.

'I should be the one apologising,' says Lucy.

'No,' says Greg, turning around and looking at Lucy. 'I shouldn't have said what I said. I know it's a tough time for you, darling, and you need my support.'

'Better late than never,' says Lucy with a teary sort of half-smile.

There's a momentary quietness in the car as we all collect our thoughts, until eventually Matt breaks it.

'Okay, seriously, can everyone stop crying now? It's my birthday. The tears are really putting a dampener on things.' We all look at Matt disapprovingly. 'Sorry, too soon? Fine, I'm going to pop back inside, grab some CDs, and then we can go for a drive.'

Matt gets out and leaves us all in the car. It was strange to see Greg break down like that. It isn't like him, but it made me happy. It was like the time Holly opened up to me. I'm happy because as much as I love my family, we aren't the best communicators. I'm not saying I'm perfect, far from it, but I've always tried to be open, honest, and share myself. If only everyone else was the same. If only Holly had told me about being a lesbian earlier or Lucy had confided in me over her affair, maybe I could have helped them. If Greg talked to me instead of keeping everything in, perhaps our marriage wouldn't be in such terrible shape. Sitting in this car though, crammed together, I feel a sense of change. It feels like we're finally connected as one. Maybe for the first time in years.

'There's definitely a funny smell in here,' says Matt, getting back in again.

'I thought that too,' says Holly.

'There's no funny smell. It's been professionally cleaned,' says Greg.

'It's sort of like that old person smell,' says Matt. 'Remember the smell at Gran's home? Mothballs and sadness.'

'Yes, that's it,' laughs Lucy. 'Mothballs and sadness.'

'Mum used to hate that smell. The smell of death she called it,' says Greg smiling.

'Maybe someone died in this car,' says Holly.

'Maybe a murder,' says Lucy.

'Perfect,' says Matt. 'You bought me a murder car.'

'It's not a murder car. I think that would have been reflected in the price,' says Greg.

'Look, a blood stain,' says Holly, pointing to a small stain on the back seat.

'That could be anything,' I say.

'It's definitely blood. You bought Matt a murder car,' says Lucy.

Matt, Holly, and Lucy start laughing, and I look up at Greg and he's smiling too. Matt starts the engine again, puts in a CD, then turns to me and says,

'Oh, and Mum, even when I move out, I'll still be back for Sunday roast. I'll still need my washing done, and you know Saskia's American and can't make fish finger sandwiches like you. I might be sleeping somewhere else, but you haven't got rid of me completely.'

'Just drive the murder car,' I say with a smile.

'I knew it was a murder car!' says Lucy.

And this time we all laugh together.

Stella Blackwell's invited me to another retreat. I'm excited after the last one, although a little apprehensive as Stella said this one's even more intense. When I asked her what she meant, she just smiled and said, "Oh, Lizzy, it's going to change your life". Do I want it to change my life? Is my life so bad? The last retreat really opened my eyes, and although I haven't indulged in any more self-pleasuring (still waiting for Greg), it definitely changed me.

Being a mother and a wife isn't the whole of me. Sometimes it's easy to fall into the trap of becoming the woman the world sees - the doting parent and nice middle-class wife - but is that all I am? The total sum of my parts? Of course not. Within me, under the layers of normalcy and suburban housewife, there's passion and ambition and a determination to live a full and adventurous life. I'm not happy just going along quietly, slowly getting old and then gradually declining in a retirement home like Joan, or dying like my own mother, without anyone noticing she was gone. I don't want to be like them. I want to do exciting things. I want to be remembered for more than just raising a family.

I suppose it's every woman's greatest struggle. Balance. All this, we can have it all nonsense, just means we aren't doing anything properly. I see women with powerful, demanding jobs, who also try and be super mums, but what are they really doing? It's women playing at being men and doing it badly. I gave up having a career to raise my family because I wanted to do it right, but now they've all grown up, it's time for me to do something for me. And I have to do it right. No half-measures. I'm going to go on the retreat, I'm going to write my novel, and I'm going to enjoy the holiday in Turkey. I'm finally going to have it all.

'Let's get this show on the road, shall we?' says Matt from the front of the car, finally putting the car into gear, and I think that yes, maybe it's finally time to get the show on the road. Time to change gears.

September Roast

Holly

'I don't understand. I thought we were happy,' I say.

'I'm sorry, love,' says Mum, holding me tight.

We're on my bed and I'm crying my eyes out. I've been crying since I got back from church where Charlotte told me she isn't going to Manchester after all, and that, actually, she's decided to take a gap year and wants to take a step back from our relationship.

'What does that even mean? A step back? Are we on a break? Are we done for good? Are we still friends?' I can't stop the tears that keep coming. 'I know this is all about her parents. They're probably sending her away to a religious camp to stop her from being a disgusting lesbian. Heaven forbid she drags their good Christian family name through the mud. I'm so angry, Mum.'

'I know, love, and you have every right to be.'

'If this is what religion does to you, I don't want any part of it. It hurts, it really hurts.'

I sink into Mum and cry into her shoulder. I can't believe that after everything Charlotte and I have been through and everything we've talked about, she ends it like this. It's so weak and pathetic. She doesn't even have the courage to tell me the truth. The worst part though is that I've lost my girlfriend and best friend all in one. I'm starting to question everything. Was Charlotte really a lesbian at all? Am I? For years and years I've always felt different. I've always been searching for answers, trying to find out who I am, and finally I thought I knew. I thought Charlotte and I made sense, but now I have to start all over again.

It was only last week that everything seemed so perfect. It was the day we got our A Level results. We met up early for a coffee before going into college. We were both so excited and nervous. This day was going to determine the next three years of our lives and maybe the rest too. Despite the wrecking ball of nerves that was swinging backwards and forwards in my belly, I was coping because I was going through it with Charlotte. We'd grown up together through school and sixth form, and now finally we were on the verge of going to university together too. It was chaos as hundreds of students gathered in small groups or by themselves to open their results. Charlotte and I opened ours at the same time and within seconds we both knew we'd done enough. I'd actually done better than expected with two As and a B, and moments later we were both screaming and jumping up and down and hugging each other. We'd done it. We were going to university together.

After ringing our parents we headed to the pub. It was lovely and sunny, and we sat outside on benches with the other students, all celebrating as one, toasting the present while our minds drifted off towards the future. Soon we'd be heading off to every corner of the country. It was a truly wonderful moment and it felt like something really monumental. Maybe the first big moment of our adult lives. Going to university meant leaving home, growing up, being independent, and I was doing it with my best friend and my first love. Charlotte and I were both so happy. The next day Charlotte and her family left to go away, and I didn't see her again until this morning.

The moment I saw her at church I knew something was different. Wherever she'd been and whatever had happened she was changed. The smile had been replaced with a sad frown and the excitement and love replaced by a sullen silence. All through the service we sat next to each other without saying a word, singing the hymns quietly, her family looking on with their usual expression of disapproval. Afterwards I asked her what was wrong and that's when she told me she wasn't coming to Manchester, and she was taking a gap year instead to get her head together. We were so happy, so in love, and now we're not. Suddenly I'm back to square one, only more confused, angrier, and without a best friend to talk to about it.

'Listen, love,' says Mum. 'I haven't told anyone about this, not even your father, so it's strictly hush hush, but maybe it will help.'

I'm still cuddled up next to Mum so I pull away a little bit so I can see her. I wipe the stain of tears from my face with the sleeve of my top.

'Do you remember the women's retreat I went on with Stella Blackwell?'

'The one Matt called your lesbian feminist crusade?'

'Yes that one. Well, it changed me, Holly, in ways I can't even begin to properly explain. I thought it was all a bit new age at first; a group of middle-aged women chanting and talking about their feelings in a field was a bit too annoyingly sixties, if you know what I mean. But once we began the actual activities, I started to believe. It was wonderful, Holly, really and I can't believe I'm going to tell you what happened.'

'Do I want to hear this? Am I going to be scarred for life?'

'I hope not, love. We did lots of things during the weekend, but the one that really changed me was at the end. It was called self-exploration.'

'Oh God, I don't think I want to know about this.'

I suddenly get all of these images of a naked Mum, chanting, and running around a field covered in mud with a bunch of other wrinkly old women.

'It was mind blowing, Holly, and I know it's a bit—'

'Weird? Disgusting? Embarrassing?' I say, hoping it isn't as bad as I think it is.

'Maybe, perhaps, but it was also quite beautiful. It meant something to me. We all masturbated together, Holly, and I know it probably sounds a bit weird to you right now—'

'Oh my God, Mum, why are you telling me this?!' I say in complete horror.

'Because it's important, love. The whole weekend was about one thing. Independence. For years and years I've relied on other people to be happy, but this was about making me happy. And not just sexually before you say anything. It was empowering, about feminism, and not needing men. Trust me, it's the last thing I ever thought I'd be doing too, but it really changed me.'

'But Mum, really?' I say in a state of complete shock. 'You masturbated in a field?!'

'Well, yes, love, but like I said, we all did, and it was actually quite beautiful.'

I think my head's going to explode. My uptight, boring old Mum, who's never done anything vaguely exciting is telling me she's into group masturbation. I don't know whether to be proud of her or disgusted.

'Fine,' I eventually say because this is too weird to get my head around. 'But how does you doing that relate to me exactly?'

'Because you need to realise that you're stronger and more resilient than you think. I know this break up is hard, I do, and I know you think you need Charlotte, but you don't. True happiness comes from within.'

'It's easier said than done, Mum.'

'I know and I understand, but until you truly love yourself, then no one can love you back.' Mum looks at me and smiles a warm Mum smile. She wraps her arms around me and gives me a hug. 'You're off to university soon. You're going to meet new people, have new loves, and you're going to grow up. Just remember it's you that matters. Be happy with you. Follow your dreams.'

Then I notice she's sobbing, and I feel her body quivering gently against mine.

'You all right, Mum?'

'Yes, love, just having a mum moment,' she says, with a half-laugh, hugging me even tighter. 'I can't believe you're off to university. Sorry. I know this isn't about me.'

'It's all right,' I say, and it feels good to cuddle up to Mum. It makes me feel like a little girl again. It makes me happy. 'I just thought it might have something to do with

Dad.'

'Why do you say that?'

'Mum, please, you two haven't said a word to each other since Turkey. Did something happen over there?'

Mum goes quiet, then she looks at me, smiles, and strokes my hair softly.

'It's nothing for you to worry about, love. Now we'd better get downstairs. Everyone's waiting for us.'

I've always hated the way my parents will never talk to me about anything. They're happy to discuss my problems, my issues, and I'm grateful, I am, but when it comes to them and their relationship they won't say a word. Like I'm just a kid (always the baby of the family) so I can't possibly help them or offer them a different perspective. They're both the same. Dad goes off to his shed and spends hours writing, while Mum blows everything off like it's not a big deal. It's so frustrating. Since their holiday to Turkey things between them have been really bad. Dad's been locked away writing, while Mum's been spending more and more time with Stella Blackwell doing whatever it is that middle aged women do (masturbating in fields presumably). They're both acting suspiciously and neither of them is talking about it, although Dad started drinking early today and is already pretty pissed, so maybe he'll actually say something meaningful for a change.

And that's the thing, isn't it? Something meaningful. It's the same with Charlotte. Why won't she tell me the truth? Why won't she say something meaningful and real instead of, "Let's take a step back"? I still don't know what she means. And I don't know what's going on with Mum and Dad because they aren't saying anything. The only person I can trust and rely on is me and maybe that's what Mum was trying to tell me before. If no one else is willing to be honest with me, then the least I can do is be honest with myself. I'm the only one I can rely on to make me happy.

'This is nice. Isn't this nice?' says Mum, looking around the table with a big smile.

Matt and Saskia are sitting on one side, while I'm next to Lucy, and Mum and Dad are in their usual positions. It's strange now Gran's gone because she used to always sit next to me. Gran dying hit Dad hard, even though he tried his best to pretend it didn't. What is it with men? Why can't they feel? I cried when Gran died because it was sad and she's a part of my family. I grew up always having her in my life and I know she was old and maybe ready to go, but it's still sad. Dad couldn't even muster a tear at the funeral. Then he broke down in the car, which was good I suppose, if not a bit uncomfortable, but at least he finally let himself go. He hasn't said anything about it since. I guess that was his big emotional moment.

'It looks amazing,' says Saskia.

I like Saskia a lot. She's just what Matt needs. I do love my stupid big brother and its definitely time he got his act together. All that moping about for about a year because of that silly girl Lindsey. I was so happy when he brought Saskia home. She's super cool and stylish. I wish I looked like her. She always wears such nice clothes and has the best accessories. I'm so jealous. I think I have a little bit of a crush on her. Nothing weird, she's my brother's girlfriend and I know she isn't gay, it's not like that, but I think if I could find someone like her I'd be happy.

'You're very welcome,' says Dad, slurring his words. 'Anyone need more wine?'

'I think you've had enough,' says Mum quickly as Dad starts to get up.

'I think I'll be the judge,' Dad starts to say and then falls over his chair leg and pathetically stumbles around for a moment.

'Maybe hold off on the wine,' says Matt to Dad. 'Just while we eat.'

'Fair enough. Anyway, today's all about Holly. Let's talk about Holly,' says Dad.

'How about a toast? To Holly, my incredibly brilliant daughter, who got amazing A Level results and will soon be off to study at Manchester University,' says Mum.

Everyone raises their glasses and toasts me and I'm smiling, but all I can think about is Charlotte and it's all I can do not to start crying again. I take a deep breath to compose myself.

'So Hols, when do you officially leave?' says Matt.

'Term starts the first week of October and I have to go up a few days early to get settled into halls.'

'Ah, halls, fresher's week,' says Lucy. 'You're going to have the best time.'

'I hope so. I'm a bit worried.'

'You'll have Charlotte though, right?' says Lucy.

'Umm,' is all I can say and it's probably obvious from the look on my face that something's wrong.

'She isn't going after all,' says Mum pensively. 'She decided to take a gap year instead.'

'Bloody religious nut job parents probably,' slurs Dad.

'Not helping,' says Mum sternly.

'I'm just saying, it's probably the parents. We know they didn't approve of the whole thing from the beginning.'

'Let's keep our opinions to ourselves, shall we?' says Mum.

'This is probably better anyway,' says Matt. 'The last thing you want at university is a girlfriend holding you back. Go on your own, play the field, have fun.'

'Is that what you did?' says Saskia.

'Maybe a little,' says Matt. 'But now I couldn't be any happier not playing the field. To be honest, even if I thought about playing the field again, I wouldn't know where the field is.'

'Good save,' says Saskia.

'Dad's right though. Her parents are religious nut jobs,' I say.

'See,' says Dad, and Mum rolls her eyes at him.

'Does that mean your dalliance with the church is over?'

says Lucy.

'If they can't accept me for the way I am then yes.'

'Good for you,' says Saskia. 'My family were religious when I was growing up, but I've never been bothered by it. It's too hypocritical, too many people are excluded, and I'm sure if there is a God, he wouldn't approve of that.'

'Exactly,' I say with a smile and Saskia reaches across the table and gives my hand a squeeze.

'Things will work themselves out, they always do,' says Saskia. 'You know, I was thinking about leaving England when this one came walking into the cafe.'

'This one?' says Matt with a smile. 'Who's "this one"?'

'How much longer are you staying now?' says Lucy to Saskia and as she does, Matt and Saskia look at each other and it's obvious from the tension that they have news. Matt isn't good at hiding his feelings and Mum is the first one to spot the crack.

'What is it?' says Mum.

Matt reaches across and holds Saskia's hand.

'We have something to tell you,' says Matt. 'Since we're engaged and Saskia's visa is almost up, we've decided,' Matt stops and takes a deep breath. 'At the end of September we're leaving to travel around Europe and then we're going back to America together.'

'For how long?' says Mum, suddenly flush in the face.

'Not sure,' says Matt. 'At least three months, but who knows, it might be forever.'

'Oh, fuckety fuck,' says Lucy suddenly.

'What?' says Matt.

'You stole my thunder.'

'What thunder?' says Matt.

Mum is slowly sobbing into her napkin and Dad is swaying from side to side with a pissed look on his face.

'I had some news too, but you've just ruined it,' says Lucy.

'Sorry,' says Matt. 'I wasn't going to tell everyone yet but then you piped up with your "how much longer are you staying?" comment, so really it's your fault.'

'What's your news?' says Mum.

'Yes, darling, what's the thunder?' says Dad.

It's Lucy's turn to take a deep breath and then she looks at us all and smiles.

'I've got a job.'

'That's brilliant,' says Dad.

'Oh yes, wonderful,' says Mum.

'That isn't all. It's another media job, a really brilliant one, actually, so I'm super excited. The one catch is that it's in Edinburgh. I leave in two weeks.'

'You're moving to Edinburgh?!' says Mum, on the verge of a complete emotional breakdown. Tears are flooding down her cheeks and her makeup is a mess. She looks like a strange, twisted Tim Burton version of Mum.

'I'll do my best to get back as often as I can,' says Lucy.

'Matt's moving to America, Holly's moving to Manchester, and now you're moving to Edinburgh,' says Mum. 'I'm not sure I can handle all of this.'

'I'll get some more wine,' says Dad. 'Oh, and congratulations, darling. We're very happy for you.'

Dad walks off towards the kitchen, zig-zagging his way through the dining room around invisible objects, while Mum sits sobbing. Matt and Saskia sit together in silence, and Lucy is next to me not saying anything. It's been an emotional day. Dad eventually comes stumbling back and plonks two bottles of wine on the table. He sits down and begins filling up Mum's glass and then his. We all sit together, no one saying anything. The only sound is Mum sniffing up tears. Despite being the youngest, it's left to me to break the ice.

'Cheers you two, I thought today was supposed to be all about me?' I say with a smile, and then I take a long swig of my wine, emptying the glass. 'Fill it up, Dad.'

Dad smiles and fills up my glass.

'You're right, I'm sorry,' says Mum, shaking her head and rubbing her eyes. 'Today is about Holly. All the other stuff will have to wait.'

'To Holly,' says Matt, raising his glass in the air with a big smile.

'Holly,' everyone says joining in.

Sitting with my family right now feels sort of funny. I will always be the little kid of the family, the youngest Wilde, the mistake that shouldn't have been. I do feel young and yet I feel this ripple of something else coming towards me. It's like when I'm by the sea. You know when you stand on the edge of the beach, and you look out as far as you can at the waves building in the distance and they seem so far away. You watch them growing and growing and then eventually they crash, and the waves roll in until they arrive at your feet. This is how I feel at the moment. Like I'm standing looking out at the waves, waiting for them to get to me, waiting to feel the water rush over me. It's coming and I'm excited, but right now I'm still on the beach, my feet dug hard into the sand, holding on to everything behind me because I don't know how powerful the waves are going to be when they finally reach me.

Lucy

'Edinburgh,' said Richard.

He'd asked me to meet him for a coffee at a cafe in Soho. The same cafe we used to come to when we started the affair. It's a tiny place tucked away down a back alley. You wouldn't even find it unless you either knew about it or were completely lost, which is how I felt seeing Richard again. Lost. I used to adore that cafe. It was our place, our little secret, but being there again the magic was gone and it felt all wrong.

I wasn't sure I wanted to go at first. The last time I'd seen him was just before I left the BBC, and I didn't know what frame of mind he was in now. I knew he was back living with his wife, but maybe he still held a torch for me. Perhaps he wanted more than just a cup of coffee. The thing was, and despite everything, I was missing him, and I was worried I might fall back into old habits. Faced with him again, sitting opposite me over steaming lattes, a cheerless monotone fog outside, would I be able to stop myself? I was going through a difficult phase of trying to move on. I was fragile and vulnerable and the last thing I needed was to see Richard, but something made me say yes. Just one last time I told myself on the tube over and over again.

'Excuse me?'

'The jobs in Edinburgh, Luce, and it's yours if you want it. I put a word in for you.'

'I don't need charity, Richard. I can find a job myself,' I said, a bit more indignantly than I'd intended.

'I know you don't, but I felt bad about how things ended with us. I want to help.'

'That's it? No strings attached?'

'No strings attached.'

I looked across at him and I still fancied him like crazy.

A part of me would always want him. There was just something between us I couldn't describe or even see, but it was there and as strong as always. I had no intention of moving to Edinburgh though. My life was in London. I had my flat in Notting Hill which I'd spent ages decorating and making just about perfect. I loved my life, and my family was here. The best jobs were in London and without his help I'd find one soon enough. It was only a matter of time.

'Thanks, but no thanks.'

'Lucy,' said Richard, looking across at me intently. 'I think you should take the job.'

'Richard, we're done. You don't have to worry about me anymore. I'm a big girl, I can take care of myself.'

'I know, but this is a wonderful opportunity for you. It's a promotion. You'd basically be me. You'd be in charge, and you could work on whatever projects you want.'

'But my life's here, Richard. My family, my friends, my flat, everything. I don't know anyone in Edinburgh. I've only been there once for the festival.'

'And that's exactly why you should take it. Listen, Luce, London's great, the place to be, I get it, but this is a chance for you to spread your wings, work on some incredible projects and establish yourself. I didn't recommend you because of us or because of some misplaced sense of guilt, I did it because you're really good at what you do. You have the potential to be great and I think going to Edinburgh will be the best thing you've ever done.'

The job was an amazing opportunity and thanks to Richard I already had it. They'd also pay for me to move and help me find a place to live in Edinburgh. I could rent out my flat until I got back, which would pay the mortgage, so that wasn't a problem. The truth was, I was scared. I'd lived my whole life in London. I felt secure. I had my safety nets, but in Edinburgh I had nothing. All I had was a job Richard had arranged for me.

'Can I think about it?'

'You have until Friday,' said Richard. 'But, Luce, please

think about this properly. Give it a shot, you're young, you have nothing to lose.'

'And what about you?'

Richard took a long, slow sip of his coffee, then he looked across at me with that smile - the one that had started this whole thing off in the first place. Only unlike the smile that had changed my life, this smile was sad, crestfallen, and resigned.

'I'm stuck, Luce. I have two kids that go to a very expensive private school. I have a wife who might never forgive me for cheating on her. I have a mortgage that's probably going to be buried with me, and then there's you, the girl I love so deeply it hurts me every second of every day. That's it for me. I don't have the freedom to get up and leave, but you do. Life doesn't last for as long we'd like and being young lasts for even less. Enjoy it while you can, before you get stuck because trust me, one day you will. One day you'll be settled, and you won't have this opportunity again. Grab it, Luce, grab it with both hands and don't let it go.'

Richard looked at me with a terrible melancholy in his eyes and in that moment I knew I had to go to Edinburgh. I didn't have a choice. A part of me still loved him and he obviously still loved me, but we couldn't be together. I knew what he was doing even if he didn't. Edinburgh was the life he dreamed of for us. It was the only way he could feel like he was still a part of me and even though it meant me being so far away, I knew in his mind he could imagine us in Edinburgh, in our own little flat, working together, being in love, just the two of us. He knew he couldn't have it because like he said, he was trapped, but by giving me the chance to be free, he was freeing a small part of himself too.

'I suppose it isn't that far away,' I said, and Richard smiled.

'So you'll take it?'

'If it makes you happy.'

'It's not about my happiness, Luce.'

'If you say so.'

We sat staring at each other in silence before we left. The thing was we had nothing to say to each other because all we wanted to say was that we loved each other and wished it could be different. It might not have been a great love story, but in those five minutes we sat staring at each other, occasionally dipping into smiles and then almost dissolving into tears, I knew Richard would always hold a special place in my heart. If only we'd met under different circumstances, we could have been everything to each other. As it was, we said goodbye, and as I walked along Dean Street, past all of the other faces going somewhere, coming back from somewhere, each with our own lives, our own secrets, back towards the tube station, I knew I'd never see him again.

'Dad?' I say, knocking on the shed door. 'You in here? Dad?'

'Here,' Dad mumbles after a moment and I walk in, closing the door behind me.

'What are you doing?'

Dad's staring blankly at his laptop. He's far too drunk to be writing anything. After all the news, and with Mum still crying, Dad left quietly and headed out here. I thought it might be a good chance to have a chat and see what's going on with him and Mum. Since Turkey they've been at each other's throats and when they aren't arguing they're not talking. Mum's doing her usual bullish "we're fine" routine but maybe Dad will spill the beans. As usual, Matt is keeping out of it, and Holly has enough of her own problems, so it's up to me to sort this out. Eldest child syndrome. I can't help but be involved.

'What does it look like, darling?'

'It looks like you're staring at an empty screen.'

'Exactly.'

'Sorry, I'm lost.'

'It's nothing, never mind, darling,' Dad says, then he takes a sip from the glass of wine that's sitting on the desk next to him.

I look at Dad and suddenly he looks old. I've never thought of my parents as old before. To me they've always just been my parents and despite me, Matt, and Holly getting older, they never really have. I have friends whose parents are the same age as Mum and Dad, and they already seem so old. They're already stuck in ruts, they've lost their spark, they no longer seem to have anything important to say, but I've never felt that way about my own parents. Maybe it's because of Dad's job working with students, but he's always kept a facade of youth, and Mum's always had an energy and a spark, but now Dad seems to be fading. His eyes are glassy and red, his stomach that's always had a slight middle class paunch, is now fat, and even the laughter lines don't seem so funny anymore.

'What's going on, Dad?' I say, sitting down on the bench at the back of the shed.

'What do you mean, darling?'

'With you and Mum. What happened in Turkey because it's obvious something did?'

Dad spins his chair slowly around and looks at me.

'I'm going to miss you, darling.'

'Don't change the subject.'

'It's just—'

'And don't give me some crap story about how everything's fine because I know it isn't. I don't want to leave knowing something's wrong. Talk to me. I'm not your little girl anymore.'

'You'll always be my little girl,' says Dad, with a faint, hopeful smile.

'But I'm not and I want to help. Please, Dad, tell me what's going on.'

Dad sighs, looks down at the ground for a moment, and then looks back up at me.

'I'm a failure, Lucy. A complete and utter failure.'

'What do you mean? A failure at what?'

'At writing. This screen's been blank for months. I have

nothing to say. I'm empty.'

'But I don't understand. What have you been doing all this time?'

'Nothing, darling. Just staring at the same blank screen. I thought I could write another bestseller, but as it turns out, I can't write a thing.'

'Oh, Dad, I'm sorry. Give it some more time. Maybe you're putting too much pressure on yourself.'

'That's what your mother said.'

'And she's right.'

'But it doesn't matter now.'

'And why's that?' I say, and then I see the first tear slip out and fall down Dad's face. 'Dad, what is it?'

'It doesn't matter because I've lost your mother. She's going to leave me and so none of this matters because without her it's all pointless. I've been such a fool, Lucy. Such a prize idiot and your mother's had enough, and I don't blame her. You're leaving, Matt's leaving, Holly's leaving, and I'm going to be alone. Alone, darling.'

'Is it because of what happened in Turkey?'

Dad looks at me, his eyes wet and sad, before he tells me about Turkey.

'I kept your mother waiting for her holiday for such a long time, she was so happy to get away. I should have been too. I should have treated it like a complete break, but I didn't. All I could think about was the stupid book I couldn't write. I was so down, Lucy, and your mother didn't know about the book. She thought I was doing great.'

'Because you told us you were.'

'I was embarrassed. I thought it was what I should be doing, but then I came to do it and I couldn't. We got to Turkey and your mother was so excited, but the happier she became, the worse I felt and for some reason I took it out on her. Like it was her fault I couldn't write. I was mean, Lucy, and angry. I didn't want to be, but I couldn't help it.'

'And what happened?'

'It was the day before we were due to fly home. Every

day we'd done the same thing; argue and bicker. Your mother had gone to the pool by herself most days or the beach, while all I did was mope around the hotel, drinking, and trying to get some inspiration for the book but nothing was coming, and I was getting more frustrated. So, that day, your mother met another couple at the pool, and she arranged for us to have dinner together that night. I'd been drinking all day and by the evening, I was ready to explode. All the frustration and anger had been simmering below the surface and it had to come out.'

'So you took it out on these friends of Mum's?'

'Worse. I took it out on your mother. I was horrible, Lucy. "A monster" your mother called me. She didn't speak to me again after that.'

'Did you apologise?'

'I've tried, Lucy, but she doesn't want to know. I went too far.'

'But Dad, she's still here. Tell her how you feel, how much you love her and that you can't live without her. Yes, you were a top-class prat, but it isn't over Dad, it can't be.'

'I don't know. I think this is it.'

'Do you remember what you said to me when I told you about Richard?'

'Not exactly,' says Dad. 'Old man memory, I'm afraid.'

'I'm not going to quote you verbatim, but it was something about my mistake not defining who I am. You've made mistakes, Dad, but you can't let those mistakes define the rest of your life. What defines us is not how many times we fall, but how many times we get back up again. You know I'm right.'

'You always were too smart for your own good.'

'And who did I get that from?'

'Definitely not me. Your mother's always been the smartest one. Did you know she got a First at university while I only got a 2:1?'

'Mum told me,' I say and Dad smiles.

'Of course she did.'

The door to the shed suddenly opens and Matt pops his head inside.

'I need you both back inside pronto, I'm taking a family photo.'

'We'll be in soon,' says Dad. Matt smiles and walks off leaving Dad and I alone. 'I'm so proud of you, Lucy. You know that, right?'

'I always have.'

'And whether you're in Edinburgh, here, or Timbuktu, and whether you like it or not, you'll always be my little girl.'

Dad gets up and gives me a hug, his whole wine-soaked body enveloping mine and he holds me, just like he did when I was a little girl, but this time I think it's him that needs to feel safe and protected against the world and not me.

'Lucy, you stand there,' says Matt, pointing at a spot to the right of the fireplace. 'And Holly you stand next to her there. Mum, Dad, you're there, Saskia, baby, you go next to Dad, and I'll be on the end.'

'Okay David Bailey, get on with it,' I say.

'I'm trying to get it right,' says Matt. 'Just like that old photo we have of us when we were kids, remember?'

'Christmas,' says Mum. 'Lucy you were about fourteen I think, so Matt you would have been about eleven, and Holly was just six years old. God, it doesn't feel that long ago.'

'It feels like yesterday,' says Dad, looking across at Mum with a saccharine smile.

'Maybe we could fish out the dungarees Matt was wearing,' I say, and everyone laughs.

'They were the fashion,' says Matt defensively.

'What were they again? Extra baggy acid wash?'

'I have to see this photo,' says Saskia.

'It's a beauty. Matt was going through his rap phase and if I remember, didn't you have tramlines shaved into your hair?' I say, as Matt goes ever increasing shades of red. 'And there was definitely some bling.'

'Again, it was the fashion,' says Matt.

'Maybe in downtown Detroit,' I say, and Saskia laughs.

'Can we please just get on with the photo?' says Matt.

We all shuffle into position as Matt takes his time setting the shot up properly. Matt's annoying at times, lazy, difficult, argumentative, but he's my little brother and I'm going to miss him terribly. I look across at Holly too, still so young, and yet the past six months she's been through so much. I can't begin to imagine how difficult it must be to tell everyone you know you're gay because, despite how far the world's come, it's still something some people frown upon. I don't care though, she's my sister and I love her dearly.

As we're stood here together, Matt making his final adjustments, I start thinking about Matt and Holly. Growing up we spent every second together, whether we wanted to or not, we were siblings, so we were each other's lives. We played together, went on holidays together, had the same friends, and shared so many moments that it's impossible to separate our lives. When I think of my childhood, I think of theirs. Yet now we're about to go our separate ways and I don't know when I'm going to see them again. From being everything in my life to passing ships, it's a strange feeling. I understand now why having the Sunday roast is so important to Dad. It's his way of keeping us together. Only now it's at an end, for the time being anyway, and it's sad, but at least we'll have this photo as a reminder.

'Okay, everyone,' says Matt, standing next to the tripod. 'Ready?'

'Ready,' we all say apart from Holly, who's doing something on her phone.

'Seriously, Hols?' says Matt.

'I'm live tweeting this to the world.'

'But you need to be looking at the camera and smiling,' says Matt.

'Unlike you old people, I can multi-task,' says Holly.

'Fine,' says Matt, who pushes a button on the camera and then joins us next to Saskia.

We wait for a few seconds, looking at the light on the camera that tells us when it's going to take our photo. We're smiling. We're together.

'Okay, it's coming. Say cheese everyone,' says Matt.

'Fromage,' says Dad quickly.

'Don't you mean organic, free range, vintage fromage,' says Holly, and we all laugh as the camera snaps and then flashes.

October Roast

Greg

As humans we're always clinging on. We're clinging onto our youth, memories, places, hopes, and we cling onto our children. We have them knowing that one day they're going to leave us, hoping that when they finally do they don't fly too far from the nest. There were times when the kids were young when it felt like they'd always be with us, as though their childhoods would go on forever, but now on the verge of losing them all in one fell swoop, I'm clinging onto every last second.

It's bearable though because despite the pain of watching them all leave, at least I knew it was coming and had time to prepare myself. The one thing I never expected though was to be clinging onto my marriage. Yet here I am, desperately hoping Lizzy isn't going to leave me, because of all of the pain I've suffered in my life, nothing is as excruciating as the thought of losing her. I can't believe it's even come to this. As cliché as it sounds, I really didn't realise until it was too late. It's the last Sunday roast before Matt leaves for Europe, and so from now on it's just going to be Lizzy and me, and if I can't convince her otherwise, it might just be me.

Last weekend Lizzy went on another retreat with Stella Blackwell and came back in a strange mood. I've already tried talking to her about us. I've apologised a hundred times for what happened in Turkey, and I've told her I want to change and put us first. All she keeps saying is she's heard it all before and she's tired of the same old rhetoric. When Lucy left for Edinburgh she told me to keep trying to make it work, and Lizzy's still in the house, so despite her frostiness and the general lack of love between us, there's still hope. When I asked her what goes on at these retreats, she laughed and said I wouldn't understand, and it got me thinking that there's a lot I don't understand about Lizzy these days.

Lizzy and I drove Holly up to university a few weeks ago. Sitting in the car in relative silence, none of us seemed sure what to say. Lizzy had been crying intermittently all morning. Holly was nervous, worried, and had been on the verge of tears for days. Eventually we arrived and walked Holly to her halls of residence. We carried her bags, dropping them off in her small room before taking her out for lunch. We ate in a pub, caught somewhere between not wanting to leave and knowing the longer we stayed the more difficult it would be. When we got back to her halls, another nervous young girl was moving into the flat with her own pair of sad looking parents trailing her like scalded dogs. We all smiled at each other before it was time to cut the apron strings. Lizzy and I left, tears streaming down the girls' faces, while I tried my best to keep it together for as long as I could. Lizzy cried all the way home, while I sat driving in silence.

When we got home, I hung the car keys up in the hallway and stood for a moment. A million memories came flooding back. Holly, Lucy, and Matt all charging up the stairs, and Lizzy or me shouting at them to be careful, before screams, laughter or tears, and them charging back down again. The house was always so loud when they were growing up and there were times when I wished for some peace and quiet, but now with the fading noise, all I crave is to hear their voices again and the stomp, stomp, stomp of their feet on the stairs.

I'm in the middle of cooking the roast. I've gone all out for the last one; traditional roast beef and Yorkshire puddings. The beef is free range, organic, and is sourced from a family run farm in Lincolnshire. I'm making goose fat roast potatoes and have a nice bottle of red for the gravy and a selection of seasonal vegetables. I know my family laugh at me for my obsession with food for the roast, but I don't think they understand how important it is to me, or how important I want it to be to them.

The roast is the meal that brings us together. It's one of the few traditions we can still cling to that keeps the family tree connected. When I'm in the kitchen, I think of my mother stood in our old kitchen every Sunday cooking a roast. Mum in her apron, whirling around the kitchen tasting the gravy, checking on the potatoes, and me waiting impatiently watching television to make the time go faster until the best meal of the week. I remember Dad outside mowing the lawn or washing the car with all the other dads on the street, proper Sunday activities, and then sitting around the table together. It feels so real I can almost touch it and I want my children to feel the same. I want them to be able to look back when they're my age and remember the roasts we had. I don't obsess over the quality of the food because I'm a middle-class snob (as Matt has claimed), or because I'm going a bit mental (Holly), or because I care more about that than my marriage (Lizzy), but because I want my family to remember these days.

'Matt just rang, they're almost here,' says Lizzy, walking into the kitchen. She rattles through a cupboard and pulls down four wine glasses.

'Right,' I say hesitantly. 'Lizzy, look, I was wondering—'

'Not today, Greg,' she says, before I can finish.

'Then when, Lizzy? We need to talk.'

'I need to say goodbye to Matt. Please let me have this day.'

'Okay,' I say, and she walks out with the wine glasses and into the dining room.

Since we got back from Turkey I've been trying to write, but it's not going well. My mind is on everything else, and I can't focus on the book. I feel like I'm drowning. I'm holding onto too much baggage. My father, my mother, the kids leaving, my marriage, and me trying to pretend everything is fine when it quite clearly isn't. Pretending, as it turns out, is a lot more difficult than actually admitting you need help.

When Dad was diagnosed with Alzheimer's, Lizzy made me promise that if I needed anything, if it all got too much, I'd ask for help. I told her of course I would and promised I wouldn't shut her out. I guess she knew me better than I knew myself because as Dad began the final journey towards death, I was still dealing with it on my own. Too afraid, too proud, and too stubborn to ask for help. When Mum died I sank into the same place. Only this time I haven't managed to escape. I broke down in the car on Matt's birthday, but that was it and to be honest, I'm still holding onto far too much pain. I need Lizzy to rescue me, but I've spent so long pushing her away that I don't know if she can, and more importantly, I don't know if she wants to.

'Dad,' says Matt, bounding into the kitchen and giving me a strong pat on the shoulder. Behind him I can see Saskia talking to Lizzy in the hallway. They're smiling and even from here, I can see that Lizzy is trying her best to keep herself together. 'Smells delicious. I'm going to miss these,' says Matt.

'One last game of table tennis later?'

'Of course. I have to beat you one last time before we leave,' says Matt, and surprisingly I'm struggling to hold back the tears myself, so I smile instead, pushing the lump back down my throat.

We're all sitting around the table, although unlike in the past, it's just me, Lizzy, Matt, and Saskia. The numbers are rapidly dwindling. The empty seats reminders of the people who aren't with us. I helped Lucy pack up her flat and move to Edinburgh. We drove up on a Saturday, Lizzy waved goodbye from the front door, tears streaming down her face, while Lucy and I took it in turns to drive the eight hours to her new place. We talked and bought service station coffee and it was nice spending one last day with her.

I left her in her lovely new flat, sitting on the floor surrounded by boxes. I offered to stay for a few days and help her unpack, but she said she wanted to do it by herself. We kissed and hugged, and I got back in the car and drove home alone.

'Now I'm moving out there's a few things you should know,' says Matt. 'Some things I did growing up I wasn't entirely truthful about.'

'Is this about the vase you broke and blamed Lucy for?' says Lizzy.

'You know about that?' says Matt in disbelief.

'Of course we did,' I say. 'It didn't seem likely that Lucy broke the vase while using it as a swimming pool for frogs. For a start, Lucy was terrified of frogs, and secondly, there were red fingerprints all over the vase. The same day you painted that picture of the red frog.'

'But why didn't you punish me if you knew?'

'We were hoping you'd feel guilty and confess,' says Lizzy.

'I suppose you know about the marijuana too then?' says Matt.

'Actually, no,' I say. 'Although now you've mentioned it, you might as well tell us.'

'The night you caught Holly smoking weed in her bedroom. It was actually mine.'

'How old were you when this happened?' says Saskia.

'I was twenty and Holly was fifteen,' says Matt. 'She'd never smoked before and wanted to try it and so I thought better at home with me than out with God knows who. I was trying to be a good brother. Just before Mum and Dad came upstairs, I ducked out to get some more Rizlas, so all they saw was Hols smoking. They went ballistic and she was grounded for a month.'

'I'm so disappointed in you,' says Saskia.

'Me too,' says Lizzy.

'I was young,' says Matt. 'And stoned a lot of the time. Speaking of which, on a completely unrelated topic, the dent in the car.'

'I knew that wasn't Mr Johnson from next door,' says Lizzy.

'You blamed a disabled man for hitting our car?' I say.

'To be fair, he wasn't really disabled,' Matt says to Saskia. 'He had one of those stickers on his car, but he just had really bad eyesight. It wasn't like he was a paraplegic.'

'Quite the crime spree,' says Saskia. 'Should I be worried?'

'I've grown up a lot since then,' says Matt.

'It's true. He changes his underwear nearly every day now,' says Lizzy with a smile.

I look across at Lizzy and her smile instantly changes to an uncomfortable frown. My smile fades too and I look down at my plate. I'm not hungry. I have too much on my mind. I'm moving my roast potatoes around the plate, dabbing them in small puddles of gravy, but I can't eat a thing. I'm like one of those background actors on television who's pretending to eat without actually eating.

I'm going to miss our Sunday dinners so much. I know life goes in stages. There's childhood, adolescence, university and the early twenties, before adulthood comes along with all its trappings: marriage, mortgages, careers, children etc. The thing is all the other stages are relatively short when you think about it. Childhood is twelve years. Adolescence is seven years. University and the early twenties are maybe eight years if you're lucky. However, we've been parents for twenty-eight years. That's longer than all of the other stages combined. It's a long time and when you come out the other side so much has changed. Lizzy and I have both changed, the world is different, and now we're supposed to start one of the last stages of our life. The retirement years. We have the time and the money to do anything we want, but we've spent so long focused on our family that I'm not sure we know what we want to spend the time and money on. When Lizzy and I first got together, all I wanted was to be with her. I was just me and she was just her and we spent every second getting to know each other. But we've drifted so far apart since then it's like we're acting out the roles we think we should be playing. She's the dutiful wife and stay-at-home mother and I'm the provider father. They aren't who we really are though, and now Lizzy's discovering who she is again and I'm finding out that maybe I'm not who I thought I was, we're struggling to be us again.

'I'll help tidy up,' says Saskia when we're all done.

'Good, we can have a good chat,' says Lizzy.

'Table tennis?' I say to Matt.

He smiles and we get up and go out to the garage. Our last game. There's also something I want to say to him that I should have said a long time ago.

Matt and I walk into the garage where the table tennis table is already set up. Matt walks around and picks up his paddle. I grab us both a bottle of beer from the small fridge.

'Here you go,' I say, passing a bottle to Matt.

'Cheers,' says Matt, chinking his bottle against mine. 'I'm going to miss this. I know we've only started playing again this year, but I like playing table tennis with my old man in the garage. It feels sort of—'

'Cathartic?'

'I was going to say nice, but yeah, cathartic will do.'

'I'm going to miss it too,' I say, picking up my paddle. 'And your mother's awful at table tennis.'

Matt looks at me and smiles before his face straightens up.

'Are you and Mum going to be all right?'

I think it's the first time he's ever asked me about us. Matt doesn't like to get involved in our relationship and I always thought it was because he didn't care, or didn't feel like it was his place, but maybe it's only now he finally feels grown up enough to ask. Either that or he's more worried about it than he's letting on.

'Yes, of course, son. We'll be fine.'

'Good,' says Matt with a smile. 'Because it's shit playing table tennis by yourself.'

'Matt, are you using table tennis as a metaphor for life?' I say.

'You're the English lecturer, Dad, I'll let you figure it out.'

I look down at the paddle, at the faded tape that's wrapped around the handle. The same one I used against Dad growing up. I must have wrapped new tape around this handle so many times over the years. Even now one of the ends is coming away and it looks a bit ragged. There's so much history in these paddles. So many memories, and looking across at Matt, I hope there's more to come. I imagine myself standing here with my grandchildren teaching them how to play. Three generations of Wildes together. Dad would have been so proud. I know that might sound a bit sentimental, but you know what I've realised. Sentimentality isn't just a saccharine emotion kept purely for Richard Curtis films and romantic poetry, it's what happens to our memories as we get older. Sentimentality is us clinging onto our past hopes and dreams because they mean so much to us. Age gives us perspective and the thing I'm realising more and more is the only thing that matters in life is relationships. The relationships between parents and children, and husbands and wives. It's the one thing that connects us all. Holding this paddle keeps a piece of my father alive and creates new memories for me with my son.

'Play for serve?'

'Sure, son, but before we do there's something I want to say.'

'If it's about money, we're fine. I have money from the cafe and Saskia has plenty.'

'It's not about money. It's something else,' I look across at Matt for a moment, smile slightly uncomfortably, and then take a deep breath. 'It wasn't always easy being my father's son. I'm not like him. He was fun, light-hearted, and you always knew how he felt about you. I always wished I was more like him, but I'm not, and I know there's been times when you've probably wished I was different too.'

'Dad, it's fine, really,' says Matt, but I raise my hand to stop him.

'You're going away, Matt, and I don't know when I'm going to see you again and honestly, it terrifies me. I'm scared because I'm not going to have so many opportunities to tell you how proud I am of you and how much I love you. Having you here every day for the past twenty-odd years, I've taken it for granted, but suddenly you're leaving, and I don't want you to go without me saying it. And that's the thing, Matt. I am so proud of you, and I do love you a lot. You know that, right?'

'Of course I do.'

I can feel the tears again, bubbling away inside of me, but I realise as I look at Matt that the tears aren't just for him. They're for Mum, Dad, Holly, Lucy and Lizzy too. It's taken me far too long to realise that holding onto all of these emotions has done nothing except tear me and my marriage apart and drive a wedge between me and the people I love.

'Before I left home and moved in with your mother, Dad gave me some advice and now you're moving out, I want to give you the same advice,' I say.

'If it's about the birds and the bees, Dad, I'm good. I have all the main moves down.'

'It's not about that and I have no idea what the main moves are anyway, and before you tell me, I don't want to know,' I say and Matt laughs. 'My father told me this. Happiness is never far away, as long as you're looking in all the right places. What he meant was, you need to follow your dreams. Whatever they are, go after them and make them a reality. You'll never be happy if you aren't being true to yourself. So go out there and be you, be proud to be you.'

'Thanks, Dad,' says Matt, and I can see the beginnings of tears in his eyes too.

'I've never told you this before, but you remind me a lot

of my father,' I say and then I walk over and give Matt a hug. I embrace his whole body, pulling him close and slapping him strongly on the back. My son.

'One last time?' I say, picking up my paddle.

'One last time,' says Matt.

So we do. Me and Matt. Father and son. And I don't let him win because he's grown up now and can beat me on his own.

We play for thirty minutes and during the last few points, I get a sudden thought. It's more of a realisation actually, and I put my paddle down.

'What's up?' says Matt.

'I have to go. There's something I have to do.'

'Is this because you're losing because that's really sad,' says Matt, but I'm already rushing out of the garage and into the house.

I run upstairs and pull the ladder to the attic down. I climb the steps and turn the light on. I walk carefully between the wooden beams to the far corner where a small pile of boxes is stacked against the wall covered in an old blanket. I pull the blanket off, get down on my knees, and start rifling through the first box. I know it's here somewhere. I go through the second box and then the third. Finally I get to the fourth box and as I do I see the envelope and a smile spreads across my face. I reach in and pull the envelope out, quickly opening it up and pulling out two pieces of old, dog-eared paper. I look down and immediately see Lizzy's writing on one piece and my own on the other.

I remember the exact moment when Lizzy gave me her letter. It was the day before our wedding day, and I was dropping her at her parent's house. She was spending the night with them, and I was staying at a nearby hotel. It was the last time I was going to see her before we were married. Before I left she slipped a piece of paper into my hand and told me to read it before I went to bed. As soon as I got back to my room I read the letter. She told me how much she loved me and that she would be patient with me, grow with me, respect me, and she'd never forget how she felt right now. She promised me that no matter what happened, no matter how difficult things were, she'd always be by my side. What I've never told Lizzy is that I wrote her a response that night, but for one reason or another, I've never given it to her. It's been stashed away among my boxes ever since. I'm hoping this letter might save us.

I'm so excited and nervous as I climb down the stairs from the loft. I'm going to finally show Lizzy the letter I wrote so long ago. I get to the top of the landing, my heart racing, my hands sweaty, and I start walking down the stairs. I can hear Lizzy's voice in the living room talking with Saskia and Matt. Her sweet voice. The voice I love so much and have loved ever since I met her. I reach the bottom of the stairs and that's when it happens. A pain shoots up my back, my head is suddenly dizzy, my chest's tight and I can't breathe. It feels as though someone has reached into my chest and is squeezing my heart as hard as they can. Then a pain shoots down my side and up my arm and I notice the ground moving towards me as my heart explodes in my chest. I try to speak, to say Lizzy's name, but the words won't come. My back hurts and I'm lying on the ground looking up at the ceiling. My breath is getting tighter and slower and my vision's starting to fade.

As I'm lying here a montage of memories flicker through my mind. My father and I fishing when I was little, sitting together on the riverbank on a warm afternoon, talking, and fishing as though the day would never end. Meeting Lizzy at university, our first date, moving in together, getting married, our honeymoon. Fast forward to Lucy being born, Matt small and crawling around on the floor. Then Holly is turning two and it's her birthday party. A family holiday in Scotland, the time we drove in the car all the way there and stayed in that cottage by the loch. Lucy graduating from university, Matt getting engaged, and Holly sitting with me in the shed. We're just talking, and I realise how alike we are and how much I'm going to miss her when she's at university. My first dance with Lizzy at our wedding. Then I'm a small boy again and I'm in the back of our old car driving somewhere, Dad's whistling and Mum's handing me a sandwich. A flurry of memories and then they stop.

'Greg!' screams Lizzy.

I can hear her voice and then I see her face. It looks terrified, but it makes me happy. She's kneeling over me, and Matt is next to her.

'It's okay,' I say, but I don't think they can hear me. 'I love you so much.'

'Greg, stay with me. Please, don't close your eyes,' says Lizzy, and she's crying, and I want to reach out and hold her, hug her, and tell her it's going to be all right, but nothing works. I feel her tears fall on my face and then slowly my eyes close and it's black. For a second I hear a noise and it's Lizzy's voice and then that's it. There's nothing and I'm sure I'm dying. And then I see my father.

Lizzy

At first, I thought it was nothing. My initial reaction was that he'd just fallen down, maybe bumped his head, and at worse had a concussion. That's what our brain tells us because it can't or perhaps doesn't want to imagine the worst-case scenario. It's nothing. It's going to be all right. How was I to know that Greg was dying? That his heart had stopped, given in, and that the letter he was holding in his hand could have saved our marriage. I didn't know any of this, so as I stood over him with Matt next to me, time seemed to literally stand still because I couldn't believe what was happening. I looked at Matt and for a moment all I felt was complete and utter horror as I realised what was happening. That my husband was having a heart attack.

Our holiday to Turkey was the last straw. I really thought it was going to be the turning point for us. Greg had made such a big song and dance about how much he wanted to go away with me that I felt like there was still a chance. He obviously wanted to put the work in and fight for our marriage, and then when he broke down in the car on Matt's birthday, it gave me hope that there was still enough emotion, passion, and enough of the Greg that I fell in love with left. I started to believe we had a future and Turkey was going to be the start. Then we went away, and Greg was awful, worse than he's ever been, and I knew then that our marriage was over. I still loved him, but I didn't like the person he'd become. I didn't want to admit it or even talk about it, but in the days and weeks after we got back, I started making plans to get away. Stella Blackwell agreed that I could stay in one of her three spare bedrooms for as long as I wanted, so when the children were all gone, I was going too.

Greg tried to talk about what happened and he tried to

apologise, but I was done with his apologies. There are only so many times someone can say sorry before you realise that they aren't actually going to change. That the words are just hollow, meaningless token gestures from someone who doesn't understand why they keep doing the same thing over and over again. Greg and I were done and that was it. I accepted it. But then Greg goes and has a heart attack and none of it matters because all I can do is hope and pray that he makes it. That my husband doesn't die before we have the chance to fix everything and be happy again. They say that when someone dies, their life flashes before their eyes. As I'm sitting next to Greg, waiting for the ambulance, holding his hand and crying my eyes out begging him not to die, our marriage flashes before my eyes. I remember everything in a split second; the good, the bad, and the ugly. I remember the day we met, the day we got married, and everything else up until this moment.

'It's going to be okay. Dad's going to be all right,' says Matt. He looks at me and then puts his hand on my shoulder and gives it a strong squeeze. 'He's strong, Mum.'

'But what if he's not?' I say, looking at Matt. 'What then? I just can't imagine a life without your father.'

We're in the hospital waiting room. Matt, Saskia, and me. We don't know what's going on and they won't tell us anything. Back at the house they came in and I was ushered away from Greg while the paramedics went about their work. Matt held me in his arms, and I cried. Saskia looked on with horror as Greg was taken in the ambulance, and then we followed in Matt's car. The car we'd bought him for his birthday that now felt so long ago. The car Greg cried in because his mother had passed away and now Greg could be gone too.

Matt looks off down the corridor where Saskia is getting us coffee from the drinks machine. Matt rang Lucy and Holly and they're on their way. I wasn't sure we should call them, but Matt said, "just in case" and the whole thing felt so surreal, as though we were acting out roles in a television medical drama. We even said the same cliché lines and used the same hackneyed expressions I'd heard so many times, and all of it felt unreal because it couldn't be happening. Things like this didn't happen to people like us.

I took the letter from Greg's hand and held it so tightly. I read it as soon as we got here, and it made me cry even harder. The letter. I'm still holding it now and I don't want to let it go because it feels like it's somehow helping to keep him alive.

'Sorry, this is all I could get,' says Saskia, putting three cups of watery looking coffee down on the table in front of us.

'Thanks,' says Matt, and Saskia sits down next to him. The three of us sitting together in silence. Waiting.

As we're waiting I start thinking about a life without Greg. It's ironic because until a few hours ago that's exactly what I'd been planning. It's what I wanted. I suppose I always thought that when a marriage ends, it's with a big bang, but the reality is that Greg and I slowly fizzled out. After my disappearance and his affair things just weren't the same between us. I was all ready to walk away and start afresh but seeing Greg today and the thought of losing him forever changed everything. I can't lose him and especially not like this. I also need to know about the letter. It's obvious he wrote it the day before our wedding day, but why didn't he give it to me then? And why was he bringing it to me now? I have so many questions, but more importantly I have a new perspective. Maybe this is a second chance to make us work, but all of it rests on whether Greg makes it or not.

The doctor walks towards us and I'm trying to see from the look on his face if it's good or bad news. My eyes are stinging, red, and painful from the tears, and I have to squint to see the details on his face. He's in his fifties, has a kind, gentle face, and he's probably done this a hundred times before. His face, full of wrinkles and laughter lines, doesn't give me anything. I see a wedding ring on his finger and for a moment I imagine him going home to his own family; wife, children, maybe a dog, to someone who asks him about his day, and he has to tell them about me. About the wife who broke down when he had to give her the worst news in the world. I imagine him hugging his wife and holding her close because he can't imagine losing her. Tears are already waiting behind my eyes and I have a deep pain in my heart. The nearer the doctor gets the more the pain throbs and a few tears leak out and down my face. I get up, wiping the tears quickly away as the doctor finally stands in front of us.

'Mrs Wilde?'

'Yes,' I say, barely able to say the word out loud.

I see the name badge on his white coat. Dr Wilkinson.

'Your husband's had a severe heart attack. He was resuscitated twice in the ambulance, but we've managed to stabilise him—'

'He isn't dead?!' I say, suddenly awash with relief.

'He isn't out of the woods yet. The next twenty-four to forty-eight hours are crucial.'

'But he's okay?' I say.

'For the moment, yes.'

And this is when I break down. The pain in my chest stops and releases me into a fit of tears and Matt holds me in his arms. Greg is all right. He isn't going to die. Not yet anyway. The doctor looks at me and smiles and I thank him over and over again from the bottom of my heart because he's saved my husband's life. Saved our life.

'Can we see him?' says Matt, tears glistening in his eyes too.

'Of course, but be careful, he's still very weak. He needs rest so maybe just for five minutes.'

'Thank you,' I say again, and the doctor leads us through into Greg's room.

I've never liked hospitals. Everyone says that don't they? I don't suppose anyone likes hospitals because why would you? You're either there because you're sick or because somebody else is. The smell, the way they look, the machines that do things I don't know about or understand, and the tubes that keep people alive. Greg is attached to a machine that's beeping and there are tubes and monitors everywhere. He looks awful. He's awake though and as soon as he sees us all standing over him he smiles.

'You scared the life out of us,' I say, smiling between the sniff of tears. 'You must promise me you'll never have another heart attack again, okay?'

'Promise,' says Greg, his voice is gravelly and rough. 'Love you.'

'Love you too,' I say, and I just want to get in bed with him and hold him, but I can't because he's too fragile. 'I have the letter, Greg. The one you had in your hand. I read it.'

I show him the letter and he smiles again. He tries to say something, but he can't get the words out, so I tell him to be quiet and rest.

Matt says hello, gives Greg a kiss on the head and tells him he'd better get well so they can finish their game of table tennis. After a minute or two a nurse comes in and starts fiddling with the tubes and checking the machines. We say goodbye and let Greg rest. Matt, Saskia, and I go back to the waiting room then they go off to get some food. As soon as they're gone I get the letter out of my pocket again. I unfold it and look at Greg's handwriting on the page. The familiar scrawl, the big looping letters, and the backwards slant I always found so funny. I smile to myself before I read it one more time.

"Dear Lizzy, my love. It feels almost unbelievable that by this time tomorrow you'll be my wife. I can't even begin to tell you how happy and excited I am. Thank you so much for your letter today. I just finished reading it and it inspired me to write this letter back to you. I know I'm not the most emotional person in the world which frustrates you at times, and I'm sorry for that, but it doesn't mean I don't love you with every ounce of my being. You've given me so many letters since we met and I haven't given you any, so this is it.

It's so hard for me to write this because your letter was so touching. It's one of the reasons why I love you so much Lizzy. You've never been afraid to tell me how you feel or show all of yourself to me. You're so open and honest and it used to terrify me because I didn't know how to deal with it, but now it makes me want to be better. You see that's it. When you meet the one you're supposed to be with they complete you. They fill in the parts you're missing. You fill in all my parts Lizzy and it may sound trite and cliché, but you do complete me.

There was a moment when we first we met. It was a sunny day, and we were walking together with some friends. I can't remember where we were going, but there was a few of us. I remember one moment when you were ahead of me talking to Kate, your old housemate at university, and I was watching you and I knew then that I wanted to spend the rest of my life with you. You were talking and laughing and just looked so beautiful, but above everything, I had this feeling deep inside of me that I needed you. That I needed you to be a part of my life, a part of me, and from that moment on something inside of me changed because I knew something I had never known before. I knew what true love felt like.

I know I have my faults Lizzy, but it hasn't stopped you loving me, and I hope it never does. Maybe at some point in the very distant future you'll have enough of me, but if that ever happens, please don't give up on me. You see the thing is I'm not that strong of a person. I try to be. I pretend to be. But I'm not. I need you Lizzy and I always will. You make me so happy and since you agreed to be my girlfriend and now my wife, my life has been infinitely better. I love you so much and I always will. Your husband, forever, Greg."

Part Four

(Eight months later)

Lizzy

There are so many different kinds of happiness, but I suppose I've never been very good at finding it myself. In my teens I was too insecure. I thrived at university, but I was still trying to figure out who I was. The happiest I can remember being was when Greg and I were living in our first flat together, but even that was tinged with a slight uncertainness. We didn't have much money, and despite my grand literary aspirations, once again I was racked with self-doubt. When we moved to this house and started a family, I was content rather than completely happy because it wasn't the life I'd imagined over and over in my head. It's like I said, there are so many different kinds of happiness. I've always been happy in part, as if the jigsaw pieces that made up my life were almost in place, but there were gaps. Pieces were missing so the whole picture couldn't be seen, but finally it feels complete. This is, as far as I can see, as near to pure happiness as I've ever felt. And yet it all could have been so different.

When I found Greg on the floor, I thought he was dying. When his eyes closed and he wouldn't wake up, it felt like my heart stopped too because I thought I'd lost him. I thought the love of my life was gone, but since then everything has been so different. For weeks after it happened, Greg spent most of his time in bed recuperating. We talked about everything, and Greg was so different, so open. Its cliché, he said it himself, but almost dying completely changed him and gave him a new appreciation for life. As death so often does, it put everything in perspective for the both of us. During those weeks we talked about our dreams, wrote bucket lists, and put a plan in place that would make us happy. Not just me or him, but us.

Greg took early retirement and now he writes full time, and our life is so changed from what it once was. We take breaks whenever we want, we spend each morning together, lying in bed, having a cup of coffee or tea over breakfast, enjoying life and each other like never before. We have the security of money and the time to really enjoy it. The children might be gone, and it's a huge hole in our lives, but we've managed to fill it with each other, with our writing, and with travel. I have a literary agent and my first novel is finished and ready for submission. Greg's latest book is finished too. It's been a rollercoaster few months, but the reality that I'm going to be a published author is getting closer and the dream I had sitting in my bedroom as a teenager is starting to feel tangible. The main thing is though, and maybe this is just the by-product of our new life, Greg and I have never been closer. We've fallen in love again. We've turned the corner and I know we won't go back to how things were. It feels like we've finally remembered why we got together in the first place. And the sex has been phenomenal. My life is like Fifty Shades of Greg!

I'm upstairs packing for a four-day mini break to Paris and Greg is downstairs cleaning the kitchen. We went to Paris a million years ago, before we had kids, and we haven't returned since so I'm really excited because I have such fond memories of our time there. We even managed to book the same hotel we stayed at all of those years ago. It feels sort of cyclical as though we're going back to where it all began.

I'm packing bags, specifically Greg's toiletries bag, because he's absolutely useless at it. I'm making sure his travel toothbrush is here because I know Greg and he'll forget it and then we'll be forced to buy a new one in France. So instead of wandering hand-in-hand through the beautiful streets of Montmartre, we'll be in a pharmacie with Greg moaning that none of the French toothbrushes are soft enough for his delicate, middle-aged gums.

Packing's always been my job. Whenever we went on

holiday, my role was to pack for me and the kids, while Greg did his own. Once, during the early years of parenthood, we went away for a week to Scotland. I wasn't feeling well so Greg, trying to be the dutiful husband, offered to do it all. It wasn't until we were in Scotland, at the cottage we'd rented miles from anywhere, that the true horror of his incapabilities became so terrifyingly clear.

We were staying in northern Scotland, in early March, and Greg forgot wellies for the kids, rain jackets for us, umbrellas, and toothbrushes. He'd packed each child four pairs of socks for a seven-day trip and Lucy had fifteen pairs of underwear to Matt's five, which meant that towards the end of the week Matt was wearing pink knickers with Disney princesses on them. After that Greg was banned from packing for the family again. I have a theory he'd only done such an awful job so he wouldn't have to do it again, such was the complete and utter patheticness of his attempt.

'You aren't done yet?' says Greg, walking into the room with a smile. 'I could have packed, read half of that guidebook to Paris, and done a hundred sit-ups by now.'

'Yes and you would have forgotten half of what we need, and let's not pretend that you could ever do a hundred sit-ups. Especially with your pathetically weak heart.'

'Fair enough,' says Greg, walking over and putting his arms around my waist. 'This time tomorrow we'll be in Paris.'

'I know,' I say, pulling his body closer to mine. 'Wandering around the Louvre.'

'Or getting a baguette from that little patisserie around the corner from the hotel. With cheese and ham, sitting down by the Seine and watching the world go by.'

'No cheese for you, Greg, it's not on the cardiac diet,' I say with a smile.

'Fine, killjoy. A salad baguette, followed by a stroll around Sacre Coeur, before back to the hotel for—'

'For what?' I say. 'All that walking and the only thing I'll want is a foot massage.'

'I'll give you a foot massage,' says Greg, who starts to run his hands up my waist towards my chest. 'At least for starters. What's French for first course?'

'Premier Cours.'

'For Premier Cours,' says Greg in a terrible French accent.

'Not quite as sexy when you have to ask for the translation. Okay, you'd better go because we still have lots to do before we leave,' I say, pushing him away with a smile. 'But as soon as we get to Paris—'

'I can't wait,' says Greg, turning around and walking slowly out of the room.

'Love you.'

'Love you too,' says Greg, stopping at the door. 'Oh, and don't forget my toothbrush. You know I need my soft one otherwise my gums will bleed.' I just give him a look. 'What?' says Greg in mock incredulity.

When we returned from Paris the first time we found out I was pregnant with Lucy. I remember the joy we felt that we were having a baby, but I also remember feeling a sense of loss. Paris has always been a fantasy of mine. I've always dreamed of living in a small, top floor flat in Montmartre. It would have a little roof top terrace where I'd sit and write on warm days. I'd walk around Paris as though it was a giant film set, the star of my own Woody Allen movie. Paris was the dream, but after we left and learned we were about to have our first child, I knew that dream would never become a reality. And so it's sat at the back of my mind ever since, a fragment from another life. But going back now, finally a writer, it feels as though it's possible again. Maybe the dream's changed slightly, morphed into something a bit different, but it's still there and it makes me shiver with excitement.

I finish packing and I sit down on the bed for a moment listening to the silence. Today's Sunday, which always makes me think of the kids. Sunday was always a family day and despite it often driving me crazy, I miss Greg's roast dinners, sitting around the table once a month with the kids. It may have led to many an argument, but I understand why it meant so much to Greg. It meant a lot to me too, and although we try to see the kids as much as we can, it isn't the same. But it's all right because time has moved on and we've all moved on too. So now I look back with wistful nostalgia at all the wonderful moments from the last thirty years, but forward with wonder and excitement at what's to come. Speaking of wonder and excitement, Greg and I are about to go on our first couples retreat with Stella Blackwell and her husband, which should be interesting. I don't think Greg really understands what he's letting himself in for, but I can't wait to see the look on his face when he finds out.

Part Five

(Eighteen months later)

Greg

I'm fiddling with pigs in blankets that I'm already regretting. It's impossible to get all the little toothpicks in before the bacon starts to unravel. It looks so easy in the book. I'm already dreading the stuffed dates. I should have gone simple. Jamie Oliver is simple. Gordon Ramsay is fairly simple, so I ask you, why the hell did I decide to go with Nigella?

For the past few months I've been working on my new book and getting the house ready for Christmas. With the whole family plus new partners and baby Josh staying, Lizzy went all out with the decorations. She finally got around to buying a big, sparkly new Christmas tree because we've had the old one since the kids were little and to be honest, it was pathetic. It wasn't the best tree when it was new from Woolworths twenty-something years ago, but over the years we've lost two of the branches and because it was so old it didn't fit together properly anymore and leant to the left. We've updated the rest of the decorations too and I ordered the most expensive free range, organic turkey I could find, which is currently going through a twenty-four-hour brining process. Lizzy thinks I'm going a bit over the top, but this will be the first time we've all been together in over a year, so I think it's worth it. At least I hope the brining is worth it. Nigella seems to think so.

Holly's already here with her girlfriend Chloe, who's absolutely lovely, and Matt and Lucy should be here soon. We have festive music playing, there's nuts and mulled wine on the table, and according to the forecast there's a good chance of snow. In other words, it's the perfect Wilde family Christmas.

'Do you need a hand?' says Holly, standing in the doorway with Chloe.

The kitchen is awash with vegetables waiting to be chopped, bottles of wine waiting to be drunk (not by me anymore unfortunately) and there's plenty to be done. In years gone by I loved locking myself away in the kitchen while my family played games and watched television, but not anymore. I look at Holly and she's so grown up and not just that but happy too. I'm so pleased for her. After the whole Charlotte mess she went off to university sad and desperate and I was so worried about her. She's always been my most difficult child. She always asked the most questions, created the biggest problems, and challenged me more than Matt or Lucy, but I always felt as though she was the strongest too. She's opinionated, firm in her beliefs, and quick to attack, but after Charlotte she changed and suddenly seemed a shadow of her old self. Then she met Chloe and her whole being changed. I've never seen her so full of confidence and life. Chloe is studying Drama too. She's smart, funny, and it's obvious she's completely head over heels in love with Holly.

'I'd love a hand,' I say, but before the girls have the chance to chop anything the doorbell goes and its chaos as Matt, Saskia, and baby Josh arrive. I hear the doorbell and the next thing I hear is a high-pitched squeal from Lizzy.

'Oh my God!' squeals Lizzy. 'They're here everyone! They're here!'

Holly, Chloe, and I rush out of the kitchen towards the front door and stood there are Matt and Saskia who's holding a very tired looking baby Josh.

Josh is six months old now. Lizzy and I managed to get out to America when he was born, but we haven't seen him since. We were shocked when Matt told us that Saskia was pregnant, but like everything else about them, it happened quickly. They were married in America soon after they moved there and now they have their own house, Matt's photography career is taking off, and they have a son. It's incredible that barely three years ago Matt was still living at home, single, unemployed, and looking as though his life was drifting towards mediocrity. I was worried I'd be spending my retirement years still cleaning up after him, moaning about his nail clippings in the sink, and begging him to get a job, but now he's got his own family, his own life, and I couldn't be prouder of him.

'Dad,' says Matt, leaning in and giving me a hug. He looks so grown up now. The scruffy hair, two-week-old beard, and manky clothes have been replaced by smart chinos and a shirt, his hair is short, and his face is clean shaven. Even the whiff of poor undergraduate is gone, and he actually smells quite good.

'Son,' I say, and then I'm hugging Saskia, and Lizzy is hugging poor Josh like he's never been hugged before. If he wasn't so tired and hadn't spent the last twelve hours on a plane, he'd probably try and wriggle free, but instead he just sinks into her. Lizzy's crying, Matt's hugging his sisters, and then from behind them Lucy appears with her new boyfriend Tim, and there's more tears, hugs, kisses, and our front door becomes the stage for a big family reunion.

Lizzy is sitting on the sofa with baby Josh on her lap. He looks just like Matt did when he was that age and it's like being in a strange time warp. I feel like I'm a young man again watching Lizzy holding Matt in her arms. He has the same eyes and the same cheeky smile. He's a real smasher as my Mum would have said.

Tim and Lucy have only been dating for a few months, but they seem very happy. Tim is Scottish, tall, thickly built, with a mop of blond hair, and blue eyes. They met in Edinburgh, and I know she's never been happier. After everything that happened at the BBC, I'm so relieved she's turned things around. I get everyone a drink before we settle in to catch up.

'You didn't tell me he was so handsome,' says Lizzy to Lucy, looking towards Tim.

'I didn't want it to go to his already huge head,' says

Lucy.

Lucy's sitting on the floor next to Tim and she smiles at him, before giving him a kiss on the cheek. Holly and Chloe are sitting together on Mum's old chair, and Matt and Saskia are sitting on the sofa next to Lizzy, who's probably never going to let go of baby Josh.

'I don't have a huge head,' says Tim. 'She's always mistaking confidence for arrogance. In my line of work you need to have a certain confidence.'

'And what do you do?' says Chloe.

'TV presenter. I present a couple of shows in Scotland, although I'm looking to get something down here soon.'

'I definitely approve. Especially if he gets you back to London,' Lizzy says with a smile.

'A real-life celebrity in the house,' says Holly.

'I thought you already had one of those,' says Tim, looking at Lizzy. 'I loved your book.'

'Oh, thank you, but I'm hardly a celebrity,' says Lizzy coyly.

'Didn't you just do a big interview for The Telegraph?' says Matt.

'Well, yes, but that doesn't make me a celebrity. Anyway, enough about me, how about more drinks for everyone?' says Lizzy.

'I'll do that. I should probably finish cooking dinner anyway,' I say, and I'm about to leave the room, but Matt stops me.

'Dad, sit down, you aren't doing anything else today,' says Matt. 'Lucy, Holly, and I will take care of everything.'

'I'm fine to cook. I just had a full medical and the doctor said I have the body of a twenty-year-old,' I say.

'A twenty-year-old who had a heart attack recently,' says Lizzy.

'It doesn't matter,' says Matt. 'You sit down and get to know your grandson. We're hijacking Christmas.'

I'm about to argue the point and insist on doing something, but before I can Matt's moving me onto the sofa next to Lizzy and Josh, and Matt, Holly, and Lucy walk into the kitchen. Within minutes I hear them arguing and shouting at each other, but I ignore them and carry on playing peekaboo with Josh, while Saskia, Tim, and Chloe compare notes on their Wilde family partners.

When I thought I was dying, I had this moment when I thought of the future, of all the things I was going to miss out on. I thought of my children growing up, of them settling down, having their own children, and of all the time I should have had left with Lizzy. The pain of that moment has stayed with me ever since and that's why sitting here with my family isn't just special, it's everything. Every day I'm alive feels like a gift. Life is precious and without warning it can all change in a second so I'm going to enjoy every wonderful, silly, difficult moment from now on because who knows when it might be gone.

The table looks like something from a glossy magazine spread. There's a beautiful golden turkey in the middle of the table, the rest of the food is piled around, and we each have our Christmas cracker paper hats on. I'm sitting in my usual seat and Lizzy is opposite. Josh is sitting in the old highchair we had in the attic. We kept it after we had our own kids and it's been up there gathering dust ever since so it's wonderful to see it in use again, although it needed a really good clean and Saskia is worried it doesn't meet today's rigid safety standards (which it doesn't). Holly is sitting next to Chloe, Tim is squeezed in next to Lucy, and Saskia is feeding Josh the baby food they brought with them on the plane.

'What's brown and sweet and glides around an ice rink?' says Lucy, reading off her Christmas cracker joke. 'Bourneville and Dean.'

We all groan and shake our heads.

'I don't get it,' says Saskia, the only non-British person at the table.

'It doesn't matter,' says Matt. 'It's an awful joke.'

'Its tradition though, isn't it?' says Tim. 'Bad cracker jokes.'

'Not in our house,' says Chloe. 'I had pretty religious parents who banned anything that wasn't strictly by the book, and by the book I mean the Bible.'

'What is it with you, Hols?' says Matt. 'You only fancy religious nutters?'

'It's why we bonded. Chloe was trying to get over religion and so was I.'

'And nothing beats getting over religion like getting under a lesbian,' says Matt.

'Matt, really?' says Saskia.

'What?' says Matt. 'I was just—'

'Being your usual inappropriate self,' says Lucy, and we all laugh.

I look across at Lizzy and she smiles and without having to ask, I know this is the right moment. I tap the side of my empty wine glass with my fork.

'Your mother and I have announcement,' I say when it goes quiet. All the children look at each other quizzically, then they look back at me. 'We sold the house.'

'What?!' Matt, Lucy, and Holly say in unison.

'We just accepted an offer,' says Lizzy.

'But why?' says Lucy.

'Because it's the right time,' I say, looking across at Lizzy. 'You kids are all grown up and have your own lives. This house is too big for us.'

'But what about all the memories?' says Matt.

'We'll still have those,' says Lizzy, and there's a disbelieving silence around the table, which is eventually broken by Lucy.

'So where are you going to live?' she says.

All heads turn to look at me and I look at Lizzy, who's holding a glass of wine in her hand. Her cheeks are flushed, and she's never looked more beautiful.

'For the next year, Paris,' I say. 'And after that, who

knows.'

'Well this has blown my mind,' says Matt.

'Me too,' says Holly.

'Me three,' says Lucy.

It was a hard decision to sell the house, but it's time. This is a family house. It needs children, laughter, tears, and everything else that comes along with it. We sold to a young couple who already have one child and another on the way. Lizzy's always wanted to live in Paris, so we've rented a two-bed flat in Montmartre for a year. So this is the last Sunday roast dinner in this house. It's the end, and the beginning, and I suppose in so many ways it's what life is all about. It's the delicate balance between holding on and letting go.

The next few hours are wonderful. We eat, talk, and drink, while outside the snow starts to fall across London. It feels like we're in our own little bubble, separate from the rest of the world. Josh sits with us and is as good as gold. He must be so tired from the flight, but you wouldn't know it. Tim tells us how he met Lucy and spent months stalking her until she finally agreed to a date. Apparently my daughter is quite a difficult catch, although I can't help but wonder if all that business with Richard played a big part in that. Saskia tells us all how much Matt has changed, grown up, and become a successful photographer. Although the bit that warms my heart the most is when she tells us how much importance he places on making a roast dinner every Sunday.

After we've cleaned away dinner and Josh is down for his nap, we all sit in the living room, and Matt gets out the board games. Lizzy and I sit on the sofa while everyone else starts playing. We're happy to sit back and observe. I'm not sure my heart would appreciate a board game with my kids. They choose to play Monopoly and begin a two-hour marathon game. As they all get drunker the game becomes littered with laughter, backstabbing, petty squabbles and mistakes, the bank (Matt) starts to lend money willy-nilly, and then eventually runs out completely. The dog piece goes missing for a few turns, and Chloe's shoe is in jail for a very long time. Eventually there's an argument, accusations of cheating, and the game is abandoned with no clear winner.

As the afternoon turns to evening, the drinking starts to accelerate, Josh is awake again before bed, and the party spreads out across the house.

'Let's pop out to the shed,' I say to Lizzy when we get a moment alone in the kitchen.

'Why? It's freezing out there,' she says.

'Just for a minute,' I say, so she begrudgingly agrees, and we grab our coats and head out to my shed.

Once inside, I hold Lizzy's hands and look into her eyes. She's shivering from the cold, and so I lean down and give her a kiss, and when I pull away she looks at me with a knowing smile.

'What?' I say.

'Are you replicating the night we went to Uncle Colin's house and were caught kissing in his shed?'

'Maybe. Only this time there's no Uncle Colin to tell us off.'

'And we can sleep in the same bed afterwards without the fear of being labelled fornicators!' says Lizzy and we both start laughing.

I look across and on the desk there's the photograph of us on Brighton pier. It was a hot summer when Lucy was nearly two and we'd driven to Brighton for the day to escape the heat of London. We sat on the beach and had ice cream and then we took a walk on the pier. I asked a passing stranger to take a picture of us. Lizzy and I looking so happy and carefree. After the photo was taken, I remember we got fish and chips and we sat on a bench on the edge of a park so Lucy could play. We talked about having more kids, the future, how happy we were, and I remember to this day the feeling I had sitting on that bench. It was one of pure wonder and excitement at the life we had created and the life we were going to have.

'There you are,' says Matt, opening the door. 'It's picture

time.'

'We'll be there in a minute,' I say, and Matt smiles before closing the door.

I look at Lizzy, at the love of my life, and then I kiss her again.

'Happy Christmas,' I say.

'Happy Christmas,' says Lizzy, and the music from inside the house mingles with the faint sound of songs from nearby as the snow continues to fall. It's Christmas all across London and people in thousands of homes just like ours are celebrating. They're happy, drunk, falling in love, with their family, friends, and after everything that's happened, I'm just happy to be one of them.

'Mum, you're here,' says Matt, pointing at a spot underneath our wedding photo. 'Dad, you're next to her.' I walk across and stand next to Lizzy, and we're flanked by Holly and Lucy. Saskia's holding Josh, and she's next to Tim, and Chloe's on the other side. 'Brilliant,' says Matt, who pushes the button and joins us next to Saskia.

I look across the line. Lucy is stood smiling next to Tim, his arm casually around her waist and hers around his. Holly and Chloe are cuddling up and grinning, both happily drunk. Matt and Saskia have their arms around each other, and they're both smiling, and Josh is happily cooing away between them.

'Say cheese,' says Matt.

'Cheese,' we all say as the camera snaps and flashes.

'We have to take it again,' says Matt.

'Why?' I ask.

'Because Lucy smiled and it ruined the photo,' says Matt.

'Hilarious, Pissy Pants,' says Lucy, reaching across and hitting Matt on the arm.

'Pissy Pants?' says Saskia.

'It's a funny story,' says Holly.

'It's not funny,' says Matt. 'Southend is a really long pier, and I really needed a wee.'

'Says Pissy Pants,' says Lucy.

'Right, that's it,' says Matt, and he lunges at Lucy, but she quickly ducks out of the way and runs off. Matt starts to run after her, but Holly trips him up.

'Whoops,' says Holly.

'You're going to get it too,' says Matt.

Holly joins Lucy and they run off with Matt chasing them. Seconds later I hear them running up the stairs, the thump, thump, thump of their feet, the girls screaming.

'Are they always like this?' says Tim.

'Since they could walk,' I say with a smile.

I listen to them running around upstairs, before they run back down again, falling onto the sofa laughing. Lucy, Matt, and Holly, my kids, all grown up, with their own lives, their own loves, their own families, and yet still my children. Lizzy and I sit down on the sofa, cuddling up to them. Tim grabs the camera and takes a shot of the five of us, laughing, smiling on the sofa Lizzy and I bought together so many years before. It's one of the only original pieces of furniture in the house. A big brown leather sofa. The leather is cracked in places and despite having it professionally cleaned a few times, there are still stains from when the kids were little. Every spot, every square inch holds so many memories and happiness radiates from it; a family life well lived.

'Quick, get in Tim, Chloe, Saskia, baby Josh,' says Holly.

They all join us on the sofa and Holly gets out her phone and holds out her arm, pointing the phone at us all.

'A quick Christmas selfie,' says Holly.

'Everyone say masturbation!' says Matt and gets a punch on the arm from Lucy.

'Inappropriate,' says Saskia.

'Oh, she meant that sort of selfie. Got it,' says Matt.

'Ready everyone?' says Holly.

'Ready,' we all say, and Holly clicks the button on her phone.

Summer 1984

Greg

'I can't believe it,' says Lizzy, standing next to me. 'Our first house.'

'I know, it's a bit—'

'Overwhelming?'

'A bit,' I say. 'So what do you think, right here?'

'Sure,' says Lizzy.

I'm stood next to Lizzy in our new living room looking at our new sofa. It's the only piece of furniture in the room, but it's beautiful. Big, brown, and made from the finest Italian leather. I saw it in a shop last week and from the moment I set my eyes upon it, I knew we had to have it. It cost a fortune, but it's like I said to Lizzy, we're going to have it for the rest of our lives. I remember seeing a sofa like it in a film. If we have nothing else in the living room except this, I'll be happy. It's not just a piece of furniture, it's art - that's what the salesman at the shop said and Lizzy rolled her eyes, but a part of me believed him.

Lizzy and I sit down on the sofa and look around at the sparseness of our new living room. The only other thing we've done is hang our wedding photograph over the fireplace. Lizzy and I outside the church where we were married, smiling and so happy. The best day of my life.

'We'll get more furniture soon. I promise,' I say.

'And maybe a television?'

'Why do we need a television? I thought we'd read books, talk, drink wine. It's the dream, remember?'

'I remember,' says Lizzy. 'Although from time to time I'd like to watch a bit of telly.'

'Fine, we'll get a television.'

'And a dining room table.'

'And a dining room table. A nice big wooden one that sits six people.'

'Six people? How many kids are you planning on having?' says Lizzy.

'I don't know, love. Maybe four,' I say.

'Two?' says Lizzy.

'Three, last offer?' I say.

'I'm having these kids, remember. You know I have my own dreams too, right?'

'I know and just because we have three kids, it doesn't mean you have to give up on your dreams. We can have it all. We're the new generation. It's going to be different for us.'

'And what's the new generation having for dinner because I'm starving?' says Lizzy.

It's Sunday and the first day in our first house. For the last two years we've been living in a dingy rented flat, but we want to start a family soon so we dived in. We found this house almost as soon as we started looking. A three-bed, fixer upper in Muswell Hill, we couldn't believe our luck. It was above our price range, but with some help from our families, and with my job at the university, we decided to risk it. The house just feels right. At the moment it seems enormous, which is partly because it's empty and partly because only Lizzy and I are in it. One day it's going to be filled with life.

'It's Sunday, we should have a roast,' I say.

'A roast? And how's this roast going to magically appear?'

'I'll make it.'

'Excuse me? Mr I Can't Boil An Egg, is going to make me a proper roast dinner?'

'Why not? Maybe it will be my thing from now on. On Sundays I'll make a roast.'

'That's going to be your thing? I thought the other thing was your thing?'

'They can both be my thing,' I say smiling, and I reach across and grab her, cuddling up to her and giving her a kiss. My Lizzy, my wife, and then all thoughts of the roast and eating are thrown aside, and we lie on the sofa, in our new house, and make love.

Acknowledgments

I'd like to thank the following people for their help with this book and their ongoing support. Firstly and always my wife, who puts up with me and my writerly ways; stopping mid-conversation because I have to write something down, waking up in the middle of the night to work (and then being a grumpy bugger later), and always having a glazed faraway look on my face because I'm thinking about my book. I have to thank Ariella for helping so much with this book and also my ex-Editor and good friend Harriet, who keeps supporting me and helping me, and takes me out for amazing pizza! A huge thank you to Aimee Swann, my Editor-in-Chief, who did an amazing job with this book. I hope we keep working together on many more books to come.

I'd also like to thank all the people on social media who keep me going, encouraging me, supporting me, and telling me how much you like my books. I'm not sure if we tell our readers enough, but without you we'd probably be the most depressing bunch of people in the world. So thank you.

Lastly I'd like to thank my parents, who as I said in the dedication, gave me so many happy Sunday roasts growing up. I feel so very lucky that I grew up in an age when everyone did have a roast on Sunday. I look back on my own childhood, and maybe it's with rose tinted glasses, but it was wonderful, and I have my parents to thank for that.

Be sure to follow Jon on Twitter *@JRance75*, on Facebook *@JonRanceauthor*, and check out his website *www.jonrance.co.uk* for all the updates on his latest work.

Thank you for reading. I hope you enjoyed *Sunday Dinners*.
Do leave a review if so on all your preferred platforms to help spread the word!

Thank you!

Printed in Great Britain
by Amazon

28864685R00169